TINY
INFINITIES

TINY INFINITIES

By J. H. Diehl

chronicle books
san francisco

To Jackson, Sandy, and Caroline

Library of Congress Cataloging-in-Publication Data available.
ISBN 978-1-4521-6335-2

Manufactured in China.

Design by Alice Seiler.
Typeset in Prensa, Gotham Narrow, and Frontage Condensed.

10 9 8 7 6 5 4 3 2 1

Chronicle Books LLC
680 Second Street
San Francisco, California 94107
Chronicle Books—we see things differently.
Become part of our community at www.chroniclekids.com.

The fireflies, twinkling among leaves,
make the stars wonder.

—Rabindranath Tagore

PROLOGUE

BACKSTROKE

HARRIET SAYS I am a backstroker at heart, which is true. I have won more medals for freestyle than backstroke, but when I am swimming on my back, counting strokes while my arms pull down the pool, I am racing but relaxed. Fierce but smooth. I am as sure as there is dry air above my face that once I slide under the blue-and-white flags at Cherry-wood Pool I'll need five more strokes to touch the wall. Flags—five strokes—the wall. Every time. What I love most about backstroke is, it proves a person doesn't need to be looking straight ahead to know exactly where she's going.

1

PIPER

HEADLIGHTS WOKE ME: shining down the path through the bamboo forest, between the upper and lower parking lots at Cherrywood Pool. Luckily the glare didn't reach the bench where I'd fallen asleep. Like a tide that rolls up a beach and drops back short, leaving your towel dry, white light flooded one end of the walk but kept me in darkness. I slipped to the ground, hugged my swim bag to my chest, and squeezed in among the tall, gray-green bamboo poles. I was cold. My Sharks team suit, T-shirt, and shorts were still damp, and the air temperature had dropped. I didn't remember falling asleep, but I remembered not wanting to go home after swim practice and not knowing where else to go to avoid watching my dad move out.

A car door opened. Loud static clipped on and off from a radio. The words were too fuzzy to make out, but the cloudy syllables said clearly: *police cruiser.* According to older kids on the team, high-schoolers liked to party here. So I waited for the police to decide there were no teenagers and leave.

The trouble teenagers could get into—the kind police might be looking for—was about as unclear in my head at that point as the sounds of the radio, even though I was going to turn into a teenager in only two weeks, the day after school got out, in mid-June. All I cared about now was to avoid people and questions keeping me from carrying out the plan I'd come up with. People I knew, who'd say, "Alice, what are you doing alone at the pool in the middle of the night?" And people I didn't, who'd ask the same thing. Especially police, who—of course—would make me go home.

Each burst from the radio, the dark air absorbed like a sponge. This went on a couple of minutes. Burst and sponge. Burst and . . . sponge. Finally the volume turned down or maybe off, and I imagined they were listening from the car.

New sounds seemed to rise up to fill in the quiet: a hum from the eight-lane Washington, D.C., Beltway bordering the pool property, below a steep hill; a pulse of crickets chorusing nearer—an uneasy, uneven insect music that played the mood I was in better than I could have answered what it was in words—and footsteps.

Someone got out of the car without closing the door.

Swimming trains you to discipline your breathing and enlarges your lung capacity. I controlled my inhales and exhales to make them silent while a flashlight beam waved over the bamboo. Then, carefully, I backed away from the bench. Deeper into the bamboo, down the slope toward the lower parking area, flattening myself as much as possible in the slim spaces between the poles.

A stump the size of a quarter pressed into my right cheek. The ground smelled of dust, dirt, and mold. I lay, mostly on top of dead peapod-shaped bamboo leaves, wondering two things: why were the bumps on your skin when you got cold called goose bumps—why goose and not chicken or swan or pigeon—and what if they found me? If I ended up home, if I had to witness my dad go, it felt like I'd a little be saying it was okay. And it was not. I didn't agree. I would not be present. I refused.

A few inches from my face, a firefly blinked its own tiny searchlight—greenish yet completely unconcerned with me. *Unk*—the door shut rudely. The engine rumbled on, and the car pulled around to the lower lot and stopped again. I sat up.

The flashlight reappeared through the deep screen of bamboo, pointing into the chain-link fence by the toddler pool. Someone I couldn't see shook the locked pool house door, and a man called, "Hello? Anybody there? Hello?" in a voice performing a duty.

Thankfully, a few minutes later the car headed off down the access road into the neighborhood. Now I could sneak back in through the hole in the fence every kid on the team knew about—behind the big azalea near the snack bar—and spend what was left of the night sleeping on a lounge chair.

I circled the pool entrance, to the picnic area, and crawled through the fence, as easily as finding my way in my house blindfolded.

The outdoor clock, mounted on the back wall of the pool house, said 2:37. But the lounge chairs, where I'd planned to sleep, looked like a herd of creepy cows in shadows on the grass. The peeping crickets seemed to be passing signals back and forth about me, for unseen watchers. It was as if the air had filled up with spooks, even though I didn't believe in ghosts or magic. Even though I knew I was alone.

The last thing I felt like doing was sleeping on one of those chairs.

The best way to get warm was to swim.

As fast as I could, I pulled off my T-shirt and shorts. Dove into the lap pool, sprinted a length to shed the feeling of being watched. I kept my eyes shut except once or twice to stay straight with the black lane lines on the bottom of the pool, because I'd forgotten to put on my goggles.

After that I set a slow, even pace. I could do this steady freestyle stroke until dawn, I figured, like those people who swim the English Channel. And I did, for twenty minutes or so—until my left arm crashed on something hard in the middle of the pool. *Fwack.* Stinging.

I mashed the water. Pounded it to shove up a wall of liquid like a shield, raced in the opposite direction and threw myself out onto the cement deck. Grabbed my bag, ran to the roof overhang at the back of the pool house, only then turned around.

On the water floated a plastic mute swan. Lifeguards set it in the pool to keep Canada geese away. How had I missed that?

Shivering and spooked, in the cold shadows of the pool house, it felt as if I'd crossed a portal away from the world I knew and needed to go back. I scrambled into my clothes, crawled under the azalea bush, and started running.

Two blocks from my house, while I was concentrating on keeping my flip-flops from slipping off my feet and my body ahead of spirits that weren't following, I saw her.

A little girl in pink-and-white-striped pajamas. Alone, in the middle of the road, standing inside a circle of light cast by a streetlamp, barefoot. A car was approaching.

I stopped a few yards away with such a jerk that my flip-flops smushed sideways under my heels, my toes burned, scraping pavement. "Hey, watch out!" I called. The nearby houses were dark. The front yards were empty. The girl ignored me.

The car's headlights threw forward around us, and the girl's gaze seemed to shift to the grass they illuminated on her left. The driver's eyes might be on his phone, I knew, or the dials of his dashboard or a drink in the cup holder or out the side window.

All this I took in in a second or less, and in the same moment recognized her—from the transfixed look on her face, and her mess of shortish, blond-white curls— as a stranger I'd seen yesterday afternoon, in the backyard next door to mine.

Swimming teaches you how to dive without hesitation at the start of a race. Fast, I crossed the space between us, hooked my arm and hugged her close. She was easy to lift, light and bony. She didn't protest, and we fell where I aimed, onto a patch of lawn above the curb at the far side of the street. Just in time, it sounded like, from the tire screech.

A porch light came on at the house next door.

"Sorry," I said urgently, turning my face to hers. I couldn't help thinking I had gone from attempting to escape ghosts I'd spooked myself with to saving a real little girl from an actual metal giant.

Her miniature nose, lips, cheekbones, and eyebrows seemed to have been outlined with a fine-tipped pen. She looked me in the eye with a blank expression I couldn't make out.

"What were you— Are you all right?" I asked in my big-sister voice as her chest rose and fell gently, catching her breath.

"Don't be scared," I said. "I hope you're not hurt." She kept looking at me but made no sound. "Can you hear me? Do you speak English? *¿Habla usted inglés?*" I tried, hoping the Spanish I learned at school might work.

I don't know if I expected an answer. "My name's Alice," I went on. "I live next door to you, I think. Your family just moved in, right? Did you see me waving at you yesterday? You pretended not to, but I thought you did. Can you give me a thumbs-up you're okay?" I couldn't seem to stop asking her questions.

Honestly, I didn't need to be asking her anything. The grass-covered ground was soft. I was used to giving piggyback rides to Mike and Josh; I'd been in charge of games for twenty kids, watched them fall, cry, helped them get up. I was fine and she probably was too, I was guessing, when the driver's door of the stopped car opened.

I'd been hoping the car would just go away. My swim bag where I'd dropped it was caught in the low eyebeams of a teal-colored sedan with a bash in the rear door and a PIZZA DELIGHT sign on top.

"Hello? You people all right?" called a man standing in the street with his hands in the pockets of his jeans. I couldn't say how old he was. Sounded like he was asking a question he didn't want to but had to, which is how I felt about answering. Had to, didn't want to, like I didn't want to be with this girl or on my way home. There were no other choices, though—no good ones. There was nowhere I wanted to be. Only places I didn't.

The light from the nearby house went off.

"Yes," I said.

He picked up my bag, laid it a few feet closer to us, in the gutter at the side of the road, then quickly raised his hands as if I'd pointed a gun at him. "Don't worry, I'm not going to hurt you," he said. "Just making sure everybody is okay. You girls are very late to be outside." He lowered his arms and took a step closer. "Is she hurt?"

I stood, to make it easier to run if I had to. The girl scrambled up and started to move away, to the darkened yard. "Thank you. It's my cousin who's visiting. She sleepwalks. I'm taking her back to my house," I said quickly, feeling all at once responsible for getting her home.

"Close one." He shook his head as if he was watching an instant replay of the near miss, like he hadn't been involved.

"We live right down there." I pointed vaguely toward where he'd come from. "My parents will be out in a minute to help us," I threw in. *Just leave*, I pleaded silently.

"Well, if you're sure you're okay," he said, "I can watch until your people come or you get into the house . . . but where is she going?" The girl was marching across the grass, away from us.

"It may take me a few minutes," I said, not sure what I meant. But he seemed to buy it. He gave a little formal nod and returned to his driver's seat. I don't know who was more relieved, him or me. I paused just long enough to watch him draw out his phone to look at it. Then I picked up my bag.

I found her at a corner house lot, on the part of the lawn by the other street, where it was darker. She was sitting near a small, new-planted tree, with stakes and wires attached to hold it in place. I reached for her right hand to pull her up to walk home, without realizing it repeating what the man had said: "I'm not going to hurt you."

"*Eeeyee-eeyee-Eeeeyeeeee!*" she yelped. My heart jumped a mile, and I felt a thin wetness in the web of skin between her fourth and fifth fingers. Blood.

I whipped off the T-shirt covering my swimsuit, to wrap her wound, but she curled her small body around her hand and refused to let me touch it. My fingers were smeared with blood now, too; I hadn't noticed any on her before, though I remembered she'd been lying on that hand when we fell to the ground.

Now she was clutching it to her stomach and lay kicking the air like a bug on its back. "*Eeeeeeem-raaer-eeyeeee!*" she cried, loud enough for lights to come on and neighbors to rush over. I thought so, anyway, but maybe they mistook her for a cat or a coyote, because no one appeared.

All I could think of was a trick that worked with my brothers. I lay down and imitated her. "Ahhhhh," I whisper-yelled, and kicked and waved my legs. If anyone came out now, they'd probably go right back, I thought, that's how crazy we looked. But she did stop; her body quit moving, and she shut her eyes.

"Listen," I said, sitting up on my elbow. "I'm really sorry about your hand. I can wrap it up. Like this—" I folded the shirt around one of my hands and made a thumbs-up with the other. "It'll feel better."

She didn't start yelling again, but she didn't open her eyes.

"This is maybe a stupid question," I said, "but I'm wondering if you hear me talking, or if you might be . . . deaf?" Probably she was too little to even know that word, I thought. She looked about four. What else could explain the car or her sounds, and no reaction, now, to mine? I wished I knew sign language.

"If you do hear me"—super-stubborn was a possibility, I decided, or super-scared or both—"could you just say your name? Or show fingers for how old you are? I'm almost this many." I held up ten fingers and then three more above our faces against the night sky. Her eyes stayed closed.

Well, that was enough chitchatting. With some struggle, because she squealed and kicked, I managed to wrap her like a burrito in my wet towel while keeping the part around her right hand as loose as I could. I clutched her in front of me like a wriggly worm, my bag slung over one shoulder. It was awkward. But I intended to finish this night with at least one thing done right.

In the first block, I had to stop to re-grip a couple of times while she squirmed. By the second block, she seemed to have accepted the ride. But I slowed down as we neared my house. A police car was parked in front, and there were lights in the living room windows.

If I hadn't been carrying a large bleeding package that was likely to run off or scream when I set it down, maybe I would have snuck around to the back. Instead, I rang the bell with my elbow. My dad opened our front door with an expression on his face that morphed from bleached surprise to relief. "Oh thank God!" Two police officers behind him immediately started tapping numbers into their phones.

"But Alice, you're covered in blood! And who's this? Is she hurt, are you hurt? What happened?" He attempted a hug, as if he needed to make sure I was real. But the towel bundle was already slithering out of my arms, and I slipped from his. "You're wet. You *were* at the pool?"

"I'm fine," I said, bandaging up, for the moment, the raw awfulness of being home—with my plan failed and him about to leave. Because of course this girl needed actual bandaging, and as soon as possible. "That's hers, from carrying her," I added about the blood on my arms and T-shirt.

She had pushed off my swim towel and was sitting on our wood hallway floor, cradling her right hand between her stomach and knees.

"That new family moved in at Mr. Salgado's, and she was in his yard yesterday. I don't know her." I didn't answer about the pool. "Is Mom upstairs?" Nobody answered me either.

"Hi there, I'm Officer Gina." The woman's black gun stuck out at her hip as she squatted to eye level with the girl. As much as I'd been determined to do the right thing and bring her home, I couldn't help feeling mad that I'd had to. I'd ended up exactly where I didn't want to be.

Officer Gina was small and compact, while her partner was practically double her size and much younger. He'd rushed out to their cruiser and was coming back in the door with a large white box with a red cross on it, which he held open for her. Officer Gina was clearly in charge.

"Officer David and I are going to get you home safe to your family," she said. "We want to make your owie feel better. Show me that hand."

No surprise to me, the girl did not respond. "I forgot to mention, I think she might have a hearing problem,"

I said. "She was in the middle of the road, just now, by herself, at Summit and Oak." I left out why I also happened to be there. "She almost got hit by a car. It seemed like she didn't hear it. I had to grab her out of the way."

"Got it." Officer Gina nodded as if I'd given her helpful information. "Kiddo?" She patted the girl's knee. What a mistake. The girl leapt at the door, like a squirrel flying from the ground to a branch, and yanked the knob with her good hand.

Officer David reached over to flip the deadbolt. "Let's not try that—Hey! Whoa!"

Wham. Wham. She banged her head on the door. Like she wanted to crack it to make more blood come out. *Wham. Wham.*

"Take it easy, there!" Officer Gina said.

Words were pointless, so I jumped up and squatted by her to try the trick again: moving parallel, pretending to hit my head on the door, too. It worked. The girl stopped, eyeing me suspiciously. *Yes.*

"Oh my God," I heard my dad mutter. I couldn't tell if he meant he was annoyed or amazed.

She sank back to sitting, her injured hand behind her knees.

"Good grief," said Officer Gina. "Which side are they on?" Meaning the new neighbors.

Dad pointed an index finger toward Mr. Salgado's. The look on his face reminded me of a balloon after you've blown it up almost too far and then let the air out, when the rubber gets stretched thinner than it's supposed to. Officer Gina was smart, I thought, watching her leave by the back door in our kitchen.

"Can I borrow some gauze?" I asked Officer David. He frowned as soon as I started winding the bandage around my own hand.

"See? This is what they want to do." I held my wrapped hand out in front of her face. She shut her eyes.

Someone pounded outside the door then, and the girl startled me by standing up when I did. By now I very much doubted she was just pretending to be deaf. But was she imitating me, like I had with her, or something else? Maybe she felt vibrations through the wood door?

Officer David had barely unlocked the door when it shoved open a few inches, and the girl started to squeeze out. A man wearing sweatpants and no shirt scooped her up into his arms. "Piper!" Finally she had a name.

He was taller, balder, and younger than my dad. Obviously Officer Gina had told him about the hand because he looked at it and me and demanded, "What did you do to her?"

"Nothing, I—" I realized that my shirt had blood on it, and I hadn't washed the smears off my arms and hands. My appearance must have looked not exactly innocent.

"Mr. Phoebe, let's step into the living room to continue this conversation," interrupted Officer Gina. "It's too cramped for all of us here." Our front hall was a narrow rectangle between the door and the kitchen, with an arched opening to the living room at the side.

But Mr. Phoebe, whose hearing seemed fine, ignored Officer Gina and started trying to pry open the fingers of Piper's injured hand. She let out another one of those jungle animal sounds that would have woken up my brothers if they hadn't already moved to our cousin Guy's house.

"Piper!" Mr. Phoebe lifted her above his head, trying to catch her eye. "Will you stop!" She was kicking the air like a wild version of exercises the swim coach sometimes had us do on land, bicycling our legs. When Mr. Phoebe quit trying and lowered her into a hug in his arms, then she did stop.

"I'm sorry. She doesn't hear me." He glanced nervously at the police officers and gently rubbed Piper's back to console her. "It's sometimes beyond . . . frustrating."

My dad stepped forward. "I'm Sam Allyn," he said in the voice he used these days to talk to my mom, filled with disapproval. "My daughter, Alice, found your daughter wandering in the street."

"I understand that's what she says," replied Mr. Phoebe, whose expression changed quickly to a stuck-up smile, as if he was used to being lied to. He turned to me. "How did her hand get hurt?" he asked in that same tone, like he was too smart to believe my answer. "How long was she with you, anyway?"

"You must be Mom," Officer Gina called over his shoulder, to a woman in pajamas and slippers who'd appeared on our doorstep. This whole scene was so much crazier than I'd thought this stupid night was going to be.

"Hello, yes! Joanna Phoebe." Behind her stood a teenage boy, and she carried a sleeping toddler with the same white-blond hair as Piper's. Joanna Phoebe readjusted her load and shook the policewoman's hand. "Thank goodness you found her! What a night. . . . Hello, hello there," she added, greeting the rest of us.

The boy stayed outside the screen door, on the steps, with his hands stuffed in the pockets of his jeans. He wore a black T-shirt that said in large pink letters, I AM SUSHI, YOU ARE SUSHI. I liked him right away for that, and I wished he'd come in, too. He looked like he was in high school. Was that how teenage boys slept, in their jeans?

"We got lucky, didn't we Eric?" Joanna Phoebe beamed at her husband with happy relief. Seeing her, his smirk melted, his shoulders relaxed. Without another word between them, they swapped kids. He settled the toddler on his shoulder, and Piper, whimpering only a little, held out her hand. "Oh, darling, ouch."

I could see in Joanna's eyes she was more worried than her voice let on.

Officer Gina said, "I'm going to suggest you have her checked out at the nearest emergency room, in case she needs a stitch or two. For the record, does your daughter suffer from a disability?"

Joanna and her husband looked at each other again, and somehow between them agreed who would answer.

"She doesn't hear words," said Mr. Phoebe, nodding. "She does hear some sounds—birds, doorbells sometimes. But not people."

I knew it, I thought, pleased to confirm my near-perfect record of figuring out screaming little kids, thanks to Mike and Josh.

"She used to, didn't you, beautiful?" said Joanna, rubbing noses with Piper as she fixed a piece of tape on her hand.

"Right after our little guy, Timmy, was born." Mr. Phoebe patted the boy's back. "From a perfectly normal kid to—worse and worse." He shrugged, like he had no answer to a question. "Every doc has a different explanation."

Officer Gina was tapping notes on her tablet. "And you and your wife were where this evening?"

"The house," Mr. Phoebe said. "We moved in less than twelve hours ago. We were asleep when you rang the bell. No idea she could get out."

"How scary," Joanna said to Piper, who, her hand taped in gauze, had settled in her mom's arms. "Thank goodness you're safe." Joanna looked up at the officers. "We are so grateful for your help. I can't bear to think what might have happened."

"Well, it was Alice here who located your daughter . . . ," Officer Gina began.

"And who we don't know anything about," Mr. Phoebe interrupted. "I'd like to be clear where things stand and if she's responsible for that injury."

"I am not!" I said, unable to listen to Mr. Phoebe any longer without getting mad. "She was almost hit by a car! She would have been, if I hadn't saved her! I'm sorry about her hand, but . . ." Didn't they understand, without me it would have been so much worse? I hated Mr. Phoebe, I thought.

"Alice, we'll sort this out," my dad said. "Calm down."

"I didn't see when her hand started bleeding," I protested. "All I did was try to help her. And compared to what could have happened. She could have been hit by a car!"

Officer Gina raised her right palm, like she was directing traffic in the middle of an intersection. "Alice, give us a minute," she said.

"Let's let it go for now, Eric," said Joanna. She looked nervous, a little worried he might not.

Officer David's phone beeped, and he and Officer Gina stepped into the kitchen. My dad handed me a fleece shirt to put on. Mr. Phoebe shifted Timmy to his other shoulder.

"You know," Joanna continued to her husband, "on our way over here, Owen showed me the back door was open, and it turns out the lock's broken. That's got to be how she got out."

Owen. That was his name. He'd disappeared from the steps. Embarrassed, I opened our screen door, in case Owen was in the yard, to see if I could tell if he'd heard me. He wasn't.

"Alice, where are you going?" my dad asked.

"Nowhere," I said.

"But your hand's hurt, too!" Joanna exclaimed.

"What? No. That's—I was only showing Piper what they wanted to do to help her." I waved my gauze-wrapped hand for her to see. This time Piper gave a little giggle at it.

"Joanna, it seems to me we need more answers from this girl," said Mr. Phoebe. I stepped away from Piper, closer to my dad.

"Sir, the priority is medical attention for your daughter," said Officer David, coming back in the room.

"We've got a car waiting out front. To show you the way to the nearest ER, since you're new to the area," Officer Gina said.

"And it's late." Joanna stood up to go, with Piper on her hip.

Mr. Phoebe glanced at my dad and me and said, "All right," and walked out.

"Bye, it's been way too exciting meeting you," I told Piper, with another wave of my gauzed hand. "Hope you feel better."

She turned her face into her mother's chest, like a baby playing peekaboo, and Officer David followed after them. Joanna gave Dad a sympathetic smile.

He shut our front door, looking irritated and tired, as if he'd just put up with watching ten awful TV ads in a row, and now we were back to a show he didn't like anyway. "If you'll excuse me a moment," he said to Officer Gina, "I need to fill Alice's mother in on the events. Triple A, as soon as you're done here, go up and show Mom you're all right, and then to bed. We'll talk in the morning."

The police officer resumed typing on her tablet. Usually my dad's trips to visit my mom resulted in screaming or sobbing. It was eerily quiet. Officer Gina wouldn't be here, I realized, if he hadn't decided to move out and the Phoebes hadn't decided to move in next door. I couldn't help thinking what a waste of time it was, for so many people to go to so much trouble to pack up and switch the places where they lived. Why couldn't we all have stayed right where we were?

Then Officer Gina looked up at me. "Alice, please come with me to the kitchen." Her face was grave. "You and I need to chat."

2

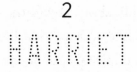

"AGE TWELVE. ALMOST THIRTEEN, I see," Officer Gina read off her tablet.

The clock on the stove said 4:08. I sort of nodded-shrugged, nervous she was about to accuse me of something. I didn't think it was a crime, though, to be outside at a pool even if you were supposed to be in bed. "I don't know why Mr. Phoebe said it's my fault. It was the opposite of what he thinks!"

There was a pause before she looked up. "Alice, I hear you. We'll get to all that. First, help me out with a few details. Is it fair to say you came across our friend Miss Piper after you decided to return home from the pool?"

The mention of returning home, and her saying I decided to, thudded me, like Piper banging her head: I was back to where I started before I left for swim practice. Actually, given that I was being interrogated by the police, my situation was pretty much worse. I gave Officer Gina the same nod-shrug, because I didn't really want to think about any of this.

"By the way," she added, "that hand should be fine after they get a couple of stitches into it, just so you know. Tell me something, were you planning to run away tonight, and now you're back? Or was it more of a thing of you staying out late without your parents' permission?"

The one window in our kitchen had turned into a dark rectangle with no view of the backyard, only a reflection of the table. I felt walled in. For some reason, I noticed the fake wood pattern in the tabletop. Why didn't my parents own a real wood table?

"Alice, please answer the question," Officer Gina said.

"I don't know," I replied, because I got the feeling she could give me a ticket or something if I didn't answer.

Then Officer Gina asked if I had met up with friends, or a person I might have contacted on the internet. Crazy questions. "Well? Who else did you spend time with while you were out this evening?"

"Nobody!"

"And you recognized Piper when you saw her, and knew where she lived, because you two girls had met before?"

"Kind of," I said. "We waved across the fence, in the afternoon."

Dad had asked me to meet him at home before swim practice. I'd been waiting for him on top of the picnic table on our back patio, cross-legged, with my back to the house, the way I liked. I do my best thinking in Cherrywood Pool, and my second-best thinking on top of that table.

The lawn, swing set, bushes, woodpile, our vegetable garden: they'd looked the same as always. I'd been thinking what a relief this was, because so much inside our house was changing, when I caught sight of a tiny girl staring through the chain-link fence from Mr. Salgado's yard.

Loose curls hung around her head like flowers. They were so blond they seemed to glow with their own light. Even from that first moment, though, there was something else unusual about her besides her hair. A blank, emptied-out look on her face, as if she'd been hypnotized.

I followed the path of her eyes through the fence and decided she must be watching patches of sun shifting over the grass. Light was glittering onto the ground through branches of the tulip tree. Without raising her head, she lifted a hand and wiggled her fingers.

But this new girl wasn't saying hello, it turned out, when I waved back at her and got no reaction. Just wiggling her fingers like she might be trying to figure out how fingers move. Or what they did to the sun on the grass. A lot of shy kids pretend other people aren't there, I knew from experience. Then my brothers and Guy burst out the back door, which meant Dad had arrived. Next time I looked, Piper had vanished from Mr. Salgado's yard as if someone had edited her out of a picture.

It was after the talk with my dad, when the point-lessness first started to irritate me—of him moving out and a family moving in next door practically the same day—that I had decided home was the last place I wanted to be the next morning when he packed up and left. So in a way, you could say it was because of seeing Piper in the backyard that I knew where I was headed that evening: someplace else.

"I don't think she remembered me tonight," I told Officer Gina. I described how I'd seen that strange look on Piper's face for the second time, in the street, like she was under a spell. How hard she was to talk to and wrap in my towel.

"All right, Alice." Officer Gina typed a few more seconds, shut her tablet cover, and regarded me solemnly.

"Please listen while I say a few things I generally tell kids your age in these situations. I'll be brief, since it's quite late, and I hasten to add I know very well that every person and every circumstance is different, okay?"

"Okay," I said, because was there much choice?

"Your dad tells me you received upsetting news yesterday," she said. "And I want you to know that going off without telling anybody is not a responsible way to deal with your troubles. Officer David and I were here talking with your parents and making phone calls for two hours, and we had a second car out looking for you. That's two cars and four people who, because of your actions, you've taken off county streets. . . ."

Great. I would have been a better use of her time if I'd been lying in a ditch.

"When you have problems at home, you need to address those. Talk with family members or another adult you trust, maybe your counselor at school. Here's my card. You can call my office anytime, and we can put you in touch . . ."

I stared at where the backyard would be, if I could see out the window. The dark glass was like a warped mirror. How had I suddenly transformed into a person who needed to carry around the phone number of a police officer? I didn't want to be the girl in that mirror.

In bed, I watched the empty ceiling, and couldn't sleep. I kept thinking about yesterday, when Dad had tacked his new address to the refrigerator with a magnet, like it was something to be proud of.

"Now, I know this is happening fast," he'd told me. "But it's not a surprise. The surprise is the when part."

"It *is* a surprise." He was moving the next morning, Saturday. Whatever space feelings take up inside you, I emptied out and inflated with blank air, so there would be no room to feel that he was leaving. I'd heard my parents argue about it. But those were words that came and went. That wasn't actually happening.

Aunt Ruthie had stopped by, which I hadn't expected, and she gave me a smile like a hook on the end of a fishing line. I refused to let her catch my eye and held my gaze at my swim bag, lying open on the floor. Usually, I was glad to see Aunt Ruthie. She was my mom's younger sister and had been helping us out for months. There was already a plan for Mike and Josh to live with her during summer vacation.

What wasn't a surprise was that Mom hadn't joined us. I'd picked up another prescription for her at the pharmacy on my way home, and she'd probably taken one of those pills and conked out.

"My apartment is a few blocks from work," Dad said. "That's too far in the mornings for you kids before school."

I kept staring into my bag, at the ordinary items I counted on for swimming: towel, goggles, cap. At home, I counted on my dad. My dad being here was ordinary. The idea of that not being ordinary shocked me.

"Mike and Josh are going with your aunt a couple of weeks early," he said.

"I'd love to have you, also, Alice, if you'd like to come," she said. "Tonight."

"No thank you," I replied, because I wanted nothing to do with this plan. "It's too far from the pool." Which was actually true.

Ever since I joined the team, the summer before first grade, I'd been trying to get my name on the Cherrywood Sharks record board hanging outside the lifeguard's office. There was no way I was slacking off this year. My goal was to attend every afternoon workout and Saturday morning practice until school ended. Then, during summer, when our regular meet schedule started, I'd do the two-a-day weekday workouts in the early mornings and late afternoons.

Aunt Ruthie's house was twenty minutes by car from Cherrywood Pool. From home I could walk in ten. Plus, someone needed to help take care of Mom, I thought. "Can we be finished?" I said. "Practice is about to start."

Aunt Ruthie nodded at my dad as if to say, *You know how Alice is about swimming.* Aunt Ruthie could make a nod do that.

Out the kitchen window, the boys had climbed to the top of the rope ladder on our swing set. If I were seven, I thought, I could be jumping off that ladder for no particular reason, like Mike. I might still believe that if I found the right enchanted stone I could cure my mom and she would go back to being her old self. It would never have occurred to me that the five members of my family had turned into pieces of a jigsaw puzzle, pulled apart and flipped over on the wrong side.

"That's all you have to say?" My dad fidgeted with change in his pocket. "I'll call a lot," he said, "and stop by."

The kitchen was silent except for his jingling. Being quiet isn't magic, but it was the power I had.

"Triple A"—that was his nickname for me, my initials, for Alice Amary Allyn—"I came here on purpose this afternoon to talk to you. You know this falls into the category of Unsatisfactory Parent-Child Interactions at Superimportant Moments."

Putting things into made-up categories was a tradition he and I had.

"Practice starts in ten minutes," I said, and I didn't cry, because I couldn't help thinking that letting people see you feel sorry for yourself at super-important moments fell into the category of Lame.

Now, eleven hours later, at four-thirty in the morning, still unable to fall asleep, I heard Mom's weeping start up from down the hall. I realized I'd forgotten to do like Dad asked and check in.

"Knock, knock," I said, and rapped on the frame of her open door, to be sure she heard.

"*Eh-heh-heh-heh-heh-heh-heh.*" She lay on her side in the dark, facing the opposite direction. That was her way of crying: "*Eh-heh-heh-heh-heh-heh-heh.*" The sounds were dry and soft like kitten fur; always seven beats repeating, from high to low.

I'd hear this when I woke up in the morning, when I came home from school, at night. There was something almost machinelike about it, so that now, even if it might be partly about me going away in the middle of the night, I knew it wasn't mostly about that.

In the six months since Mom had come home from the hospital, she'd just about lived in her bedroom. My dad liked to say this state of affairs fell into the category of Mind Over Matter. The Matter, meaning her back, had mostly healed from the car accident that started the whole mess in our family, the way I saw it. The Mind part had to do with the fact that, even though her back had mostly healed, she spent nearly all her time in bed.

"Why'd you do that, Alice, when things are already so bad?" she said without turning around. "You scared us half to death. Police, that's the last thing we need."

"Well, I'm here now. Everything's fine," I said. "There's no need to worry."

There were a couple of reasons why I'd believed I could get away with sleeping at the pool. I figured that if I didn't appear with her dinner tray, she'd decide I was busy and heat up the leftover mac and cheese I'd made the night before. Dinner was often the only time we talked, so she wouldn't miss me the next morning. My mistake was that I'd assumed my dad would be sleeping at his new apartment.

Mom rolled over and switched on the bedside light and squinted. "Go back to bed now, Alice."

Go back to bed. As if this was any other day. It was like telling me to sleep in my room after a tree fell through it, with punched out walls and branches hanging through the ceiling. So I carried my quilt and pillows outside and slept on top of the picnic table, until the sun woke me to a note from Dad that I should meet him here after the Saturday Sharks practice. If he was going to go away, I thought, just do it already. This good-bye was starting to feel like trying to swim the Chesapeake Bay with both feet tied to bags of bricks.

Coach Bowling had been assigning me to the 13–14 lane, even though my birthday was two weeks away, since league rules said I had to compete in the older group all summer. This time there was a swimmer in my lane I'd never seen before, who looked eleven, maybe ten. To be polite, I waited for her to finish a set before pointing out her mistake. "Excuse me, Coach B likes us to swim by age group—Eleven-Twelves are over there."

"I'm aware of that fact," she said, and pushed off.

Since school hadn't ended, some kids were still too busy to start summer swim team and the lane wasn't crowded. Oh well, I thought, she'll learn. I watched her a little: okay at butterfly, nothing special with freestyle or backstroke. But a really strong breaststroke that powered her down the pool. Pretty much the opposite of me.

We ignored each other the rest of practice.

"Alice, you met Harriet?" Coach B called from the end of our lane before we climbed out. "Fill her in on the team and the Saturday and Wednesday meets. She's just moved to Cherrywood, and you guys are the same age."

She walked off to speak to a parent. Harriet looked unenthusiastic.

"We don't have to," I said, since I didn't want to.

"It's fine," she said.

"Okay, well, I'm Alice. Coach B is nice."

"I'm aware of the fact that you're Alice."

"Want to see the record board? There are some really fast times." The closest I'd come to getting my name on it was last summer, when I missed breaking the 11–12 Girls 50-meter freestyle record by six-tenths of a second.

"I've seen it," said Harriet.

"How about the snack bar?" I said.

"Yes," Harriet replied, and instantly started walking fast across the pool deck, six feet ahead of me, as if she were going there by herself.

Whatever, I thought, catching up with her by the order window. Unfortunately two of my old neighborhood friends were at a table at the far end. I'd quit spending time with those girls last winter. But I'd

known them since preschool. I forgot Charlotte and
Malini liked to hang out at the pool.

A boy I didn't recognize had his arm around
Charlotte's shoulder. I wondered what that felt like to
Charlotte—could you move if you wanted, or were you
supposed to stay still? It looked strange.

Charlotte managed to lean over and whisper to
Malini. They got up to leave, and I said, "Hey" when
they passed us waiting for our curly fries. I wondered
if it looked like I was babysitting. Harriet had pigtails
tied in hair scrunchies with little birds on them.

"Hey, hi Alice!" Malini, who was always super-
polite, smiled as if it was completely wonderful to see
me. Charlotte waved with the hand that wasn't squished
between her and the boy, and then, to my relief, they
were gone.

The pool snack bar cooked their curly fries almost
crunchy, in corkscrew twirls I loved, that came out of
the fryer orange-colored. Harriet had copied my order.
I asked where she used to live and she told me Minneapolis, where she'd swum for a team called the Loons,
and her best stroke was breaststroke.

I couldn't resist. "I'm aware of the fact that your
best stroke is breaststroke."

She glared at me.

"I watched you swim," I said.

"Not like you're competitive or anything."

"I am, but my best event is freestyle." I ate another curly fry.

She shook her head. "Backstroke."

"How would you know?" My voice sounded as annoyed as I felt, which right away I regretted since Coach B asked me to be nice to her.

"Never mind," she went on. "Once I met an Alice named after Alice in Wonderland. Were you?"

It's surprising how often people ask me that. I almost always say yes, even though it isn't true, because I'm not proud of the real truth, which is that I'm named after a dog.

With Harriet, I don't know why, but I said no and asked her the obvious question, which was, was she named after *Harriet the Spy*? When she said yes, I figured I'd discovered a third thing we had in common besides curly fries and swimming: I assumed she must be lying, since that's the lie I usually tell. But I was wrong. It turned out Harriet *was* named after *Harriet the Spy*, her mother's favorite book when she was growing up.

"Too bad," Harriet said. "I thought I might finally have met someone else who comprehends how exceedingly annoying it is being named for a person who never existed, but who everybody thinks they entirely know because they've had an intimate personal experience reading about her in a book."

Plenty of kids have big vocabularies, but I'd never heard one my age say "exceedingly annoying" out loud to another kid. Or "comprehend." It was interesting and bothered me at the same time. I didn't think I was going to enjoy having somebody smug and show-offy swimming in my lane all summer. Plus, it seemed to me that this Harriet was being too personal—it was her word—for this being the first time we'd ever met.

"Why was your team named after a bird?" I asked, to change the subject. Most swim teams I knew were named after sea creatures.

"Loons are the Minnesota state bird," she said. "They are excellent underwater swimmers, can dive to depths of more than one hundred feet, and it's not true they mate for life, even though that's a popular belief."

"The Sharks don't have team scrunchies." The black-and-white birds tying her pigtails were loons, I saw.

Harriet frowned, as if I'd said something irritating, and resumed where she'd left off. "And so people assume they know an exceeding number of facets of my personality—and of course they don't," she said, untwisting the curls of a fry until it broke in two.

"Fact one," she continued, "I am named after a stranger's idea of an eleven-year-old girl. Fact two: I am not at all like that fictional character. Evidence: I do not spend my time sneaking around looking in other people's windows or skylights or hiding in their dumb-waiters. I hate tomato sandwiches, and I love math."

That was true, Harriet the Spy hated math. I remembered that part because it was when I read that Harriet the Spy hated math that I realized I didn't. It's not my best subject, but when you're a swimmer you have to think about meters and yards while you're attempting to shave hundredths and tenths of seconds off your fastest times, and I liked making those calculations.

"Fact three: *I hate writing*," Harriet said. "All in all, I would rather be named after . . . after . . ."

I looked through the cardboard basket for the fry with the most curls. The highest number I'd ever found was eight. The one I picked up had four, and when I finished eating it she was still stuck at the pause in her sentence.

"A dog?" I filled in.

Harriet scrunched her face until her skin wrinkled and her eyes and mouth narrowed into arcs as thin as her eyebrows. "Yesssss. . . . Why not? A real dog, at least," she added.

In my head, I heard my dad saying, "Well, that falls into the category The Grass Is Always Greener. . . ."

So I told Harriet about Alice the English springer spaniel, Dad's favorite childhood pet. And then I told her how I'd been thinking of asking people to call me Amary instead of Alice. Lots of people go by their middle names, and I was proud my great-great-grandmother Amary was a suffragette.

But Harriet changed the subject back to the dog. She wanted to know all about Alice.

"Okay, well, one time, on a walk," I said, "Alice T. Spaniel got so sick from eating food off the street, a surgeon had to cut open her stomach. He came face to face with a smiling PEZ bunny head."

"That is exceedingly surreal," Harriet commented. "What is the *T* for?"

"The *T* stands for *The*," I said, and she snorted. It was pretty silly, I had to admit. "Also, she liked to roll on top of dead animals to . . . *perfume* her fur. Dead rabbits, dead squirrels, dead birds, she loved to be smelly, and—" My dad laughed hard when he described this habit. He said it proved Alice fell into the category of Loving Life, which, since it was about dead animals, had taken me a while to figure out.

"And what?" Harriet smiled, ready for the next joke.

"And nothing." I felt like crying all of a sudden. "That's the Alice story."

While I'd been at the pool, until this moment, I'd managed to push my dad's move into a box in the far corner of my brain. Like this was any other Saturday morning. I'd had months of practice, at school and other places, forgetting home for a while. But talking about Alice was like walking back over to that corner in my head and finding the box jammed full of mad, sad, and panic.

"That can't be why your parents named you for her." Harriet boinged a three-curl fry and ate it.

"Alice is how they met." My voice wavered up and down. "She pulled my dad inside a tent at a Renaissance fair, where my mom was photographing people in costumes. Alice dived at some jerky snacks in her bag, and that knocked a knight's armor into a pole holding up the tent. The tent fell over, and they met crawling out." What had happened to Mom? Who was she back then? I felt like I didn't even know her, really.

"Now it makes sense," Harriet said, although from how she kept looking at me, I knew the tears on my cheeks didn't. "But I have to say, it's a good thing his dog wasn't named Brunhilde." This was so unexpected, the lump in my throat melted and I smiled.

"Or Sophonia," she added as I wiped my face. "Or Vertilene."

Harriet kept going until I couldn't help laughing. Which was another reason I knew we were going to be friends. I felt embarrassed, but my bad moment passed.

"Your team seems okay," she said, as we walked to where she was waiting for her ride.

"Hey wait up," I said, because her speediness was keeping several feet between us. "It's your team now, too. And the Sharks are *exceedingly* okay," I added, and it was Harriet's turn to laugh.

A black Mercedes SUV sped into the parking lot and jerked to a stop with a screech so loud, a tennis player dropped a ball he was serving.

Harriet's sister gestured out the window with a nail-polished hand. "I'm in a hurry. Get in, Mom and Dad are waiting." She had ironed-flat black hair, major eye makeup, large gold hoop earrings. I wouldn't have guessed they were related.

"Reasonably prompt for Lydia," Harriet said, checking the time on her phone. "Twenty minutes late for everyone else. Need a ride?"

"No thanks," I said. "I walk."

"Plausibly the safer choice," said Harriet.

3
THE TENT

"YOU'VE REACHED SAM ALLYN. Please leave a message . . ."

"Dad! Where are you? Your note said you'd be here by now." I hung up.

A chair was gone from the living room. New boxes lined the front hall.

I felt too stirred up to wait in the house or on the picnic table and decided to loop around the block on my bike. But when I went into the garage I changed my mind. There it was: the tent.

If he was moving out, I decided, I would, too.

I dragged the roped bundle of canvas out to the driveway. It was long, heavy, and budged only a few inches at a time down our side path, across the back-yard lawn, to a spot under the tulip tree near the patio.

At the end of my mom's summer job at the Renaissance fair, she and Dad had bought this tent from her

boss. It was a large, oval navy-and-white-striped pavilion that looked like a home for a wizard or a queen.
We'd taken it on camping trips when I was little, and
I always felt proud to be sleeping in such an unusual
tent. A gold flag flew from the top, and a pattern of silver dragon's teeth decorated the edge of the roof. People
at campgrounds used to ask if we were fortune-tellers
or part of a circus.

By wedging one pole against a picnic bench while
running to a pole and rope on the opposite side, I managed to raise a wobbly room. The sun shone through,
as if I were at the center of a lit lampshade, filling me
with a happy certainty. If I slept inside the house this
summer, it would be like going along with my parents'
plan. Living here was how I'd show them I didn't agree
to it. I could still go to swim practice and take care of
my mom. Yes, I decided. I would refuse to move back
in till he did.

Dad was in the kitchen when I went in for supplies,
and my words came out like milk spilling. "I'm not
allowed to run away, but you are." It took me by surprise how mad I sounded.

"Hello to you, too," he said, and set down the
duffel he was carrying. "That's not fair, Triple A. I'm
sorry I missed your call. C'mon, give me a hug, let's
talk." He smelled like hairbrushes. My dad always
smelled that way to me. It was such a familiar smell

that I didn't think if I liked it or not, or if it was a good or bad smell.

"Talk to me, sweetie," he said again.

"Tell me the story about Alice and the knight's armor." An opportunity in How to Delay.

"Seriously?" He sounded surprised, disappointed.

I knew he knew it was to stall.

"All right." He rested a foot on the duffel, folded his arms and proceeded to tell me the shortest version I'd ever heard. "And in the ensuing chaos, your mother and I met, and the rest, as they say, is history."

That was practically as short as what I'd told Harriet. He'd left out descriptions of the other props—gowns, crowns, scepters, swords, helmets from various centuries, and the dramatic part about a small electrical fire they had to extinguish with a wool blanket. And the part about driving Alice to the vet to splint her broken paw. "Weren't there signs saying no pets allowed in the fairgrounds?" I asked, trying for more time.

"A good question. I don't remember," he said. "Now Triple A, there are a few things . . ."

"So maybe they just let you in anyway?" Again the words came out madder than I expected, as if my voice had picked a mood without consulting me.

He poured himself a glass of orange juice from the refrigerator and nodded out the kitchen window.

"Maybe the same way I'm going to just let you use the tent, even though you didn't ask first."

In the afternoon sun, our tent with the shining flag looked even more out of place, like someone had drawn a bunch of smiley faces on a sad page of a book.

Once upon a time, my parents loved telling that story, and my dad claimed he'd dropped Alice's leash because the cute photographer had mesmerized him. She'd protest no, no, he'd been clueless for a way to introduce himself and used the dog and knocking over the tent as an excuse to chat after they scrambled out. "Which, either way, falls into the category of Really Falling When You Fall in Love!" Dad would finish, while Mom rolled her eyes.

"Triple A, a few more details about the move," he went on. "First, we've had to cancel your phone and your mother's for the summer."

"That's a detail?" I protested. "Because of last night?"

"It's not a punishment, it's to save money," he said. "Also, your mother feels the landline is more reliable and enough for her, by her bed. Oodles of kids in Cherrywood own phones. You'll have no problem borrowing one. If you're at the pool and she needs you, she can call the front desk."

He'd cancelled the internet, too. My dad worked as a librarian at the main university library, where, he once told me, the internet was as necessary as air.

"What about water and electricity? How am I supposed to do homework?"

"School's almost out, Triple A, and since you prefer staying here, instead of Ruth's, there's the public library a few blocks away, full of computers. So is my office, if you visit. The apartment building has free Wi-Fi, too. It shouldn't be a problem."

He glanced at the time on his phone, which he of course was keeping, since his roommates had no landline, and kissed me on the head. "I gotta go, sweetie." He brought up three duffel bags and a suitcase from the basement, where he'd been sleeping the last few months, and loaded his luggage and boxes into his car. I didn't offer to help because, well, I didn't want him to be putting anything in the car.

"Dad?" I watched him pick up the final box. "Are we going to have to sell the house?"

He pressed the box against the hallway wall to ease the weight. "That'll depend a lot on whether or not your mother decides she's well enough to return to work. It's all about money, Alice."

The color of everything suddenly looked as if someone had turned down a dimmer switch on our whole family, our belongings, our entire life.

"Bye, Triple A," he said. "You don't know how sorry I am about . . ." It was like he was trying and failing to come up with another category. ". . . all this."

We hugged again, an ordinary, everyday hug. He shut the trunk, the front and back doors of his car.

"What category is 'all this'?" I called. But he didn't roll the window down. He waved and was gone.

It was only two-thirty in the afternoon, but felt like evening. I wished that getting to sunset wouldn't take so long. I wished Harriet and I were good enough friends for me to ask her to meet again later at the pool, but we weren't. I knew I'd have to fill the afternoon with something, but I was ready for it to be time to go to sleep.

For a while I went back and forth from the house bringing flashlights, water bottles, pillows, sleeping bags, clothes, and books to the tent. Every time I felt like crying, I concentrated on a detail: ant-proof snack containers. Extra socks. Playing cards.

On my last trip, Mom was awake upstairs.

"Alice? Are you going somewhere again? Come in here, please."

She was under the quilt, with a pillow pulled so it hung across her forehead. The lights were off and the blinds were closed; the air felt cottony, like we needed to open a window. Around her, on the bed, lay magazines, a newspaper, a box of tissues, empty water bottles, and a wood tray.

"What is it, Mom?" I said from the doorway. "Do you need coffee? Or a grilled cheese?" I made a mental list of foods I'd gotten good at making since I started sharing the cooking with my dad: oatmeal, peanut butter sandwiches, French toast, nachos, spaghetti, microwave burritos, omelets, grilled cheese.

If I talked first and asked about topics like did she need a load of laundry done or want food, then chances shrank that she'd ask one of her Code Mud questions. I named them that in my head because at school we have Code Blue and Code Red for dangerous situations, so I wanted to pick a color and who likes mud color? A Code Mud was a question that, when you heard it, you wanted to freeze up or run away, or freeze up *and* run away, if it was possible to freeze and run at the same time. When she asked a Code Mud, it wasn't the right moment to wonder what exactly did she mean by that, and it seemed urgent to give her an answer.

"Oh Alice, don't you leave, too," she said. "What a mess. Isn't it?"

The strange thing was, even though she was the one who needed help, it had been her idea for Dad to go. She had asked him to.

"I'm not leaving. I can bring whatever you need," I said. "I'm just camping in the backyard." Every time I carried in a meal on a tray or picked up medicine at the pharmacy or washed her clothes, I told myself I was helping her get better. When she did, she'd get along with Dad and be a school portrait photographer again. The five of us could go back to our regular schedule in our regular house. Everything would be how it was before our backyard barbecue on Labor Day last year. When she drove to the grocery store for extra hot dog buns and ran a red light into a truck.

Mike and Josh had been shucking corn on the patio; I was helping Dad scrape the grill, when Mom squeezed the bag of hot dog buns on the table and laughed. She'd bought them that morning, but they were already stale. That's what made her laugh. We'd all laughed. The rest of us said we'd eat them anyway, but she wanted new ones.

The corner store was closed for the holiday, so she drove to the supermarket. On the way, she crashed into a big pickup truck and didn't come home for three months, when she could walk again. I'd been so worried she was going to die that I was just happy she could walk again, ever. But she didn't seem to see it that way. Pretty much she sobbed in her bedroom after that, which scared the twins and me, before I got used to it. For a long time Dad's main explanation to us had been that this fell into the category of Extremely Complicated.

"Camping?" she said now. "What do you mean? I hope you're not planning to build fires, I don't even know if there's a working extinguisher in the house." She shook her head. "You should be in a real camp this summer instead of camping on the patio."

"Well, I'm going to have swim team twice a day," I said.

"There must be something less boring than that," she went on in a dreamy voice. "When I was your age, summer camp is where I discovered photography and decided someday I'd travel the world by steamer and elephant and hot-air balloon, taking pictures for *National Geographic*. Camp got me dreaming about the future." There was a long pause, and I felt the freeze coming as I watched her remember she'd done none of those things. "Never in my wildest dreams did I imagine it might all come down to this." She slid down a few inches on the pillows. "Do you think my life is over, Alice?"

Code Mud. "Of course not, Mom," I said. "As soon as you're better, you'll know that's not true." I wanted to get out of the house to the tent as fast as I could.

She glanced at the closed blinds, which was a cue for me to open them, so I did.

"Thanks, Alice. When you have a moment, I could use the heat pack."

I boiled her cloth-covered pad in the pasta pot in the kitchen and brought it to her wrapped in a dish towel.

"Thank you for that, too, Alice," she said, fixing it against her lower back. "I don't know what else to say about you camping. I guess I know where you are, in case I need you. Dad told you about the phones?"

Hope bounced up in me the way your knee does when a doctor taps it to check your reflexes. "He said they're cancelled just for the summer. Does that mean he's moving back in September?"

"No, no." She made a little *tsk*ing sound and smoothed the bed quilt with her hands. "At least, I hope not. We'll see about restarting your phone once school begins. If your father gets his act together he should really be able to afford his own daughter's cell phone and his rent. Either way, in the end, we'll all be happier."

"Maybe *you* will," I said. "Dad says we might have to sell the house unless you get a job."

"He shouldn't have told you that. One drop in the bucket of reasons I'm glad he's gone," she said.

"*I'm* not glad, and I don't see why—"

Mom shook her head calmly from her pillows. "There'll be plenty of time to talk. I have to rest, Alice."

She rolled over, faced away from me. That was how Mom regularly ended conversations. "Thanks again for the heat pack."

"Nobody seems to care *my* life is over," I muttered, and trudged back downstairs without waiting for her reply or, worse, to hear the silence when she didn't.

If I had to live anywhere besides Cherrywood, I thought, it would be like cutting a character out of a book and pasting the paragraphs describing her into a different one. You might as well delete those paragraphs.

My one hope now was the tent. But when I came back out, it was shaking, as if a giant bee was trapped inside. The golden flag wagged each time the canvas bulged. It took about a second to figure out. The mystery was how she'd escaped again. Nobody was in the yard next door or watching from any window I could see. "Stop!" I called, forgetting she wouldn't hear.

I dumped my armload on the picnic table and rushed in, touching Piper's shoulder as she turned from whacking the far wall. Without any sign of recognizing me or being afraid of me, either, she ran to the center pole and started tugging it with her left hand.

Out of habit, I kept talking. "Piper, we met last night. I'm Alice. How's your hand? Come with me." I crossed the space from the door to the center and took a chance on closing my fingers around hers. She didn't react to this until I lifted her around the waist. Then she let go of the pole and went limp.

I held her face forward, still careful of the hurt hand, so she could see us headed to the door. So far so good, I thought—until we got out onto the grass and she started fighting to get down.

"Piper!" Joanna cried from across the fence. Of course, *now* she came out. She was standing at the one open spot in the trees and bushes between our two backyards. If a ball or an air rocket or any other toy landed on Mr. Salgado's side, he never minded my brothers and me climbing over there, at the rosebush. Every place else he'd planted tall evergreens for privacy.

At another time of year I could have lifted Piper across, but there were too many thorny stems. I had no choice but to grab her tighter and run around the side.

"I thought we'd fixed that back door," Joanna said at the head of the path between our houses, where she took Piper from me. "This is a bad sign. Timmy's napping. My husband and Owen are at the movies, taking a break from unpacking, which I was trying to do while I thought she was watching TV."

I was just happy to quit worrying about Piper's next crazy move.

"Thank you so much for rescuing her. A *second* time," Joanna said to me. "I promise you there won't be a third! Please tell your parents not to worry about strange children wandering onto their property, especially when"—she gave a nod to our yard—"it looks like they may be hosting a party."

"The tent is just for fun," I said. "There's no party."

She smiled like she appreciated having someone to talk to, even if it was only a kid. "I knew Cherrywood would be a friendly neighborhood," she said, "and it's funny your name is Alice. When we were house-hunting, and the cherry blossoms were at their peak, I actually told Eric it was a kind of Wonderland, and we had to live here."

Whoever built Cherrywood had the idea to plant a cherry tree in front of each house. Every spring they bloomed into pink-and-white canopies over the streets.

"You know," Joanna went on, "I'm looking for a babysitter or mother's helper to play with Timmy this summer, weekday mornings, so I can focus more on this one, which I obviously need to." She nodded to Piper and looked me in the eye. "I think Fate is conspiring for me to ask you, Alice."

4
FIREFLY CAKE

BY *FATE,* it seemed to me, Joanna meant *signs showing where your life is headed.* Which reminded me of a school field trip I went on a few months after Mom got home from the hospital. Fate, or what it meant, was what I heard the day my English teacher took us to the Kennedy Center to see Mozart's opera *The Magic Flute.*

Ms. Neely liked to say, in a perfect world, she would have been an opera singer. I think she got away with the field trip by telling the principal we were studying an alternate form of storytelling. After all, she said, an opera is simply another way to tell a story; it's just that the most detailed part is the music, not the plot. People sing almost every bit of dialogue. "I forgot to brush my teeth" could be a song lyric, or "I feel a tremendous urge to blow my nose." Any little thing.

When the Queen of the Night promised Prince Tamino he could marry her daughter, Tamina, if he succeeded in rescuing her, the queen's voice hovered around high notes like a butterfly in a summer field of flowers. On and on and on it fluttered until people interrupted her to clap for her singing so many hard, high notes. That was the moment I realized life at my house had turned into an opera, except that every little bit of my parents' dialogue was shouted instead of sung.

"Is today the day to put out the garbage?" Mom would scream from her bedroom down to the kitchen.

"That was yesterday! If you made more of an effort to get out of bed, you'd know!"

Mom kept herself mostly to what Ms. Neely called recitatives, the facts and questions. Dad had some powerful, emotional arias. They'd stopped ever talking in normal voices back and forth. Every single thing they said to each other was a yell.

When the queen's servants fixed a padlock on Papageno's mouth, I wished I had locks like that for my parents. Papageno, the silly bird catcher, clowned around the stage, humming because he could not sing. They stopped his words, but not him, and the audience loved him.

I had that feeling of being different when you're the only person not laughing at what's supposed to be funny. Even if I could stop my parents' yelling, I realized, they'd still be walking around humming their anger at each other.

I happened to be sitting next to Georgia, who everyone agreed was about the nicest girl at school. She was my best friend after Charlotte and Malini, probably. At intermission, when I remained in my place, she stayed, too. "Alice, you okay? How's your mom?"

All my friends knew about the accident; their parents had taken turns bringing us meals the week it happened. But I was tired of that exact question, *How's your mom?* At school it was good to be away from the house and not think about that, if possible. And it was getting impossible to answer even simpler questions like *How's it going?* I might crumble, I felt, if I looked at Georgia, so I kept my eyes on the closed stage curtain. "Um . . . my parents might split up."

"Oh no!" she said. "Alice, that's terrible. When did you find out?"

But then Ms. Neely interrupted, handing us little bags of M&Ms, which was a relief, maybe for Georgia, too, and I couldn't blame her that she got up to go find everyone else.

I remained in my velvet seat the rest of intermission, wishing I had Tamino's enchanted flute, with its power to turn unhappiness into joy. I'd vanish my parents' fights, cure my mother—even transport my family back in time. So she could have picked out a bag of fresh hot dog buns in the first place.

After that field trip I stopped sitting with Georgia and those girls at lunch. I didn't really want to continue the conversation. The main library room in the media center was peaceful, so I started going there. By the time Dad moved out, those last two weeks of school, I had a regular routine of eating my sandwich and doing homework in a big armchair in the reading nook.

I meditated, too. The P.E. teachers taught us a unit on meditation for de-stressing before exams. We crossed our legs on mats in the gym. Closed our eyes, breathed in and out. You were supposed to choose a word or phrase to focus on—your "mantra"—to repeat in your mind to keep it off other subjects. I picked "twenty-eight-point-three-three" to say, because it was one one-hundredth of a second faster than the Sharks Girls 13–14 50-meter freestyle record. That was the time I needed to swim to get my name up on the record board this summer.

So I meditated on "twenty-eight-point-three-three" in the armchair before studying. And like Dad said, it was helpful to be in the media center to go on the internet. I spent one lunch period looking up words to write my speech for the Spanish oral exam. The subject was travel. Since I was living in the tent, I thought I could describe it well, so I wrote about camping trips we used to take.

There was a glow in my mind about those trips. Remembering them felt like opening up a drawer to look at souvenirs: how it was my job to gather kindling—*palitos*—from the woods—*bosque*—for our campfire—*fogata;* we cooked chili—easy, *chile*—that tasted like the pot—*olla*—it was heated in. How Mom held me on her lap while we toasted puffy white *malvaviscos* and Dad read out loud from his *libro* of Grimms' fairy tales—*cuentos de hadas*. Sometimes my parents sang *canciones* together.

Returning to class from lunch was like time traveling back into the present. It was awful.

Everyone stopped trying to talk me out of living in the backyard during those final weeks of school. My parents had enough of their own problems just then, I guess, and I'd decided to wait till school was over to give Dad my ultimatum: no moving back inside until he did.

If Joanna Phoebe noticed me sleeping in the tent, I gave her very few chances to ask me questions about it. The couple of times I passed by her in the front yard, she was busy strapping her kids into their seats in her station wagon. Once she stopped me to confirm what hours I'd have free when vacation started. There were no more surprise visits to the tent from Piper.

Living inside that big oval pavilion reminded me of our old trips: the sound of summer rain patting the canvas in the dark; the giant height of the striped ceiling from down on the ground in my sleeping bag. Almost every night I dreamed about Dad, Mom, Mike, and Josh alongside me in sleeping bags in the tent, at a campsite in a forest. This would only ever be a dream—we stopped taking those trips when the twins were born.

Ants woke me sometimes, crawling on my arms and face, until I learned to ignore them and pick up crumbs. After a while I was able to sleep through noises that being outdoors magnified, a siren or an air conditioner rattling on or a dog bark. Mainly I got through those nights by distracting myself with swimming. To get to 28.33, I'd have to drop more than five seconds off my fastest 50-meter freestyle time. Doing that in a summer would be like a kid skipping from seventh grade straight to ninth. Plus, a problem came up that I hadn't expected.

The Sharks swim two categories of meets. B meets on Wednesday nights, A meets on Saturday mornings.

Anybody on the team can swim a B meet. At A meets, in the younger age group, only the top six freestyle swimmers compete. Every summer until now, I'd qualified to swim the 50 Free on Saturdays. I was good—I'd won quite a few medals and blue ribbons.

But in my new, older group, only kids with the top *three* times in the 50 Free got to swim A meets. With a personal best of 33.62 seconds, I was fifth. New 13–14 girls besides Harriet had joined the team. So just to win an A meet slot, I needed to drop two seconds.

Sometimes I lay in my sleeping bag at night and imagined the start of my next freestyle race: toes at the cement edge of the pool, arms ready, the starter's whistle, take your mark, bending for the dive; the flash from the start machine almost simultaneous with the sound. And getting the dive elegant, leaping exactly with the light, all the more elegant because it's harder, because light travels faster than sound.

School ended on a Friday, and the next day was my birthday. "Happy thirteen!" said Mom that morning when I brought her a tray of coffee and breakfast cereal. She took out two twenty-dollar bills from the wallet on her nightstand. "Go to the movies! Or shopping!"

"Thank you, Mom," I said, glad she remembered but knowing I would not be doing either of those things. Charlotte was leaving that day to spend the summer in California, and Georgia and Malini were packing for sleepaway camp. I knew I wouldn't be seeing them and, in any case, by now it would have felt odd to ask. Harriet I hadn't heard from since the day we met. Her family had come to town for a few days to get settled, after her school ended in Minneapolis, and then they'd gone on vacation.

"Is this enough to get my phone back?" I asked.

"No, Alice, and I'm sorry, that's too complicated." Mom stirred her coffee. "But now that it's your birthday, do you think you could start sleeping in the house? Isn't it hot at night?"

No logic connected my birthday and where I slept. I wondered where this conversation was going. I said, "I like it," and tried to sound casual and not think about my last birthday, when she made angel food cake with chocolate icing that we brought to the water park, my whole family, with my then-friends, and Aunt Ruthie and Guy.

"I *never* liked that ostentatious tent," Mom went on. "I don't know why I let your father talk me into taking it on those awful camping trips."

"Those trips were fun," I protested. You had to wonder if a car accident could wreck a person's memories along with her back. "Thanks again, Mom." I held up the two twenties and slipped out before she could say anything.

My dad had just left his gift on the picnic table. "Sorry to drop this and run," his note said. "You must be in with Mom, and I don't want to disturb. Will call you later. Here's an all-time favorite from my shelf, plus something to buy your own favorites with. Love always, Dad."

It was his old copy of *David Copperfield* by Charles Dickens, plus a bookstore gift card. I was only on page nine when Aunt Ruthie fake-knocked on the tent door flaps by clicking her tongue.

"Alice? You in there?"

She had brought me a silver chain with a shark charm. "For good luck on the team this summer," she said.

"Thank you, I love it." I really did. I put it on and hugged Aunt Ruthie, who was padded and soft, except for the READY, SET, ART pin she always wore, a leftover from when she used to make jewelry to sell in shops. That was before Uncle Ahmed died, when Guy was a baby, and she'd gone back to school to become a fourth-grade teacher.

"How's the swimming going so far?" she asked.

"Two-a-day practices start next week," I told her. "I'm going to swim both, mornings and afternoons. I'm at the bottom of a new age group."

I've got what is known in the sport as a crummy swimming birthday. The summer league cutoff date for determining age groups falls a day after mine. Long story short: some kids in my group were turning fifteen before the end of the season, while I was turning thirteen at the beginning. I was up against a lot of girls older than me.

"You'll rise to it, Alice," said Aunt Ruthie. "That's who you are. Hey," she continued. "Later, do you want to join the boys and me for a birthday dinner? Maybe a movie?"

"Some friends invited me over," I said, like I was sweeping her words into a dustpan to clear them out of the way. What a habit this was getting to be, automatically not spending time with people. But dinner with them would only remind me I couldn't have everybody together like last year.

"I'm so glad you're celebrating with friends. That's great, honey." She hugged me again and her clunky pin pressed my arm. "I'll let your dad know. He told me to find out what you were up to."

If he wanted to know so badly, why couldn't he have stayed to ask me himself? I walked with her out front to say hi to the boys, who were watching a Harry Potter movie in her van.

"Hey, Guys and Guy!" That was my nickname for them, and as soon as I said it I missed our usual Saturday morning routines, when my cousin slept over and I helped the boys build forts.

"Alice, this is my magic wand," Josh said as if no days had passed since we'd seen each other. He waved a painted stick at a brown velvet cap on Mike's head. "I'm sorting Mike in the Sorting Hat."

"Happy Birthday Happy Birthday Alice Alice!" Mike dove forward over the seat.

"Happy birthday, Alice," said Guy. Short, chubby, with black hair, Guy compared to my brothers was like Harriet compared to me. He looked like Uncle Ahmed, while Mike and Josh were tall and on the skinny side, with freckles and long arms and legs.

"Is Dad here?" asked Josh.

My eyes met Aunt Ruthie's. "He's out, guys," I said, like I was cheerful and seven, too.

Aunt Ruthie hugged me goodbye. "You are a good girl."

"Thanks, Aunt Ruthie," I said. It was a funny thing to hear after lying to your brother.

That evening I sat cross-legged on the picnic table, until the sun sank as low as the rose stems spilling over the fence, and fireflies began to flash. I felt bad about telling Aunt Ruthie I had plans when I didn't, but it was worse not having any. I wished I had a cake, if for no reason other than so I could make another wish to roll back time.

I uncrossed and re-crossed my legs on the picnic table. I'd already said good night to Mom, so there was no place to go except the tent, and I wasn't sleepy yet. Even if it fell into the category of Pointless, I felt like crying.

Fireflies were blinking over the grass and our wood-pile and the compost heap, near the vegetable garden on the opposite side of the yard from the Phoebes'. We had a great yard for fireflies. On summer nights when Mike and Josh were babies, asleep in their cribs, my parents used to snap their fingers quietly when I cupped a fire-fly out of the air. I loved the twins, but I loved being the center of my parents' attention again, those evenings here out back.

Sometimes I'd spin circles on the grass until I felt my legs collapsing. I'd lie perfectly still in whatever position I happened to land—arms out, legs scrunched under—while the dark yard spun around me, until the ground calmed and the air got so quiet I could hear my brothers' breathing over the baby monitor and the clink in my dad's iced tea.

Thinking about that only made me feel worse, and I was not going to be Sorry for Myself. Mom pretty much owned that category, and it got you nowhere but deeper in. After all, I could have said yes to Aunt Ruthie or tried calling Dad. If I'd kept hanging out with Georgia, Charlotte, and Malini, even though it was boring and I didn't want to talk, probably we would have celebrated before they left town.

It was down to me and the fireflies. So make the best of it, I told myself. If I wasn't going to have a real birthday cake this year, why not have thirteen firefly candles? I went inside to the kitchen, dumped salsa out of a jar in the refrigerator, washed and dried it.

Twilight was nearly through. Every branch, bush, and blade of grass had darkened to a silhouette. I grabbed them out of the air, thirteen fireflies plus one to grow on, and set their jar by my sleeping bag. I listened to the crickets that sang from somewhere nearby every night and pretended, this time, the song was for me. "I couldn't buy candles like you at a party store if I tried," I complimented the fireflies out loud, and I imagined my freestyle race one time for each candle, grateful when sleep started to come so I could swap out this day for a dream.

5

TEENY TINY INFINITY

AT 6:30 A.M. the water is prickly yet smooth. It glints around you in the morning sun. After a few laps you warm up, and then Cherrywood Pool is a perfect place for figuring out problems you're having outside the blue rectangle holding up your body.

Whatever is on your mind, even if it feels like a ton, you don't stop moving your arms and legs and let it sink you. You count on the water, and when you turn, you can depend on the walls to help push you back in the opposite direction.

That first morning practice of summer vacation, I was rehearsing the lines I planned to say to Dad. He was coming to the first Wednesday night B meet in two days, and we were having dinner after. "I refuse to move back in our house until you do," I repeated a few times, until it stopped sounding like the great idea

I'd thought it was. Why should he care if I slept in the tent or indoors? "Dad, I'll stay there all fall, all winter, in the snow. Is that what you want, our family sleeping in four different places, hardly seeing each other?" Or I could try, "Dad, please come back. What about the category of Standing by Your Family? Or, Doing What's Right? Or, Don't Be a Quitter? Do you want to be in the category of Family Abandoner?"

I was swimming a freestyle set, two hundred meters, and as I reached the final arm pull, a voice shouted by my head, "Alice T. Spaniel!"

My hand splashed short of the wall, I fumbled the touch. It was Harriet. Back from vacation.

"What, I . . . I . . ." I stuttered, too surprised to get any words out.

"Yup, you hated that exceedingly. I know. It got you to look up, though. The coach whistled for people to get out and you didn't hear."

Totally embarrassed, I saw I was the only person left in the water. Fortunately, at least fifty kids had shown up for the first morning of the season, and no one seemed to be paying attention.

"Sharks!" Coach B called through her red megaphone. "Answer me now, before we start: What's my blood type?"

Harriet looked at me with confused alarm.

"B Positive!" I shouted along with the other kids, and shrugged a laugh to give Harriet her answer. Coach B's "B Positive" was one of her more bizarre psych-ups. I climbed out. I'd forgotten today was the make-up for time trials. A bunch of people, including Harriet, had missed the practice when we recorded our official qualifying times for the first A meet. Everybody was getting ready.

Harriet ran to the chairs, grabbed her goggles, and was back at the edge of the pool before I'd wrapped myself in my towel and sat down to watch. As annoyed as I felt about her calling me Alice T. Spaniel, I was glad she'd set her bag on the chair next to mine.

When the coach timed Harriet's breaststroke, she ripped the water with a single-minded want-to-win stroke. Her head and torso pushed high with each bob forward. She really crushed down the pool. It was an impressive swim, and when practice was over, Coach B declared, "Excellent breaststroke time, Harriet!"

"For a short person," Harriet commented to me in her loud voice. Still, she looked pleased.

"What's that?" Coach B was short herself. "We love our short swimmers, like we love our short coaches." She turned to a little boy who appeared to be waiting reluctantly for a private swimming lesson. "Now get in that water before the Bowling Ball rolls you in!"

Coach B had a noticeably round stomach, too, and short-cut hair, and she usually wore a baseball cap; her head looked like a small ball on top of a medium one. She liked to make jokes about it.

"Big morning," I said as we watched her rotate the boy's arms in the water, teaching him to breathe. "You heard two of her best."

Harriet's opinion was sad but true, however: in swimming, as you age up, height starts to matter. The top of her head came below my shoulder. She was as short for our age as I was tall. Though it was clear Harriet's height was the only small thing about her. Her voice was as big as a radio turned up, and she walked like a turbo engine. As a swimmer, she was a classic breaststroker—much better at that stroke than freestyle, butterfly, or backstroke. She couldn't compete with me in any other event. So I didn't mind that she could beat me at one. I admired it. Harriet's breaststroke time was fast for anybody of any height. Period.

"Girls Thirteen–Fourteen Medley Relay, with me on breaststroke and you on backstroke, definitely contends for gold at the Relay Carnival in July," Harriet announced that afternoon. We were sharing an order of curly fries in the snack bar at the end of the late practice. Our team was so big—around two hundred kids total—that there were three daily afternoon practices.

"I doubt that," I said. In my life, I'd never won a backstroke race. Given my current fifth-place standing on our team in Girls 13–14 Freestyle, the chances of me swimming anything at Relay Carnival looked slim.

"Third in freestyle's my goal for now. I just want to get into the A meet," I said. Wednesday night, at the less important B meet, I'd have one more chance to qualify for this week's A meet. I held off revealing my bigger dream. From where I was starting this season, getting my name on the record board probably sounded laughable. "And anyway, why are you so obsessed with my backstroke?"

Harriet slid her phone to me across the table. The screen showed a bunch of *X*s on a grid. "Oh right, that explains everything," I said.

She tapped open a new page. "If it doesn't make sense, try this one." Harriet had created graphs and spreadsheets for every race result for our current 13–14 girl swimmers since they had joined the team. For some of us it went back nine years. Scary. What kind of person did that, plus, how had she found our results from first grade?

"This shows the average backstroke time improvement was 13.3 percent between the ages of six and eight, 14.62 percent between eight and ten," she said. "You, on the other hand, started with slower than average times, yet improved 19.2 percent between six and eight, 24.48 percent between eight and ten. *And*, drumroll please, from ages ten to twelve, while the average improvement for Sharks girls is only an 8 percent drop in time, your time drops by twenty. *Twenty percent*, Alice."

"Improving makes no difference if the times are too slow to win," I pointed out.

"You're wrong. Our peer group is plateauing while you are radically improving. Look at your Time Trials time this year."

True, I thought. My backstroke was faster than last summer, even though I hadn't swum on a winter club team. And I couldn't say the same about freestyle.

"I predict you are the number one Sharks Girls Thirteen–Fourteen backstroker by the end of this season. Assuming, knock on cardboard"—here Harriet rapped her knuckles on the curly fries container—"you don't break your leg."

"I guess thank you? For looking that up?" I added. "Either thank you or creepy."

"Meet results are public information. What's creepy? This week I'm not in camp, I had time between workouts." Harriet pulled a stack of printer paper from her swim bag. "The older material did take some digging, but never fear for our beloved trees. I'll recycle."

"Nobody analyzes swimming by percentages, by the way," I said.

"Well they should," she said. "There will be, at most, two other girls in our division who can beat you." She had about a billion more facts about the stats for our age group. "Oddly," she added, "the info I found lists ages but no birthdates. When do you turn fourteen?"

"A year minus two days from now, unless it's a leap year," I said.

"Wait." I watched her do the math. "Last Saturday was your birthday?"

Mouth full of curly fries, I nodded.

"How was it? Did you have a party? What kind of cake?"

Was I imagining it, or was there a tweak in Harriet's voice, of being left out? I said, "No. My mom is . . . sick. My dad was busy, and my friends left town the second school ended." I was surprised how reasonable all that sounded.

"I did kind of have a cake," I continued, wondering why I was again telling Harriet stuff I'd normally keep to myself. I had to admit it didn't feel bad to hear her enthuse so much about me and backstroke, especially when my freestyle goals appeared to have sunk without a life preserver.

"We get a lot of fireflies in our yard," I explained. "Some nights there're dozens of them blinking. I went around and caught fourteen and put them in a jar. Sort of for a joke," I added, in case a jar cake and firefly candles sounded as nutcake-ish to Harriet as they did to me right now. Her eyebrows stayed pinched together like she was seriously concentrating on what I said, so I went on confessing, "But I forgot to poke holes in the lid." The fact that I'd woken up and found every bug in the jar dead was something I'd been mulling over in the pool. "It was awful. There was nothing I could do. But it was totally my fault."

I'd shaken each firefly out onto the ground cloth next to my sleeping bag, to be sure. They weighed nothing, and lay there, their little legs curls, wings permanently closed. I scooped them up and scattered them outside the tent in the grass.

Harriet had continued to listen to this story without interrupting, which I interpreted to mean she sympathized. Until I finished, and her first comment was: "Fireflies are not flies, of course. They're beetles. True flies have one set of wings, whereas beetles have two—" She stopped, as if sensing it might be odd to say *whereas* out loud to another kid. "Um—*dozens* of fireflies appear in your yard? And what kind of party did you *want* to have, if not that?"

I thought: my mom, my dad, Mike, Josh, Aunt Ruthie, and Guy singing *Happy birthday to you*. The seven of us eating cake, and boxes with bows on the couch in the living room, and sun shining through the windows.

". . . but I do like my birth *date*," added Harriet, who was still going on. "In fact, I *love* my birth date. I was born on Pi Day."

"Pie Day?" Harriet had a way of inspiring my curiosity and annoying me at the same time. What did she mean, or was this her roundabout way of getting ready to make fun of my firefly cake, after all?

"The Greek letter. The mathematical symbol. March fourteenth is my birthday, and pi the number is three point one four, you know?"

Except for swimming times, which I calculated all summer long, math always seemed to slip into a sealed folder in my brain after the last bell rang on the last day of school. It did bother me a little that she changed the subject. But I mentally un-shut that folder for Harriet and said out loud to prove I knew: "Pi equals the ratio of the circumference of a circle to its diameter."

"Right, and of course the cool thing about pi is that it's an infinite number." This Harriet demonstrated by reciting a long line of the endless digits of pi so fast, the individual numbers blurred and you had to take it for granted they were correct.

I thought: I do like this girl, I do. She *was* a little weird. However, people could argue that during these last few months, I myself had turned rather weird. For example, I'd pretended a jar of fourteen fireflies was some kind of birthday cake. Now I saw what might be an extra price of my family's trouble and staying away from my old friends: if I wanted new ones, I might be stuck choosing from oddballs.

And yet, I couldn't quite bring myself to care. There was something amusing and likeable about a person who bothered to memorize the first three hundred digits of an endless number.

"Isn't it exceedingly peculiar," she said, "not to mention lazy, that people round off pi to three point one four in lots of math problems?"

"What's your point?" I asked.

"One four!" She laughed as if we'd shared a funny joke.

"No, really. What's so peculiar about it? You have to shorten it some way. People can't take days just to *write* math problems out."

"Well, think about it," she said. "Shouldn't there be a huge difference between infinity and any number that has a definite end? Isn't it interesting that the real difference between an infinite number like pi and a finite one like three point one four turns out to be a very tiny decimal? An infinitesimal decimal, to be as exact as possible about that inexactness. So then, couldn't you say that the difference between something and nothing is the same? Like my drama teacher in Minnesota said, the closest thing to laughter is crying. Like this—"

Before I could answer, Harriet cackled at the top of her lungs. Talk about awkward. The other swimmers from the team in the snack bar, and the adults, all turned to look.

"Uh, Harriet?" I said, but even as I started to mumble, "Not so loud," her semicircular smile flattened and turned down, and little by little her laugh changed into a sob. It was a smooth transition, and soon she was bawling. Just as everybody had quit looking at her, they turned to stare again. On and on Harriet cried. Then she stopped suddenly and laughed. People seemed to get the idea this was some kind of joke and went back to ignoring us.

"Very impressive," I said.

"But you see what I mean? A teeny tiny difference or a big one?" Harriet said, like she'd enjoyed her performance.

"You made a gradual change from laughing to crying. Not every opposite is the same," I said. "The difference between hot and cold is big."

"Are you sure? Where's the point that you call *hot,* and where is the point that you call *cold*?" she asked. "When does hot switch to cold?"

"Between hot and cold you have warm and lukewarm and cool."

"Exactly! And the place you cross from hot to warm—it's a tiny one, right?"

What a friend thinks is important is not necessarily always what you think is important. Sometimes it's okay to simply nod along, I told myself. I was not in the mood to continue this conversation, so I did just that. Then Harriet got a text from Lydia, who was waiting for her in the parking lot, and I rode my bike home.

But I found myself thinking about what Harriet had said, and I had to admit there was some truth to it. What was the point at which my parents had gone from loving each other to not loving—was that a teeny tiny change, too? If so, why didn't they just decide to stay in the same house? What had made the difference between them deciding we could all be a family of five, and my dad living someplace else?

6
BALL GAMES

AT HOME I cooked macaroni and cheese for dinner and took a plate upstairs to Mom with her prescription.

"Oh, good. Thanks for picking that up." She smiled at the orange medicine bottle I set on her nightstand.

"You're welcome. I hope it's hot enough," I added, as I passed her the food, a fork, and a napkin. I had a sudden desire to ask Mom what the difference between hot and cold even was really.

"That's the one that's working," she said in a cheery voice, about the medicine. "*Mmm-mmm.* What would we do without our boxes of Kraft? Thank you, Alice, it's delicious."

She could walk well with her cane and had started getting some of her own meals. But whenever I cooked something in the kitchen, I made plenty for both of us.

"They're almost the same color," I pointed out, meaning the pasta and the pill bottle, and was happy when she let out a sharp bark of a laugh.

"Maybe the noodles will have the same effect!" She raised a forkful.

Since Dad left, she and I had been checking in with each other once or twice a day. Not at any set time, and I hadn't been coming in the house much. That's why I doubted she'd miss me when I babysat. But I had to make sure.

"Mom, remember, tomorrow I'm babysitting next door?" I said. "I won't be bringing breakfast since I'm going straight from the pool."

I was out of money. I'd spent Mom's birthday gift at the snack bar. And to avoid bothering her and Dad, I'd used up my savings to pay the Sharks participation fee. Babysitting tomorrow morning meant curly fries tomorrow afternoon.

"How many kids again?" she asked. "How old?"

"Eighteen months and four, but I'll only have the toddler," I reminded her for the millionth time.

"One baby! That's nothing for you, is it?" She chuckled. "They know they're getting a *twin* diaper-changer?"

I'd told Joanna Phoebe about Mike and Josh. "Yep."

"It looks nice out." Mom pointed her fork at her window, high in the wall facing the Phoebes' side yard. The visible sky was cloudless. Sunset had barely edged its tint in. "When I finish, I'm going to get some exercise and walk around the block before it gets dark."

Her mood seemed so up, I wondered if, with a week or two more of those pills, she might even be ready to have Dad back. For months she'd been trying out different medications, which I knew because it was usually my job to bring them home from the pharmacy. Could it be only a wrong medicine that had made the teeny tiny difference between Dad living here and Mom telling him to go?

In the basement there were flattened cardboard boxes left over from his move. What if I cut them into the shapes of knights' armor, taped the pieces together, and drew details on with Magic Marker? On another sunny evening in a few weeks, I could tie my armor to the center pole and invite both my parents to meet me in the tent. I imagined them recognizing the scene: Mom saying, "Thank you, Alice," the way she had just now; Dad chuckling, "Well, that falls into the category of Déjà Vu All Over Again." I'd never have to confront Dad. We'd go inside and my parents would each swing one of the twins into the air and I'd make mac and cheese for the five of us. Then, like *The Magic Flute*, we'd all live happily ever after.

The next morning, Joanna Phoebe led me past bare white walls through rooms that smelled like new paint instead of chicken broth and saltines. Our houses were copies of each other. Except Mr. Salgado, the old neighbor, had added a big kitchen-and-family room on the back, an open space separated by a countertop island whose picture windows offered a better view of my tent than I would have liked.

In the middle of the carpet stood Timmy, holding a blue basketball twice as big as his head. Owen, the sushi-shirt boy from the other night, sat at a round table in the kitchen part of the room with homework stuff spread out.

"My ball," Timmy announced to me, as if it was one of the more important facts on the planet.

"Hi, Timmy, nice to see you," I said. "That *is* a big ball." The easy money I was about to earn, by playing with cute Timmy, put me in a good mood, and so did seeing Owen. I AM SUSHI, YOU ARE SUSHI was, strangely, one of the few things that had seemed normal on that weird night.

He had on a boring navy polo now. But I noticed something that reminded me of the other shirt: Owen's nose, chin, and the corners of his eyes were all pointy, like they'd been cut with precision. Like little pieces of sushi, always cut precise. Maybe he really *was* sushi, though I sure wasn't. I wondered why he wasn't the helper for Timmy, and where Piper was.

"Owen, I think it will be quieter for you upstairs," Joanna warned him, but kindly. "I put a basket of your clean laundry on the bed for you to put away, too."

She winked at him about the chore, and he shot me a quick "Hey," eyebrows raised, as he got up to leave, sort of suggesting we might all be better off anyway with him out of the room. My stomach jumped with surprise, so I didn't do any eyebrows or looks back to him.

"Blue ball!" Timmy said to me.

I turned to him. "Let's see you make a basket," I said, and Joanna nodded and dragged their orange plastic hoop from the corner to the center of the family room carpet.

The only furniture was a gray couch set to face the corner shelves where Mr. Salgado used to keep golf trophies and a big television. We'd come over every year to watch the Super Bowl. A smaller screen sat there now, alone.

"I'll be in the garage, you two," said Joanna. "Thanks, Alice." And she left.

Timmy swished. I caught his ball and tossed it back. Ten swishes later I faked a shot at the last second, which Timmy found hilarious.

"My ball! My ball!" He giggled and protested.

I passed it to him under my leg, and he declared, "My ball!" reclaimed it, and immediately swished.

I zigzag-stomped across the carpet to return that one, he swished, and I caught the ball before it bounced, turned my back and popped it to him over my head. He thought this was so funny, we had to stop for a second. I was laughing too. I hadn't laughed so hard in probably months.

New game: I picked up a stuffed sea otter from the kitchen floor and asked, "Is this your ball?" We crawled around, both of us shaking with our silliness, me asking if every toy and kitchen utensil was his ball, and Timmy, holding it out, would say, "No! This my ball!" I was starting to appreciate being next door in a house where fun still lived, when we heard the front door open.

Mr. Phoebe walked in with Piper over his shoulder, faced away from us. "Hi sport," he said to Timmy, and dipped his head at me. "I forgot you'd be here."

Joanna came in and kissed Piper, kissed her husband's cheek, and smoothed Piper's hair. Timmy watched this solemnly. I felt bad for him, not getting kisses, and swept him up. "Your ball!" I whispered in his ear, and he made a cute baby giggle.

"How did it go?" Joanna asked.

Frowning deeper, Mr. Phoebe shook his head. "Has Owen finished his math?"

"I don't know, sweetheart. He *has* been working."

Mr. Phoebe started up the staircase. Piper's ringlets bounced like curling ribbons, and she stared back blankly. I waved but she appeared not to see.

"Never mind staying until Timmy's nap," said Joanna quickly, suddenly tenser, and to my surprise she held out money for two hours of babysitting.

"That's way too much." I'd been there less than half of one.

"Oh, please let me." She had this funny laugh with her whole body, like a scarecrow shaking on a pole. Maybe she realized how ridiculous the amount was, since she'd already insisted on paying me twice the going rate for babysitters in Cherrywood. I let her fold my hand around the bills, uneasy and uncomfortable for both of us.

On Wednesday, an hour before I was supposed to go to the Phoebes', I decided to cook breakfast.

"Scrambled eggs with bacon bits!" Mom's face lit up as I positioned the bed tray. "Thank you, Alice. And this coffee is nice and hot! You're my savior."

If only. "Would you like me to open the blinds? It's sunny. Or heat the back pad?"

I was determined to do whatever I could to keep her smiley phase going.

"Yes to both. Now tell me, I forget their names again, how were the next-doors?"

"Timmy's easy," I said. "I'm going there again in a few minutes."

"Two days in a row?" She looked confused. "You didn't tell me that."

"I did, Mom." I kept my voice patient. "It's a tryout this week, remember, for a regular job, being a mother's helper." I crossed in front of her bed to raise the blinds.

"Alice." She said my name like I'd done something wrong. "If you've got so much extra time, you could be helping your aunt. She wanted you to work at her camp."

The county camp where Aunt Ruthie ran the art room was the cheapest summer daycare in our area. Mike, Josh, and Guy were campers there. I'd turned down Aunt Ruthie's invitation to be her assistant, for reasons I'd gone over with Mom a few times already. Camp started in the middle of morning practice, for one thing, and I wasn't confident I could get from there to the pool in time for afternoon practice—there was only one bus, if for some reason Aunt Ruthie couldn't drive me, and it took forty-five minutes. Plus, you had to be fifteen to get paid to work there.

"Say something, please," demanded Mom.

"If I did, I couldn't swim," I answered simply. "And Mrs. Phoebe is paying me."

Mom set the coffee mug on the tray and ignored her eggs. "Yet another thing that's your father's fault, letting you stay here to swim, with this big gap in your day."

"Babysitting is good experience," I argued, "plus I like being able to walk to the pool."

"And how long are you planning to camp in the yard? Ruth and your father say I should let you do that, too," she continued, as if the pair of them were idiots. This conversation was starting to slide into the category of Everything She Could Think of That Was Making Her Unhappy Right Now.

"How long are you planning to stay in bed and keep Dad away from home?" I burst back. My mouth was sometimes quicker than my brain these days.

"Alice, that's not what we're discussing," she said. "If you won't go to your aunt's, at least sleep in your room and take down that eyesore in the backyard. Why they insist on indulging your stubbornness baffles me."

Her voice reminded me of the notched knife I'd set on her tray. She didn't need a knife for scrambled eggs and toast, but I thought the tray had looked nicer with a complete place setting. I wished, now, I'd skipped making breakfast.

Me and my plan to earn money were two little dominoes standing in the path of her dropping mood. I threw a glance at the orange bottle on her nightstand. It had been dumb to put any faith in that.

"If you move to your aunt's," she said, "you can help her out instead of strangers next door. I think you're being inconsiderate of Ruth."

"You're being inconsiderate of our whole family!" I returned fast, like when you hit a ball hard in ping-pong to win a point. "Do you ever think about *why* Mike and Josh are at Aunt Ruthie's?"

"It's my fault I was injured in a car accident?" she replied, like I'd said something dumb. The accident had been her fault, though. I didn't dare bring it up, but she'd driven through a red light; we all knew that.

"It's because of you," I went on, trying not to yell, "because you made Dad go. Now you want me to leave too? Why?" My stupid voice broke a little. She made it seem like thanking me was all a lie, and she didn't care about my help. "Well, I'm not moving. Even if you've ruined everything."

"You think *I* ruined everything?" Her shoulders wilted and her face drooped, signals that she was about to cry. Then she did, which was a relief. It was what I was used to.

I felt a strange satisfaction in having my disappointment confirmed. "Dad didn't want to leave, and you made him," I reminded her. I used to feel bad when she cried. But now I just felt icy.

"We need a change," she responded quietly.

"*You* need a change," I said, to her uncombed hair and balls of used Kleenex on the quilt, irritating markers of the hours she spent in bed. "I don't want any except Dad, Mike, and Josh moving home."

She gathered herself up against the pillows and clasped her hands in her lap. "You may be a teenager, but you're still a child. This is between your father and me. Things have been bad for many years, which we tried not to show you. I think we succeeded. Since last fall, well, I've told you before: in the hospital, when I needed him most, he got *angry* at me for being sick. Your father could not accept the fact I was *injured* and couldn't be my regular self. I'm sorry that his leaving the house has to cause you pain. For me, he left a long time ago."

A lot of that was so vague, and what I did understand, I didn't believe. Not for one fraction of one second, not for the tiniest fraction anyone could measure.

"In a year," she added, "things in our family will be better than they ever were."

"Nothing you say is true." I shook my head.

"What in heaven's name is *happening*?" Mom called out suddenly to the ceiling in this pretend-dramatic way she had, another thing I couldn't stand. She raised her palms as if she were speaking to an imaginary person. "Oh God, my husband, my daughter—does everybody hate me?"

Code Mud.

The cardboard armor I'd taped together in my head? Fallen to pieces. That scene in the tent? Not happening. In real life, the life where there were no magic flutes, your mom had a good day, said some medicine was working, and the next day she went right back to all the stupid depressing stuff she'd been saying for months. For once, I felt no urge to reassure her. What was the point? "Mom, Mrs. Phoebe's waiting for me. I have to go."

She said no more and didn't try to keep me.

It was a relief to go babysit. Shutting the door on our house was like taking a deep breath. I was disappointed to learn that the mysterious Owen had left town, though. Joanna said he usually spent the whole summer with them. "Due to our move, we lined up stays at the other relatives' this year—but do you play tennis, Alice?" She wanted him to meet other teenage players when he returned. "We hear there are some good courts at the nearby pool."

No I didn't, but I told her Noah Gaines, down the street, had a Cherrywood High Varsity Tennis Team sign in his front yard.

Lined up stays at other relatives'? What did that mean?

Joanna took Piper and a box of farm animals to play in the living room. Timmy swished five baskets before Piper dashed back in, knocked the hoop onto the carpet, grabbed the ball out of his hands, and threw it at the couch. Timmy plopped on his bottom on the floor, wailing.

"Piper, that's BAD!" The anger in my voice surprised me. I thought I'd left the Mom argument behind at home, but here it was ripping through. Timmy's crying paused; he looked afraid. For once, I was glad Piper couldn't hear me.

She picked up the ball, which I pried from her hands and gave to Timmy. Immediately, she started banging her head on the nearest wall. *Mrum, mrum mrum*—the vibrations explained why there was nothing hanging on the Phoebes' empty walls. I rushed in, wishing I had a towel to grab her burrito-style. Like a squirrel she ducked and swiveled and hit another spot before I could stop her—*mrum mrum mrum*.

"Oh, angel." I hadn't heard Joanna return to the room and felt my face flush. Without a word, she circled her arms around her daughter and stroked her shiny hair. Piper finally grew still, Timmy sucked his thumb on the couch, and I waited to be fired. No one spoke. Piper and Joanna started to play with cutouts on a felt board.

I couldn't take the silence. "I'm really sorry."

"Don't worry about it, Alice," Joanna said, to my relief. In her voice there was kindness. "It comes with the territory."

Piper moved from the board to a crate of wooden alphabet blocks as if nothing had happened, examining the six sides of each cube and placing them in a line.

By now I considered myself something of an expert on the subject of when mothers were about to cry, and—in three, two, one—slow, silent tears slipped down Joanna's cheek. "Eric and I . . . used to be proud of her . . . vocabulary." Her words fell apart like crumbs. "It's as though . . . she never learned and . . . never will."

If this had been Mom, I would have felt annoyed, but I was sorry for Joanna. Maybe because she was more sad for Piper than sorry for herself. "So she used to talk?" I was surprised.

"It started when Timmy was born," Joanna said. "If you asked a question, Piper wouldn't always answer. We thought it was a reaction to having a sibling, a stage that would pass. I didn't pay a lot of attention until she started refusing to speak. Soon if she wanted something, she just pointed. Her only word was *Mama*. Now she doesn't even say *Mama*." Joanna's voice broke again. "I knew it wasn't stubbornness. She was waking up with terrible tantrums, even though she'd always been a great sleeper, then she stopped answering when we called her name. Sorry Alice, I don't know why I'm telling you this."

I couldn't think of anything to say myself. So I went and hugged Joanna, and Timmy hugged me, and she hugged Timmy, while Piper kept on setting blocks in a row.

"We tried six doctors, each had a different explanation," Joanna said. Then Mr. Phoebe was offered his new job, and they decided to hold off on more testing until after their move. They'd found a specialist here to consult, she added, but the earliest appointment they could get was in September.

"Yesterday Eric insisted on repeating the hearing tests. If they'd said her hearing is impaired, that would explain a few things." Joanna wiped her cheeks. "It isn't, according to the tests. But she doesn't hear us. All I want is for Piper to be a normal girl, like she used to. She used to be brilliant. I don't understand how that changes."

"I wish I could help you," I told her. I felt terrible for Joanna. Little did she know I was an expert on unexpected changes.

Joanna, her eyes extra bright with tears, looked up, almost like she'd forgotten she was talking to me. "Well,

I guess you've heard enough about the Phoebe family for one day," she said. "Time for your nap, little guy."

"Mommy reads a book!" Timmy insisted, as Joanna lifted him to her hip.

"You go on home," she told me. "I'm sure you have things to do." With her free hand she switched on the TV. "Piper can be by herself for a few minutes. The back door is locked!"

But Piper had started handing me her blocks. I was placing them for her in the row. Seeing this, Joanna clicked her tongue. "On second thought, if you can stay, that's probably healthier than TV." She turned it off. "Holler the moment you need me."

As soon as they left the room, Piper grabbed Timmy's blue ball, threw it against the wall, and watched it bounce on the carpet.

I tapped her arm, sat down cross-legged, and motioned I was going to roll the ball to her. She seemed to understand, because she sat. But instead of reaching for it, she just watched the ball bump her leg. It was as if the leg was detached from her body.

My second try had the same result. On the third, though, she picked the ball up and rolled it to an empty spot. As if an invisible friend sat at a third point with us in a triangle. Retrieving balls seemed to be my main job that day. Piper and I repeated the pattern she made up—me rolling to her, her rolling to an invisible friend, me retrieving the ball, three more times. I felt sure she was aiming the ball at the empty place on purpose; she sent each roll along the same angle.

The fourth time, instead of passing it back to her, I rolled the ball to the empty spot. Piper got up and collected it, brought the ball to her place, sat down, and rolled it to me. That was the moment I decided Piper was smart. Whatever was wrong with her, she knew I understood her game, and she was playing back.

I sensed someone behind me and swiveled to find Joanna holding her hands at her mouth in awe.

"Alice! That's amazing! She's never paid attention for that length of time with the doctors we've taken her to. Or anything lately, really."

"How long were you watching?" My cheeks heated with pride. "Piper invented the game, I was just playing along."

"Gosh. I think a fairy godmother must have sent us to Cherrywood and picked out this house next door to you," Joanna said, and I felt my cheeks get redder. Piper, meanwhile, had continued the game, so I turned around to keep up.

"Oh Alice, how about we forget a trial period?" said Joanna. "You've seen how I end up ignoring Timmy when she has those tantrums. I hate that, but maybe we can avoid it with you here. Could you work a few hours, weekdays, until your family goes on vacation? I mean, mostly you'd be with Timmy. But that would give me so much flexibility, while Eric's at work, to have a few minutes with Timmy by himself. Do you think your parents would be okay with it?"

I loved how she'd said "we."

"My mom said she'd love that," I answered.

Joanna gave me a funny look, and I realized I'd made a mistake. "I mean, she already said she'd love it if I had more to do this summer because . . . I'm not in camp." The words came out like I was stumbling. "And . . . we're not taking a vacation, and . . ." Both those statements were true, I thought, and with this job, I'd have a firm excuse to live where I could walk to the pool. I could earn money for the snack bar. For my phone back! If Mom and Dad could split up our family without asking me if it was okay, I reasoned, then I could do this. "So if you'd like me to, well . . . yes," I said, and I had a sensation like I was a helium balloon, let go to the sky. "I'd love to be here."

7

OWEN

"SWIMMERS, TAKE YOUR MARK." I watched Harriet's fingers wiggle slightly as she stretched her arms in dive position. It was the first heat of Girls 13–14 50-Meter Freestyle at the Wednesday night meet. I had a clear view of her from two lanes over, where I sat in the warm-up chair for the next heat. Her lips were moving. Was she talking to herself? I thought of Mom, pleading to the ceiling. Was Harriet Barclay—who used graphs and numbers to prove her backstroke theories—praying?

EHHH—the start machine bleated like an irritated sheep. Its light flashed and parent timers clicked their watches. The six swimmers dove.

Harriet flip-turned decently at the opposite end but finished last; a parent showed her a stopwatch as she climbed out. Harriet looked happy anyway. She must have dropped her time.

A waving hand caught my eye: Dad, chatting with other team parents at the far end of the pool. My heart pounded an extra-large beat. I'd started to doubt he'd show up, even though he'd promised. We were on Event 10.

When the meet ended, I would tell him my idea, for him to move home. Mike, Josh, and I had gotten used to him living in the basement. The house was his, too, after all.

"Alice! Out of the chair!" said Coach B.

Racing was the opposite of practice—no time to think. All that was in my head was getting through the water and not messing up my turns.

EHHH.

I touched third, pretty good considering it was my first dual meet race of the summer. No chance for a ribbon, though: the heat after mine was the fastest. From down the pool, Dad gave me a thumbs-up.

I watched the final heat to confirm I'd stayed fifth for Sharks girls in my age group. Not good enough to qualify. I expected this, but it was disappointing.

In the crowded Sharks team area, when I went for my towel, the chairs had two kids on each, some three. I squeezed next to Harriet on the end of a chaise lounge to wait to check in to swim my next event.

Fireflies were blinking in the bushes by the fence, which she noticed, too. Harriet said, "I've been thinking about that cake story you told me. Why do dozens of fireflies flash in your yard, while in mine I see maybe two?"

Still embarrassed I'd told her about my firefly "cake," I shrugged and changed the subject. "Before your dive, were you talking? Your lips were moving."

"Oh." It was Harriet's turn to look uncomfortable. "You saw? Once in a while, I recite . . . sort of a poem, for good luck." She hesitated. "Well, that's not true. Not once in a while. Before every race I do it."

"What poem?"

"Did you tell anyone?" She glanced through the dusk at the swimmers and parents on the pool deck and the grass. The starter blared for another race.

"Who would I tell?" Harriet had probably figured out by now I wasn't close friends with other kids on the team. "Coach B?"

She laughed. "Fine, but I exceedingly mean it when I say please do not share this: I recite the first one hundred fifty-five digits of pi as fast as I can."

It was my turn to find out something and be polite enough not to laugh. "That isn't a poem," I said, instead of what I was thinking, which was "That is odd."

"No, it's not." She looked as if she'd prefer to be anywhere other than talking about this. I wondered if Harriet felt obligated to tell me the truth because, with my replenished cash supply, I'd told her about my dad's move yesterday over curly fries.

"Why a hundred fifty-five?" I was curious. "Why not a hundred, or a hundred and two, or a hundred and sixty-seven or a hundred and ninety-three? You told me you know the first three hundred digits."

"I want to be saying the one hundred fifty-fifth digit as the starter is going off," she replied. "I know. It's exceedingly dumb. But hey, every person has their unusual thing." She dared, "You're living in a tent because your parents split up, right?"

In an infinitesimal Harriet-ish fraction of a second, I knew I was either going to get mad or get funny. I threw my towel at her head. "Now I know why people think breaststrokers are weird."

She squirted her water bottle at me and missed. "Sorry!" she said to the little kid in the next chair. He laughed.

"Digits one fifty-three, one fifty-four, and one fifty-five are all 'one,'" Harriet went on. "That's the first time in pi that a digit repeats three times in a row, one-one-one. Isn't that interesting? *And* I think it's cool, *and* I want to come in first. So the real question is, why *wouldn't* I do it?"

She put up her hands to ward off my second towel swipe, and I offered her a Gatorade from my bag. I'd brought two.

That we both secretly said numbers was too weird a coincidence. I decided against telling her about my 28.33 mantra. My habit wasn't only about wanting to win. It also helped me to calm down about my parents, since it kept me from thinking about anything but my record. None of which I felt like explaining to Harriet.

Later that night, I did a surprisingly fast 50-meter backstroke. That is, I was surprised, and Coach B noticed. She tossed me a fuzzy mini-shark key chain, for swimming a personal best. My new time placed me fourth on the team in backstroke for girls in my age group.

"A perfect example of the tried-and-true phrase 'I told you so,'" said Harriet.

When the meet was over, Harriet, who had won the second-place ribbon for breaststroke, introduced me to her parents. Mrs. Barclay looked like a drawing from ancient Egypt. She had the longest, narrowest nose I had ever seen on a human, and straight black hair cut below her ears.

"Alice, how wonderful to meet you, finally!" she said. Her eyes stared into mine like she was on a treasure hunt and whatever she was looking for was a secret. This made me uncomfortable, plus there was the fact I couldn't help staring at her nose.

"Hello," I said, uneasy that I was being both rude and somehow disappointing her.

But she continued, perfectly friendly. "Thank you for being such a *memorable* friend to Harriet. I don't know *what* she would have done at the pool without you. . . . Harriet, why don't you invite Alice for a sleepover? Dear? Meet Harriet's new friend."

Dr. Barclay looked up from his phone and shook my hand. "How do you do? Very solid team," he said. "It's a terrific community." His head was bald and shiny, and he wore narrow rectangular glasses and clothes like what my dad put on when he dressed up, a suit jacket and tie.

"Hi, Alice. Nice backstroke." And like I'd conjured him, there was Dad, in typical swim meet jeans and flip-flops. Before I could decide—do I say, *This is my father, who lives in College Park,* or simply, *This is my dad*—he extended his right hand to Harriet's mom. "Sam Allyn."

No mention that he'd never heard of Harriet. I wondered if she'd told her parents about mine.

Hundreds of people from the two teams were packing up and making their way to the exit through the pool house to the parking lot. Harriet and I walked ahead of our parents as they chatted.

"She likes you," Harriet muttered to me. "'Memorable' is how you know."

". . . and Jim got offered this truly memorable opportunity at the National Institutes of Health," Mrs. Barclay was saying. "We just couldn't say no, and here we are."

"Leaving Minnesota was memorable," Harriet said to me, "because it wrecked my life."

Our parents caught up before I could ask what she meant. It was hard to see how Harriet had a wrecked life, living with her mom and her dad and her sister together. But I felt sorry if she was unhappy. I wanted Harriet to like Cherrywood.

Dad and I drove to the nearest place for dinner—McDonald's. He ordered coffee and a fish sandwich, his usual, and I had mine, chicken nuggets and chocolate milk. We slid into a minibooth for two and he said, "You swam well tonight."

"Dad, I really didn't." He knew how it worked: the B meets gave kids a chance to swim qualifying times for the far more important A meets on Saturday mornings, when the results counted for the team's standing in the division. Since I was fifth in freestyle and fourth in backstroke, I wanted to remind him, I wasn't in the top three times, so I wouldn't be swimming this Saturday.

"Give yourself a break. Most of those thirteen- and fourteen-year-olds own a year or two of muscles you haven't grown into," he said. Speaking of growing up, I thought, it was time to find something new to order at McDonald's. The nuggets were greasy and cold; the milk was too sweet.

Dad tapped his cup in a little tune. "Triple A, you and I haven't seen much of each other in the last two and a half weeks."

"Why don't you come home to mow the grass or water the vegetables? I've been doing it," I said. "I think the snap peas are dead."

"Thanks for that," he said. "I decided not to worry about the garden this year. We have to let some things go."

Now was the time. "You should move back," I said. "Josh and Mike and I all want that. It's only Mom who doesn't. That's three against one. Our opinions ought to count, and Mom needs help. We all got used to the way it was."

"Oh? Did you actually ask Mike and Josh? *You* may have gotten used to it. *I* certainly didn't." He eyed the coffee. "And I don't think your mother did. The help she needs is not from me."

"I thought you didn't want to move."

He looked up. "No, I didn't. That's right."

"I don't get it, then. Why you left."

"Because your mother wanted me to." He seemed irritated to have to explain.

"Just like that? Because she wants you to, you go?" I was talking to him in a way I never had before. I thought it was only Mom I was mad at, but I was mad now at Dad, too.

"That's not how things work," he said quietly.

"How do they work, then?" I said. "This sucks."

"Alice, don't use that word."

"It's in the dictionary."

"I don't care if it's in the dictionary, it's not polite." His voice softened. "Plus, it's not very interesting. You can be mad in a more interesting way. You can say disappointing, disheartening, sad, bummer. Why are we talking about this?"

"You own half the house, why can't you live in half of it?" I didn't want to argue, but I didn't want him to go.

"Look, Alice, this is one of those things between your mother and me. I felt I had no choice. Your mother felt I had no choice."

"In my opinion, you had a choice," I said. "You still have a choice. If you don't come back, it's because you don't want to."

He crumpled up the sandwich wrapper and his napkin and set them on the plastic tray and glanced out the window at the parking lot, then met my eyes seriously. "I know that may be how it looks to you. But that isn't how things work with adults. You kids know your mom one way and I know her a different way and, frankly, I've been holding things together for a long time. You gotta trust me on this one, sweetie. I've been trying."

"I can cook more," I said, since I thought he meant he was tired of filling in for stuff she'd quit doing. "Next fall, after school, I'll take care of Mike and Josh. Don't give up, Dad."

"Triple A, you've been great," he said. "That isn't what I'm talking about. You kids are doing more than great, you seem happy—that's been my goal. But your mom hasn't—isn't, and I . . ." He broke off and stared again out the window.

In the reflection of us on the glass, we looked like ghosts superimposed on the nighttime of the parking lot. So he was trying to tell me their real life, his and Mom's, wasn't how it appeared. What did that make our family? As much confused as mad, I said, "So you and Mom have been just . . . acting?"

He sighed. "I'm sorry, Alice. That's all I want to say for right now about my choice, as you put it. I don't expect you to understand, which I don't say to make you feel bad, but it's . . . something you'll understand with experience. Just . . . life. Right now I don't want you to understand. My advice is to stay a kid as long as possible." He shook his head.

"Don't you love Mom?" If he answered no, I thought I'd feel as squashed as his fish sandwich paper.

"That's not quite what's at issue here," he said. "I do, but let's just say I'm trying to make the best of our current circumstances, and I hope you will too."

"I only have one thing to say about our current circumstances."

He looked at me.

"This sucks." As soon as we got up from this booth, I thought, our pictures were going to vanish from the glass. It was as if he was saying our family was that. Something I'd seen because I looked at a certain angle, like a reflection on glass. But it didn't really exist.

Under a spotlight lamp in the parking lot, a family with two parents and two kids was getting out of a van.

"In any case," he said, piling his tray on top of mine to clear the table, "Mom tells me you're still sleeping in the backyard."

"Did she tell you she wants to get rid of me, too, like you and Mike and Josh?"

"If you mean Mom thinks you'd have a better summer living with your aunt, yes, she did share that opinion. But what I was going to say," he began again, "was that I don't mind about the tent, as long as you stay in the yard at night and leave the back door unlocked in case you need to get inside quickly."

"I'm living there until you move back home." I waited for his reaction.

"Well." He sighed, as if he'd come to a wall he wasn't going to climb over and realized it was time to change directions. "If you're ready to go, I'll drop you off."

A strong feeling came over me, that I did not want him to drive to our house, stop the car, let me out, and drive away to sleep someplace else. "Please take me to the pool. I'd like to ride my bike home. And I mean it. I won't live in the house until you do."

"It's dark, Alice," he said. "Last time I looked, there's no light on your bike. Let's load it in my car and I'll give you a ride."

"You're always telling me what to do!" I said, louder than I meant to. He was only worried cars wouldn't see me in the dark, and I was making a big deal out of a small thing, but I couldn't help it. "Just because you think I need a light doesn't mean I definitely need a light. I could ride to our house from the pool blindfolded. And how do you know I won't end up walking the bike? I want it for tomorrow morning so I can ride to practice."

"Okay, okay—just be careful." He sounded tired of me.

Dad waited in his car at the pool parking lot while I unlocked the bike. Then he waved, I lifted a hand back, and we headed off in opposite directions.

Raising a breeze as I rode home raised my hopes. There's something about pointing the handlebars, pushing the pedals, squeezing the brakes, being in charge. You get a result that you direct. You're making your own way happen. When a set of headlights flashed by, I wondered if they were his, checking on me. Or maybe Dad had changed his mind and was driving home? But it was a station wagon, and our house was dark.

Next door, in the upstairs window that was Piper's room, a single light shone. As I slowed to a stop at my driveway, I noticed a person sitting on the front steps in the dark: Owen.

There was no way he wouldn't see me. The houses were close together with side-by-side driveways separated by a thin strip of grass. "Hey," I said, because it seemed awkward to be so near without saying hello, when we were the only two people around.

"Oh hey, how's it going."

"Piper's up late," I said, pointing at her light.

"Dunno." He shrugged. "I've been out here on the phone."

"Joanna told me you were gone," I said.

"They like to keep me busy," he agreed. "Tomorrow, it's off I go, camping with the grandparents."

"Already? Where do you live the rest of the year, with your mom, I mean?"

"Denver," he said.

"Did your dad used to live there, too?"

"No. You ask a lot of questions," he added, as if I'd amused him.

"Sorry," I said.

"Don't be. I'll ask you one: What's up with the party tent?"

"I sleep there," I said, remembering the view from their family room windows. It gave me the creeps to think Owen might have been watching.

"And not in your house, because . . ." He paused, as if I were supposed to fill in a blank.

"I feel like it," I said, getting brave, because if he'd been looking, maybe he was curious about me. "I got kind of upset when my dad moved out a couple of weeks ago, so I . . . moved there."

"Ah! My turn to say sorry." He sounded surprised.

"Weren't you upset when your parents got divorced?"

"No, because they didn't. They were never married. They dated maybe a day."

"Oh," I said, embarrassed I'd asked.

Owen laughed. "I'm an accident my mom decided to have. I've always lived with her or my other grandparents and with my dad during the summer. Probably a big mistake on her part, given what it did to her life."

"She told you that?"

"Why not? My mom is a very honest person. When I was five and bugged her about why I flew on airplanes to visit my dad when most kids had one at home or didn't have one or whatever, she gave me a version of the story."

"Sorry I asked," I said.

"Doesn't bother me," Owen said. "The bike sleeps in the tent, too?"

"Yes, it makes things easier." I'd been keeping my bike in the tent at night to keep from having to go in and out of the garage. The more I could minimize noise, the less my chances of waking up Mom. My freedom was at stake. "Well, good night."

"See you," he answered, and I walked quickly down the side path, listening to the wheels click as they turned over the flagstones.

The light had gone off in Piper's window. I parked the bike in the tent and lay outside on the grass, which felt pricklier at night than during the day. It was too late to see a first star to make a wish on, about Mom and Dad. I figured no one could see me in the dark, even from the Phoebes' back deck, and I'd hear their sliding door if it opened. The yard belonged to the crickets, ants, fireflies, mosquitoes, and me.

I reviewed my weeks in the tent: I'd never walked outside it in my underwear; didn't talk to myself. Couldn't think of anything I'd done in the yard that was too stupid-looking.

A cicada swished close by; another car passed on the street. Overhead, between the treetops, little brown bats fluttered in crooked lines, as fast as butter-flies. I imagined that if I could grab a bat out of the air, I would find myself clutching a tiny hunchbacked witch, with webbed arms, squirming to remount her broom-stick. I could picture the choir of crickets in green-and-cream-colored robes, hidden in the grass. The secret life of my backyard at night, that I liked to make up, never scared me.

"I can't stand this. You've got to do it!" From next door, Mr. Phoebe did, though, as his shouts sliced the dark air.

"Oh, please don't start!" Joanna's words were prick-lier than the grass.

A window *thunk*ed shut next door.

I was used to adults arguing—but in the tones of my parents' voices. I liked Joanna, and I didn't like Mr. Phoebe. But I didn't want him to be the next father to move away. How could he get so mad when she had to take care of such a hard child as Piper, plus Timmy, plus Mr. Phoebe was the one who already had a son and Joanna helped take care of him too, plus she had moved to Cherrywood for *his* job. I didn't see what he could possibly have to be mad at her about.

The angry sounds tumbled on, muffled by windows. I was thankful it was impossible to understand much else. But I didn't move. I wanted to know the argument had ended, and there was no place I felt like sleeping. Not on the grass or in the tent or at the pool. Not at Aunt Ruthie's or my dad's apartment or in the house, where I'd probably be lying awake listening for my mother starting to cry.

Things could be worse, of course. Owen's life sounded worse, even if he didn't sound like he minded. I thought: if this was what it was going to be like, being a kid as long as possible, well, it sucked.

8
HARRIET'S HOUSE

"HAS MY FASHION-FORWARD female parent made an incorrect gear purchase?" Harriet sounded amused by this possibility.

Like her, I'd arrived at Cherrywood Pool in time for 7:30 a.m. warm-ups for the first Saturday A meet. I'd worn my racing suit, even though I wasn't scheduled to swim. Each team gets a few scratch entries for no-shows. No luck. Every Girls 13–14 Shark swimmer showed.

"She got it right," I said. "That's this year's, mine's old."

My team clothes were a little small. I didn't care. They were wearable, and I liked the design better, with SHARKS across the back.

"You'll be swimming next Saturday, by my calculations," Harriet said. "Backstroke!"

"Whatever," I said. It was not fun to get hopeful and then discover hopefulness was a mistake. "Where's your family sitting?" I asked.

"Lydia deposited me," Harriet said. "My parents don't usually come. Ma-*mahhh* wanted Pa-*pahhh* to see the pool, and he happened to be free only last Wednesday. He travels exceedingly. He most likely won't be at any more meets."

She plopped her bag by my feet, removed her plaid flannel pants and brand-new team hoodie with black sharks leaping over CHERRYWOOD in red letters on the front, and dove in the water to do laps with the other kids.

It was a typical crowded dual meet. Parents, officials, team siblings, and people from the visiting team crossed the deck back and forth in front of my chair. The referee, the starter, and the head timer gathered the parent volunteers, three for each lane, to practice timing a race with stopwatches.

Coach B, leaving the clubhouse, saw me.

"Alice! Paige is going to be late," she said. Paige was the assistant head coach. "Could you help with the Eight-and-Unders?"

She passed me a blue pen and winked. "Thanks, sport." It was a tradition to write event numbers and lane numbers on the little kids' hands, so they remembered their races. We had a dozen kids swimming in the youngest age group that day. When I finished, I had to make sure they got to the right benches and lane chairs on time. But even our twelve most junior swimmers were nothing compared to twin babies Mike and Josh after naptime.

A speedy meet runs a little over two hours. The average is three for the fifty events, always swum in the same order. Breaststroke is in the second half. At the ten-minute break midway through, I went and found Harriet.

She was off by herself, reading the heat sheet taped to the wall below the record board. She stood in front of it, nipping her fingernails with her teeth.

"You're seeded second," I said. Only the star Sting-ray breaststroker had a faster time.

"That's her." Harriet pointed out her competition, a girl almost six feet tall, who was near us with two of her teammates. "My mother assumes I can be dropped off at any regulation-size, cement-lined cavity of chem-ically treated water," Harriet said, turning back to the heat sheet, "and so long as she's procured the correct clothing, I'll be gung ho to swim."

Along with her new Sharks team suit, I noticed, Harriet wore her loon scrunchies from the day we met.

"Why does she think clothing has anything to do with it?" I asked. When Harriet didn't answer I figured she had pre-race jitters, so I tried a Harriet-type distraction.

"Isn't it cool," I said, "how water holds you up *and* also slips through your fingers, like it's nothing?"

"Huh?" Harriet said, as if I was cuckoo. I guessed it wasn't all that interesting an observation, but I kept on.

"You know," I explained, "how raindrops have shapes as they fall from the sky? But they soak into the earth and disappear?"

"Unless there's a flood," Harriet corrected me, "or it's virga."

"Virgo?"

"*Ver-guh*," she repeated. "Rain or snow that falls so high up in the atmosphere, it evaporates before it can hit the ground."

"Right." My random facts were not competitive with Harriet's.

"If you drive around Arizona in a summer thunder-storm, you can see showers pouring down. But the earth underneath is dry."

"Alice!" called Coach B. "Can you please tell your group it's time for cheers?"

"Cheers are dumb," Harriet said, and pulled a book out of her bag.

I rounded up all our six-, seven-, and eight-year-old swimmers from their towels, the changing rooms, and the snack bar. Sharks from every age group crouched in a circle around the coach. We whispered: "One, we are the Sharks." Raised our voices some and rose to a squat: "Two, a little bit louder." Came halfway to standing and upped the volume: "Three, I still can't hear you." We shouted, jumping in the air: "Four, more MORE *MORE!*" The team huddled down to start over, and we repeated the whole thing three times, like always. On the last "more" I caught sight of Harriet, eyes on her book, and thought, *yes, okay, cheers are dumb.* But I liked them because they were a part of swim team you could count on. They were a tradition.

I bet I was the only one who noticed Harriet's lips moving before her dive. She and the star Stingray were in the middle lanes. Harriet surfaced a third of the way down the pool after a strong starting pull. Her head bobbed with her quick, flitting strokes, and she managed to keep up until the turn, when I knew it would be all over. The taller swimmer could pull ahead with a good turn.

But something went wrong for the Stingray. Her turn was slow, and in the end the two girls appeared to tie. Harriet—gasping for breath—looked up from the water to ask her time and climbed out grinning. The other Sharks in the race hugged her. The Stingray stood panting at the end of the pool, hands on her hips, staring at the deck. I was in awe of Harriet's determination. She won by one one-hundredth of a second, which helped the Sharks win the meet by six points.

A big advantage of living in the tent was that I was probably the only kid in Cherrywood younger than high-school age whose parents weren't fussing 24/7 about where I was. Cherrywood is your basic helicopter parent neighborhood. But my dad must have convinced my mom, like he said, that it was okay for me to live out back and walk to the pool. On the landline answering machine, he left a voicemail thanking me for continuing to mow the lawn and saying he was going to be in touch, with his new schedule, to make it to another evening meet. But I didn't hear from him after that.

Days started to go by when Mom and I didn't see each other, or we talked only through her bedroom door. She and Dad knew I swam twice a day and could get team carpool rides to the meets away from Cherrywood Pool, and that I babysat next door on weekday mornings. And that pretty much covered it. If I knocked and she said to wait a minute, and I answered I had to leave right then or else be late for swim practice, she'd say, "Okay, great," without asking me to come in. Or I'd call up the stairs, "Going to the pool!" and she'd yell back down through the door, "Have a nice time!"

I spent every day trying to make Harriet's back-stroke predictions come true, and soon stopped feeling like I had to tell anyone where I was going every time I left the house, and nobody seemed to notice, and I was fine.

That week at the Phoebes', I started out playing with Timmy and ended up as babysitter for both kids while Joanna unpacked moving cartons or cleaned the house or researched schools and sign-language specialists for Piper. Mr. Phoebe was always downtown at his office by the time I arrived. Owen, shipped off to his grandparents, had not yet returned.

Piper fell into the category my dad called Expecting the Unexpected. If you expected you didn't know what she'd do next, you could sort of anticipate it. That is, I could never be sure she'd send her ball to the empty spot when we played that game, but I was ready when she did. Her eyes flicked in that direction sometimes, which tipped me off.

One day I got a rhythm going, alternating her game with returning Timmy's basketball, post-swish. Both kids laughed when, twisting between her ball and his, I pretended to be overwhelmed by the fast action. I wished Joanna would come downstairs so she could see and it would make her glad. But of course that game lasted only a minute or so before Piper climbed onto the couch with the shoebox of blocks, turned it upside down, and watched the wood cubes tumble. They clacked as they hit each other.

As an experiment, I held up the box of felt pieces from her picture board and flipped it so they'd fall. Again her eyes followed the contents to the floor. I sensed her waiting a beat—but for what? She lay down on the couch and appeared to stare into space.

"Do you like the blocks because you hear something?" I wondered out loud. "Timmy," I said, "let's spill noisy toys." I swept the blocks into their container.

"Cars," said Timmy. He tipped the toy tub of plastic vehicles, I poured the blocks, and they all hit the floor in an amazing long crash.

But there was no sign Piper heard any of this.

"My ball!" Timmy said, and swished.

"That's right," I told him, feeling disappointed. I'd thought I had a hunch, but it seemed like it was wrong.

Later, while Joanna put Timmy down for his nap, I tried teaching Piper how to wave a giant soap-bubble wand. Outside on the Phoebes' deck, I set a tray of bubble liquid and showed her how to dip and wave the plastic wand loop. But Piper was more interested in the colors swirling on the surface of the bubbles as they wobbled out and away from us into the sunlit air.

That night at the B swim meet I finally qualified to compete in backstroke the following Saturday. It was a relief to make it back into the group that got to race in the A meet, like I always had in past summers. Too bad Harriet had gone away for the week to a sleepover camp. I wished I could hear her *I told you sos* and missed her waving her spreadsheet numbers and celebrating.

The moment she appeared on the Darby Dolphins' pool deck that Saturday—she'd returned in time to swim her breaststroke race—she marched straight up to me, and before I could say, "You were totally right" or even "Hey," she asked, "Can I sleep over at your house tonight to do experiments on fireflies for my science fair project for school?"

"Hi Harriet, nice to see you, too. How was computer camp?" I replied, very slowly, to annoy her. "Guess what—"

She powered her voice over mine: "If you come to my house for lunch after the meet, then we can bring over my equipment to set up in your tent. Lydia's picking me up."

"Sure, okay, Harriet," I said, irritated to be interrupted, though still glad to see her. "But guess what? I. Am. Swimming. Today!" That got her attention. "You were right, backstroke."

She looked as if the science fair had finally moved over in her brain and freed space to remember her prediction. "Excellent!" She grinned, and then she borrowed Paige's heat sheet to enter my new seed time and our teammates' into her phone.

I rounded up the Eight-and-Unders, because Coach B had asked me to help out again during the first half of the meet, before the backstroke races started. She called us over for cheers during the Dolphins' warm-up. Harriet preferred to watch from where she was sitting on her towel. As usual I loved the total silliness of cheers: "Hubcap, hubcap on the ground! We think our team is really good!" That was it. It made no sense. Everyone who said it smiled.

"That was exceedingly imbecilic," criticized Harriet, when I returned to my swim bag to peel off my T-shirt and shorts.

"That's the point, isn't it?" I said, excited to swim. "You know, to break the tension and help you relax."

"To sound like a puerile embarrassment?" she said.

I didn't feel like asking what that meant. "Calm down. It was supposed to be silly." I grabbed my goggles and cap. "C'mon, time for warm-ups."

"You're really swimming!" Harriet's genuine happiness about it seemed to snap her right out of her cheer snobbery.

We splashed up and down, six to a lane, trying not to bump each other, warming our muscles for racing. Being with the Saturday swimmers felt like life before Dad left. I used to be considered good, and the only thing different about this year was that I was on the young end of the new age bracket, instead of the old end of the old one. Carefully, I counted my arm-stroke distance on my back from this pool's flags to the wall. Five, like Cherrywood.

For my backstroke push-off, Harriet gave me legs, which meant she stood with her back to the pool, her feet at the edge, so I could grab her ankles from the water. The rules allowed it, and the other swimmers were starting the same way. I was seeded fifth, which meant I had an outer lane, one of the worst, with the pool edge at my side.

EHHH. I arced backward, dolphin-kicked under-water—concentrating on staying under and keeping my form, arms clasped above my head—surfaced and reached and pulled; pushing water when my elbows went down under the surface, moving forward back-wards, blind to everything but sky. The flags, four more strokes, then a roll to my stomach and then the fifth arm pull to set up the turn. I flipped into the wall, kicked out on my back, and reversed to the finish, where I beat my seed time and two other swim-mers, for fourth place.

I was nowhere near the Sharks record board time for Girls 13–14 backstroke. No, I was not even close to being second on this year's team. Not yet, anyway.

But I'd made a respectable return to A meet territory. And I'd earned two points for the team, two of the ten points we won the meet by.

Harriet's house looked like it belonged to a family on television. Three stories, soft gray wood, black shutters, white trim. The house towered above its neighbors. Bringing Harriet over was going to be embarrassing, even if we stayed in the backyard and never went inside. But I was in a good mood. In my bag was a yellow fourth-place ribbon, and on it hung a new personal-best key ring from Coach B, a purple shark.

"That looks so comfortable," I said, following Harriet across a wide front porch with rocking chairs, a wicker couch, hanging flower baskets, and a swing. It was more furniture than in our living room. There were plenty of thick, oatmeal-colored cushions, and everything looked brand-new.

"My mother is an interior decorator," Harriet said. "Our house has to be 'memorable' for the clients."

She led us down a hallway hung with large, square black-and-white photos of sand dunes. The focus was so near the ripples in the dunes, they hardly looked like sand. They reminded me of the flowers and plant parts my mom used to photograph up close, because you noticed the lines and shapes more than what they started out as, petals and stems. She said that was her goal. Before her car accident, she'd done these nature photos on the side, on weekends, hoping to sell them in a gallery. We had a few hanging in our dining room. I kept myself from saying to Harriet that my mom was a photographer. I wasn't sure if she was anymore.

We passed through a room of all-white furniture, with a glass coffee table holding a silver pitcher of white tulips. It was starting to seem a little lonely, too clean, like nobody lived there. I followed Harriet up a staircase to another staircase to her bedroom, painted tangerine. "I love this color," I said.

"I didn't pick it, and it doesn't look anything like my old room," Harriet said, which I took to mean she didn't agree. Cubbies and drawers were built into the base of her bed, which had been painted to match the walls, with added purple-and-green-checked borders. The closet door stood open, revealing three times the amount of clothing I owned.

"For a nerd you have a lot of dresses," I noted.

"My mother decorates the house *and* us." Harriet turned on her laptop, the only object in the room that fit the Harriet I knew, other than a postcard tacked to the bulletin board.

"That's Tim Berners-Lee," I said, surprised. It wasn't a picture you'd find in any old thirteen-year-old girl's bedroom.

She looked up at me. "Who's the nerd now?"

I explained that my dad, a librarian, had shown me that picture. "He thinks the Dewey Decimal System is about the greatest idea ever thought up by mankind. He's always saying, 'Tim Berners-Lee's invention of the World Wide Web might be more *creative*, but I wonder if he could have conceived it without Melvil Louis Kossuth Dewey going first.'"

Mrs. Barclay appeared in the doorway to ask if she could make us tuna sandwiches. She wore white high-heeled sandals even though she was inside. I couldn't help staring a little at her nose. "Alice, I'm pleased you're here visiting. Cherrywood has been so memorable, and so welcoming. Your Sharks are a lovely team. I hope you won't mind if Harriet practices her oboe while I make you girls lunch."

"*Mother!*" Harriet protested. "I have a friend over. I just swam a meet. It's the weekend!"

Mrs. Barclay smiled patiently. "Only thirty minutes."

"What's Alice supposed to do?"

"I can read," I volunteered. In Harriet's tangerine-colored bookcase I'd spied a copy of *The Hobbit,* which I'd read four times. Might as well start on five.

"That's the kind of friend I like," said Mrs. Barclay.

"Sorry." Harriet closed her door, and I settled with the book on a pile of pink throw pillows. "I wish she'd let me have Saturdays off."

I had never seen or heard an oboe up close. The sound made me think of a green frog hopping between lily pads. In the middle of a scale, Harriet broke off. "Want to see something gross?" She stuffed a strip of purple silk down the tube, the kind a magician pulls out of a hat. "I have to clean out the spit," she said, and laughed when I looked disgusted.

Mrs. Barclay had set out plates of sandwiches, raw veggies, and a pitcher of lemonade on a table in a sunny corner of the kitchen. Everything was a pattern of pale blue and yellow, light-colored wood, and stainless steel. Harriet saw me staring. "Mother calls this Country French." She smirked.

"But everything's so . . . nice here. Why did you say moving wrecked your life?" I asked.

"Are you entirely rationally remotely serious? I had to give up *everything,*" she said. "House, room, streets, school, swim team, oboe teacher, pediatrician, dentist. I very much miss my dentist! All of which were fine, exceedingly more than fine, and I was given no choice."

But your family is the same as it was in Minnesota, I thought.

She took a bite of her sandwich and completely changed the subject, as usual. "Have you heard of cannibal fireflies?"

"I've heard of predator-eats-prey, if that's what you mean." I pointed at her plate. "Sandwich formerly known as a tuna."

"They're called femmes fatales," she said, "female fireflies that can imitate the flash patterns of other fireflies . . ."

I stopped listening, happy to be sitting at this cozy real-wood table. Everything seemed so . . . solid.

". . . basically, sneaky female fools dumb guy into thinking she's a babe of his own kind."

I tuned back in.

"He zooms over and—*chomp*—she munches him down." Harriet took a giant bite of her sandwich. "It's all about survival. There are these chemicals called lucibufagins—"

Finally! A name I recognized. "Fagin is the bad guy . . ."

". . . in *Oliver Twist*," she interrupted back. "I know, I was in the musical in fourth grade. He's irrelevant. *Lucibufagins* are chemicals in firefly blood. They make fireflies taste bad to certain spiders, so they're like protection. The femmes fatales' blood is low on lucibufagins, so they eat males whose blood contains large amounts. The femme fatales want the extra chemicals so they'll taste bad to spiders, too. But, you know." Harriet paused. "Where is the science fair project in that?"

"I have no idea what you're talking about."

She took another bite of her sandwich. "By the way, did I tell you my family doesn't eat red meat? I only eat fish. When I go to college I'm becoming vegan."

You never knew what Harriet would say. These random lectures distracted me from thinking about other stuff, which I appreciated. I hadn't told her much besides that my dad had moved out. It wasn't that I didn't want Harriet to know; it was more that if there was anything else to talk about, I preferred it.

"How do you know so much about fireflies all of a sudden?" I said.

"That would be thanks to Tim Berners-Lee. After lunch, I'll show you the websites."

"The fireflies in my yard all look the same," I said. "How do you tell which ones are the cannibals?"

She shook a piece of sandwich at me like it was a winning raffle ticket. "You. Are. Brilliant. That's our first investigation! Femmes fatales belong to certain species low on lucibufagins. They eat the males from different species, loaded with the stuff. We can identify the species in your yard. That might lead me to a winning project for the Cherrywood Middle School Science Fair."

Why was she so obsessed with this science fair? How did she even know about it, I wondered, and she must have read my mind. "My mother picked this neighborhood because the high school has the most U.S. Science Talent Search Semifinalists in the state," Harriet said, "and it's the only middle school in the county where students are required to participate in a science fair."

"Maybe so," I said, "but most kids wait to start until winter break." And most kids did experiments like mine from last year: New Year's Eve, I planted three tubs of grass and watered them for two weeks with vinegar, coffee, and tea. I guessed a few people did amazing projects that won prizes and got sent to national contests, and maybe those kids did start during the summer. But I had never been friends with them.

"If we find *Photuris* and *Photinus*, two of the most common firefly types in this region, we could even get a female eating a male *on camera*," Harriet said. "Slight problem, in that I don't have a decent camera for night photography."

"My mom might," I found myself saying. "She used to be a professional photographer. Our basement is full of her cameras. I don't know how to see if they work, though. She's never let me touch them, and she hasn't been out of bed since like winter since she pretty much just cries all day."

Why did this stuff slip out when I was around Harriet? I inhaled deeply, hoping to suck in the liquid I could feel seeping from my eyes, and Harriet looked down. Get it together, I told myself. "So slight problem in that I don't really know if her cameras will work either."

"Your mom sounds sort of like my father. Try talking to *him* during the five minutes he's home Saturday or Sunday." Harriet's face was grim. I could tell she wanted to make me feel better, even if her way of doing it half-misunderstood what I said. "One of his three cell phones rings, he tells me just a minute, claims he hates being interrupted, takes the call. Then he interrupts that call to take another one. It could be from any time zone on the planet. He's overseeing scientists working on cures for diseases that kill thousands of people. Everyone says his work is going to change the world."

"He sounds busy," I put in, "but I don't think my mom and your dad have a whole lot in common."

"However, I *have* figured out how to get his undivided attention," she went on, ignoring my words.

"When I play the oboe, he sits and listens and doesn't answer his phones."

If only I could solve my problems that easily, I thought.

"I can take my oboe to your house," Harriet continued, drawing herself up like she was performing on a stage. "You'll usher me into your mother's room." She flourished her arm, like a king's courtier. "Introduce me. Without a word, I bow"—she bowed—"and play my Mozart concerto, which is so startling that afterwards, we ask if she owns a camera with a night mode!"

Harriet was enjoying herself, and I knew she didn't know how to help me, but she at least, unlike most other people around, wanted to. I liked her for that, and in general, and even when I didn't get her. And there was a lot about a lot these days that I didn't get. I couldn't help it, I burst out laughing.

9

JUMBO SHRIMP

EACH OF US wheeled two carry-on-size suitcases down the sidewalk from her house to my tent. The bags twirled when they bumped pebbles and dipped over cracks in the pavement, like ladies dancing a tango. It turned into a game, keeping them upright, in straight lines, the entire way.

It was fun until we reached my backyard. Her house compared to here? In one of those Harriet-fractions of a second, my mood sank like a nickel in a pool. Our worn-out picnic table on the chipped concrete patio; the tent that was too weird for camping—it was embarrassing to think of it next to Harriet's tangerine room and French Country tuna.

But: "You get to *live here*?" she screeched, in a voice that fell into the category of The Grass Is Always Greener. I couldn't help thinking how the grass in Harriet's yard literally *was* greener, plus it was mowed.

"There ought to be a page in a tunic and tights announcing us with a trumpet fanfare!" she added, as we lifted her suitcases across the canvas threshold. "This is great!"

Most of the space was empty, filled only with warm golden light from the afternoon sun. I liked living bunched up in one cozy corner, to the right of the front door. She was right, it was great, and I felt better. Harriet laid all four bags on their sides, and I helped her unpack.

Flashlights, notepads, graph paper, pencils, a thermometer, a ruler, empty glass jars, a stack of clear plastic deli containers and lids, cheesecloth, a butterfly net, a roll of metal screening for a window, a microscope, fuzzy pipe cleaners, a roll of paper towels, a kitchen funnel, two pairs of scissors, rubber bands, extra flashlight batteries, six library books, collapsible milk crates, and a gooseneck electric desk lamp.

"Ah," I said, amused. "Where exactly are you planning to plug that in?"

She waved her hand. "Have you noticed what time fireflies start flashing in your yard?"

I hadn't and told her so, and we unfolded and stacked the milk crates to create a row of shelves. I set my own newest firefly container there, a coffee can with a soft lid I'd poked holes in with a fork. "I add a stick, fresh grass, and leaves for them to eat," I said.

"Adult fireflies don't require food," Harriet said. What sounded like her snapping at me was just her way of talking, of teaching things or telling me stuff, I was learning, so I didn't feel stupid now. "A little fruit nectar, maybe. An apple slice or even a wet paper towel is enough. Speaking of which, I'm thirsty. Let's get some water or something."

I'd had us come through the side yard expressly to steer clear of the house. But I realized I hadn't fully thought through her plan to experiment versus mine to keep us outside. At some point, we'd need to use the bathroom. So we went in. I didn't see how we could avoid it.

As soon as we entered the kitchen, Mom, who I hadn't talked to since yesterday morning, called down. "Alice? Is that you?"

"Be right there!" I shouted. I opened a cupboard, handed Harriet a glass, and pointed to the icemaker and water dispenser in the refrigerator. "Be right back," I told her, to make clear I was headed upstairs alone.

"Ask about the night camera!" she whispered after me.

Mom was sitting up. She'd opened the blinds; the all-news station was playing on her ancient clock radio. A good sign. When she listened to the news, it was like a crack opening up in the dungeon in her head, to let in light from the outside world. "I was thinking, if you had time, you could make me an omelet. If you don't, I'll go down, I don't mind."

The landline phone rang next to her bed. "Hello?" Mom cupped her hand over the speaking end. "It's Ruth! Hang on a sec. . . . Hi Ruth, hi boys. Alice is here, too."

The more times she repeated, "That sounds nice," to whatever Mike and Josh were saying, the more I worried that Harriet—curious, unpredictable, persistent Harriet—would wander upstairs looking for me. It didn't strike me as impossible that her oboe idea was semiserious. I mentally re-inventoried what had come out of the suitcases. No oboe—as far as I could remember.

Mom had turned our basement bathroom into a darkroom for her giant plant pictures. She worked in it for a few years, until not long before her accident, when she quit taking the plant ones because she'd only managed to sell a couple of prints. The darkroom continued to be off-limits to us kids, though. The rule was, if we played in the basement and needed to use a bathroom, we had to come upstairs.

When Dad moved down there, he packed up her gear so that he could take showers, but I was still nervous about hunting through her stuff. She had all kinds of expensive cameras. The idea of other people touching them was likely to send her off on one of her rants.

I'd have to hear for the hundredth time how terrible it was that my father had broken her old enlarger and had no respect for her things. I was glad to help Harriet with her experiments, but I didn't want to ask about those cameras unless I had to.

"I'll go make your omelet," I said, waving to catch her attention. I wished I could erect an invisible force field on the staircase, to keep her up and Harriet down.

Mom covered the receiver with her hand. "Your aunt would like to speak to you."

Oh no. I didn't feel like I could refuse without upsetting Mom or worrying that I'd hurt Aunt Ruthie's feelings, so I was stuck abandoning Harriet for what was definitely way too long. Alert for the sound of feet climbing stairs, I took the phone.

My aunt wanted to know, how was my babysitting job? I tried to sum it up in a few seconds.

"Why on earth didn't this woman research special-needs childcare in our area before she moved?" exclaimed Aunt Ruthie, who knew something about it from her teacher training. "An autism diagnosis is common enough," she said, "but the outcome can depend on getting help early in the child's life. I hope she isn't waiting too long."

"Aunt Ruthie, can I tell you more about it another time? I'm kind of busy right now."

Of course, Aunt Ruthie said, and she'd stop by soon with Chinese takeout, so we could really catch up.

"I have a friend from swim team over," I said, handing the phone back to Mom. If she heard voices, I didn't want her coming down to investigate.

"Thank goodness I have three healthy children," she was telling Aunt Ruthie while nodding at me as I left the room.

It was so quiet in the kitchen that, until the butter melted in the pan for the omelet, I assumed Harriet had gone outside.

"Where are *these* from?" she called from the dining room.

"Oh, those," I said. "My mom wanted to make photographs look like paintings by the artist Georgia O'Keeffe."

"Huh! Interesting!" Harriet's voice suggested I'd finally said something smart that she hadn't figured out herself, which felt good. If she'd found a subject to occupy her big brain, I had little reason to worry about her following me back upstairs.

"Looks great. Thank you, Alice," Mom said to the one-egg omelet I delivered on her tray.

With that thank you, it was as if she'd twisted the focus on a telescope from fuzzy to clear. For months, when I brought her food or did chores, those were times she smiled—the times she'd say thank you instead of some Code Mud. So maybe the reason I took care of her was to hear thank you. When Mom went negative, I wanted positive. So I'd found ways to get her to speak positive words to me. I couldn't help wondering if there was an oxymoron in this. It only made me feel worse, figuring that out.

Downstairs, Harriet was still standing in front of Mom's pictures. "These remind me of the ones of sand dunes at my house. You should bring your mother over," Harriet said.

"Maybe so," I said, thinking *not,* and we went out to the picnic table.

She removed a small plastic box from her pocket. Inside was a firefly she'd caught, killed, dissected, and pinned, with its various parts labeled. "A dead specimen can teach you how a creature functions when it's alive," she said.

"Killing a thing to understand how it lives," I said. "That's an oxymoron."

"Jumbo shrimp," she said agreeably. "Animal specimens aren't oxymorons. Specimens can be alive."

"I used to think an oxymoron was a person who is a moron who breathes too much," I said. Harriet looked up at me from the display box and laughed. "Until my English teacher, Ms. Neely, started oxymoron contests,"

I continued. "How many pairs of contradictions could we think up in five minutes—*sweet tragedy, terrible joy, weirdly common, horribly wonderful.* Winners got sweet-and-sour gummy worms."

"Does she teach eighth grade too?" Harriet asked. "I'd love to have her next year."

"I thought you hate writing."

"What I hate is when teachers ask you to keep journals of your thoughts. Did she make you?" I shook my head. "Journals are dangerous," Harriet said. "People inevitably find them, read the secrets, and go ballistic. Anyhow." She smiled. "It's the same difference whether I want to take English or not: it's a requirement. There's no choice. To think otherwise is a genuine illusion."

"Ha—original copy!" I said. "Plastic glasses."

She tapped her temple. "If we *do* manage to catch and identify multiple firefly species," she said, "I want to mount them in a bigger box."

"To hang in your *awfully beautiful* bedroom," I teased.

I ran back in to get us a bag of pretzels and cans of lemonade. Maybe half an hour had passed since we came home, but now, for some reason, it no longer bothered me how shabby the house and yard looked compared to Harriet's. The top of the picnic table felt more comfortable than ever. By shifting a little, at an angle, there was room for both of us to sit and see out over the lawn. We put the snacks in the middle, like a campfire. It was the first time since Dad moved that anybody not related to our family had hung out with me there, and the thing I hadn't expected was how bringing a friend to the place where I lived alone most of each day, seemed—well—oddly normal.

10
LIGHT LANGUAGE

"HERE'S A REASON your yard attracts fireflies and mine doesn't!" Harriet pointed her pencil at the wet spot by our back hedge. In spite of a drainage channel Dad had dug and lined with gravel, that part of our lawn always puddled up after rainstorms; my brothers called it "the stream." "Fireflies love moisture," Harriet said.

She was wandering around, sketching a map to help her keep track later of where fireflies appeared most. I watched her progress from the picnic table, between reading a few more pages of my book, until the sound of the Phoebes' sliding deck door caught my ear.

Owen waved hello with his calculator, sat down on the deck steps, and opened his math textbook. Without thinking, I called, "Hey, want some lemonade?"

"Hang on a sec." He stood up again and disappeared into the house. I explained to Harriet who Owen was.

"Good idea. We could use an extra person tonight," she said. "Forsythia, honeysuckle, oak hydrangeas, unidentified bushes, long grasses," she continued, reading from the list she was making, "weeds, assorted vegetables, ditto for flowers, mature trees. You have a million places for fireflies to shelter, to lay eggs, and for their larvae to grow, so—okay!"

Harriet, pointing her pencil in the air, switched to her professor voice. "First, it is a known fact that most female fireflies do not fly. Males are the fliers. Females wait in bushes, trees, or grass for males to locate them. Second, it is a known fact that constructing a new home usually involves cutting trees and bulldozing land. Thus, the yard of a new home is likely to include fewer perches for female fireflies than an older home with a lush, established garden. Thus, we can reasonably expect to see fewer fireflies in the yards of newer houses."

Lush was a polite word for my overgrown yard, but it gave me an idea. "Don't landscapers plant new sod and trees and bushes at new houses? They probably use fertilizer or weed killer to speed up the growth," I said, "to make the new yards look better quicker. And wouldn't those chemicals kill fireflies?"

"You're good, Alice."

"Thank you," I said, taking a bow. "My parents worried about me and my brothers rolling around on the lawn if they sprayed it with chemicals, so they never used any." I squatted and ran my fingers through the grass. "There's probably a ton of bugs."

"Thanks for the offer to procrastinate," Owen said, strolling in the side gate. He lifted the books he carried under his arm, to indicate his homework. He had on a T-shirt I hadn't seen before, pale blue, with an old-fashioned toaster on the front, in red. Two pieces of toast were flying out the top of the bread slots, and above them, the word WHEE!

I had the feeling that if you understood the humor in his shirt, it meant you understood something wise, or something cool, or something about being a teenager I didn't know—I wasn't even sure what. So I liked the shirt, like I liked his sushi shirt, because I didn't understand it and wanted to.

"Guess what," Harriet called from the vegetable garden, where she had circled back to take more notes. "If you crammed the seven billion human beings on Earth on the end of a ginormous scale, and piled every insect at the other end, the insects would weigh more."

"This is Harriet, a friend from my swim team," I said to Owen. "We're getting ready to do an experiment for her science fair project."

"Awesome!" He gave the word a twist, so it sounded half serious, half not, and as if it was supposed to be an answer to both her and me. Could he be making fun of us, two girls two years younger?

"Also BTW: your sandbox smells like a dog toilet." Harriet was peering under the lid.

"Good one," Owen said.

"No dogs go in there. It just needs new sand," I said, as if I hadn't heard joking in their voices. It bothered me that Dad hadn't been back to water or weed or take care of anything.

I went in for Owen's lemonade, and when I came back, he was seated at the table with his books open. "Thank you," he said. He popped the can tab. "I have to turn in a problem set and take an online quiz by midnight."

"Why do you need to do a summer math class?" I asked. I remembered hearing Mr. Phoebe say he didn't want Owen forgetting math during his vacation. To me that didn't explain being required to submit homework and sit for online quizzes.

"Spring semester I kind of messed up," Owen said. "My school says I can stay on track if I retake the course online and pass a placement test." He flipped to the back of his book to check an answer. "Wrong again." He bounced the base of his palm off his forehead, with that same twist to the tone that confused me. Was he serious? Or did he mean that even though other people took his math seriously and made him do it, he didn't care?

"Can I see?" I felt sorry for how Owen's parents kept giving him a hard time.

I slid into the seat beside him on the bench. If Owen was so behind going into tenth grade, I figured there was a chance I'd understand. At school I was in the middle track and did okay.

Wishful thinking! The problems looked like gibberish, with more variables than I'd ever solved for. "Is that algebra?" I said. Algebra was the class I would be taking in the fall.

He nodded. "Quadratic functions are impossible."

"Quadratic functions?" Harriet echoed from down the yard, as though she were a traveler in a foreign land who'd finally overheard words she understood. "Show me."

Predictable. It was the first time I was jealous of Harriet being smarter.

"Seriously?" Surprise arced Owen's eyebrows. "What grade are you in?"

I'd grown used to Harriet and almost forgotten her height and pigtails made her look ten. "She's going into eighth, like me," I said, and asked, out of curiosity, when she sat down across from Owen, "Harriet, are you taking geometry next year?" Geometry was the top math class at Cherrywood Middle School.

Harriet shook her head and glanced at the textbook upside down. "I can assist," she said.

"Honestly?" Owen laughed. "I. Am. Tanking." He pointed. "In these, how do you get the equation for the axis of symmetry?"

"Use the formula x equals negative b over $2a$. Locate the b here," Harriet showed him, "and the a there."

They began to trade his pencil and notebook paper back and forth. "You insert the value of x to find the vertex and the y intercept, like this," she said.

I climbed onto the tabletop and sat cross-legged, facing them. It was nice, I thought, how Harriet didn't brag. While she was writing, Owen looked up at me with a grin, like, *isn't this situation amusing.*

A wave of embarrassment rippled through me that had nothing to do with math. It turned into the oddest sensation, like a large, invisible rubber band had started pulling me toward him. In the same instant that it surprised me, I knew what it was. As sure as I knew—swimming on my back, counting strokes— where to find the wall.

Crush. I'd had it in first grade for Ethan Bould, who moved at the end of that year, and in fourth grade for

Max Lu, who liked Evie Lopez instead of me. I realized I'd had it but ignored it the night I met Owen with my bike.

It was like gravity, but not pushing down, not like an apple falling. It drew up, across, through, and inside me at the same time. It stayed in my arms, chest, and legs. I scooted down the worn tabletop a few inches closer to Owen's math book. His hair was picking up points of light from the late-day sun and I wished I could touch it. And yet if he could somehow see or feel what was happening to me, well, I'd either turn into stone or fall off the table. "The tent is sagging," I interrupted, and forced myself to get up. "I'm going to tighten the ropes."

The blue-striped canvas really had drooped in a couple of places, and I'd been meaning to untie and re-knot the loose cords. I took my time checking each stake. Then I volunteered to complete Harriet's map, and was glad when she told me yes, she needed the swing set side sketched in.

At seven o'clock Harriet decided they should take a break from math to watch for the first firefly flash. Owen said it was time for him to leave, though. His dad and Joanna were invited to a party down the street, and he had to babysit. Before this, I hadn't heard of Owen babysitting Timmy and Piper. Of course it made sense that he had been, all along, the days he was in town, or past summers. But what did I know? I'd met the family only four weeks ago and saw a fraction of what went on at their house, a few hours each day.

The rubber band feeling stretched as Owen disappeared up the side path.

Harriet had decided the top of the picnic table was our best central scanning position. She sat facing the back hedge. I focused on the woodpile and vegetable garden. We were ready with her stopwatches, graph paper, and map. The sky was barely beginning to dim, the way a scoop of ice cream hints it's starting to melt when its ridges go round and shiny.

"First flash, seven nineteen!" Harriet called out. "Quick, Alice! Time the interval between blinks; I'm guessing *Photinus pyralis*, the early evening firefly, one of the two most common eastern species."

She took notes while I counted, "Three . . . four . . . five seconds."

"Five seconds is perfect for a *Photinus pyralis* male," Harriet said. "If there's a female, she should flash two seconds later from the grass or a bush."

Firefly flashing turned out to be like texting friends you were trying to find in a crowd. Sure enough, a dot of light from the grass fit the pattern Harriet described. Soon dozens of fireflies were sailing low over the lawn and the garden, twinkling on and off like mini Christmas lights. I'd watched them every summer, of course, but never noticed the details Harriet was pointing out.

"See that flight pattern, that hook-like curve, a letter *J* with the blink on the upturn?" she said. "That's exactly how it's described in the field guide!"

For a while Harriet marked her map, and then, as we waited for the air to darken further, she taught me her favorite card game, Fluxx, with a deck she'd brought from her house. At sunset Harriet declared it was finally "time to talk firefly." She taught me how to blink a flashlight the size of a marker as though I were a female firefly. Five seconds later, a flash from the air answered.

And then, I got one! It had taken thirty calls with my light until, amazingly, a firefly landed on the back of my hand. Sorry for having duped the poor guy, I held still the few seconds it took him to figure out he'd made a mistake and lift off to resume his search.

"Good, we saw how that worked." Harriet sounded impatient. "I need you to go in and heat water until it's warm, but not hot, and then bring the pan with the water in it out here."

"You want to quit your experiment already?" I thought we had just started.

"Talking to fireflies was not an experiment, Alice," she said. "Tonight we're doing a few warm-up exercises to help me think up an experiment."

"All right," I said, but I couldn't resist adding, "What's the different between *warm* and *not hot*?"

Harriet rolled her eyes. "The temperature should be between eighty and eighty-five degrees," she read off her pad.

In the kitchen, no sounds came from upstairs. One prescription I picked up regularly for my mom was intended to help her sleep, so maybe she was, although it was early, or she could have been watching a movie with headphones.

To avoid making noise, I took out a saucepan in slow motion from the pot drawer. I ran the faucet at half-strength, set the pan silently on the burner and, as quietly as possible, made us PBJs. A sizzle told me when the water was ready.

Meanwhile, Harriet had collected fireflies in one of her jars, all of which had holes in the lids. She tested the pot with a thermometer and let the temperature sink to 83 degrees before planting the jar in the water, nearly up to the top.

The warm water heated the air inside the jar. The hotter air excited the fireflies, and the speed of their flashes accelerated. Harriet timed them with a stop-watch. Five-second intervals between flashes dropped to four seconds, to three point five . . . then the water started to cool. The flash cycles lengthened to five, and Harriet declared that exercise finished.

We ate our sandwiches on top of the picnic table while Harriet consulted her field guide and her phone. Was there an exact moment you could say the sky stopped appearing blue and turned its nighttime color? I wondered as I watched the dusky air. The answer had to be another teeny tiny infinity.

"So far, we've caught two of the over one hundred thirty-six species of Lampyridae, lightning bugs or fireflies found in North America." Harriet pointed to pictures in her book. "*Photinus pyralis*, with the reddish head, and *Photuris pennsylvanicus*, which is more orange."

I hopped off the table and cupped a few of the little blinkers that liked to hover over my dad's old pile of grass clippings next to the woodpile. "A third species?" I said, and Harriet happily agreed. Not only were they smaller, these fireflies had yellow and pink marks, a type not listed in her book. She immediately suffocated a sample in a small sealed plastic bag.

"Harriet, I was about to let those go—"

"Alice! Hey, Alice?" It was Owen, from the other side of the Phoebes' tall evergreens. He waved from the deck doorway.

"I was wondering," he said. "If you guys aren't too busy, could you give me a hand with the kids for a few minutes? Things aren't going . . . according to plan here."

"We'll be right there!"

The instant I said this Harriet frowned and began turning the page of the guidebook like she needed to be sure she hadn't missed something. I was already picturing how Harriet could entertain Timmy, while I looked after Piper, while Owen finished his math.

Then, clearly annoyed, Harriet looked up at me. "First of all, I've never babysat," she objected. "Or, babysitted? Second, from your description—what's her name?"

"Piper," I said. "C'mon Harriet, Owen has a midnight deadline. Let's go. You spent all that time teaching him."

"From what you told me about Piper," she continued, "the sight of a new person might upset her exceedingly, in which case Owen is unlikely to accomplish a thing. What if she gets violent because she's never seen me before?"

"We'll stay in a different room." I climbed off the table and waited for her. "All you have to do is shoot baskets with an *exceedingly* sweet toddler."

Harriet did not budge. "The thing is, the last step I need to finish is to track flash patterns here over a period of hours," she said, "to potentially identify additional species. So I can't exactly leave your yard until . . ." She checked her phone. "Dawn. I need to follow through, to optimize my chances of developing an experiment, and because I have no guarantee of a second opportunity."

There was a crash next door, like furniture falling.

"See?" Harriet said.

The fastest route was over the fence. However, the rosebush on my family's side had morphed into an enormous thorny knot. I ran around the long way.

The deck door was open, and Owen stood by the kitchen table, where his pencil, notebook, calculator, and textbook were laid out. His hands were in his pockets, as if he wasn't sure what to do next. Both kids were in their pajamas in the family room. Piper was running in circles around the couch, where Timmy sat watching TV. Each time she passed in front, blocking his view, he cried out and reached to grab her. That seemed to be Piper's game.

"My parents put them to bed before they left, but nobody fell asleep. They started complaining, so I brought them downstairs," Owen said.

The first thing I did was turn off the TV. Piper sped up, like she wanted to see how fast she could go. Timmy plopped over on his side and began sucking his thumb. I felt mad that Harriet had refused to come. I'll give Piper a minute to wear herself out, I thought.

"My father is going to lose it if I don't finish," Owen said, "since I had mucho hours to, all week. In theory, I'm also supposed to be at an all-night movie marathon at Noah Gaines's house after my parents get home."

"No worries, you'll get there," I said, wishing I could go along to watch movies with Owen, but of course it must be a high school party.

The return of that gravitational pull toward him made me feel in danger of being exposed, so it was a relief to launch into babysitter mode. "Yes, I'll play," I said, when Piper quit her track races and brought me a ball for our rolling game. I added, "Wait," and gestured *stop* with a raised hand.

Timmy looked just sleepy enough to agree to a trick Joanna used to get him to take his afternoon nap. "Hi big guy," I said, squatting to the level of his eyes. "You can bring this in your crib if you let Owen put you to bed right now." I placed the big blue ball in Timmy's hands and moved to the carpet to roll Piper's to her.

Timmy sucked his thumb and pulled the ball close, holding on firmly as Owen lifted him onto his shoulder.

"Thank you so much, Alice," Owen said. "I figured it was easier asking you than interrupting my dad and Joanna. They're only gone a couple of hours, and she kept thanking me, she was looking forward to going out so much."

"As soon as—you know—then—you know." I mimed that Owen should remove the basketball from the crib after Timmy fell asleep.

"Got it," Owen said. "Will you ask Harriet if I can take her up on her offer afterward?" Harriet had said she could help him finish the math once her firefly observations were underway. When Owen and Timmy headed upstairs, I tapped Piper's shoulder. "Let's go outside," I said, and she let me take her hand and slip her plastic sandals onto her feet by the back door. We walked together down the deck stairs, across the grass to the rosebush.

"Harriet!" I called in a loud whisper. "Owen wants your help over here in like fifteen minutes."

"Give him my phone number," she said. A few seconds later, a paper airplane sailed over the rosebush.

I picked it up. "A message from my mad scientist friend, Harriet," I said to Piper.

"I thought you said she can't hear." Harriet was speaking through the stems in the place where it was possible to see between the two yards.

"Her mom thinks maybe she can read lips."

I always followed Joanna's habit of speaking to Piper out loud. "It's either a hunch or stubbornness," Joanna would say cheerfully. "I can't lose hope."

"She talks to her to treat her like a regular person. I haven't told anyone else this." I hesitated. "But sometimes I get the feeling Piper understands my voice."

"Yours?" Harriet sounded skeptical. "No one else's?"

"I know that doesn't make sense," I said, "except, she reacts to some sounds, and to her little brother crying. If she hears tones but not words, I wonder if she hears my voice like it's music."

"But," Harriet said. "If your voice sounds like music, why wouldn't everyone's? Hey!" She pointed. "Your friend appears to be fascinated by a *Photinus pyralis*."

It was true. Piper was staring at a firefly hovering by the rosebush, on our side, in the twilight air. It was the kind from Harriet's guidebook that blinked a greenish light and dipped and flew in a *J*-shape. I caught it. Inside the cage of my fingers, it glowed orange. "Want to hold it?" I held my hand out to Piper, then turned her right palm up and opened mine to pass the firefly to her. Without moving, she watched the bug open its wings and rise in the air. That gave me an idea.

"Here's a magic wand," I said. I took Harriet's pen-shaped flashlight from my pocket, positioned the light in Piper's hand, and curled my fingers around hers. We pressed the on-off button together.

"We're going to call a firefly with your magic wand," I went on. "You'll like fireflies, because they don't use sounds to find other fireflies. Only their lights. The way they flash on and off is a code to talk to each other. So you don't have to talk, either. You can use light language."

We switched the beam on and off, two seconds after each male flashed from a cluster blinking by the rosebush. Piper kept very still, paying attention. One bug flew toward us, and I caught it for her. This time, she let the firefly crawl from my hand to hers, where it glowed once, and lifted away.

I could almost see the bug's light switching on Piper's mind. Her eyes followed the tiny blinks across the air. I would have stayed and caught it for her again. But I wanted to give Harriet's message to Owen. So I said, "Time to go in," and lifted Piper in my arms. She kept working the flashlight as I carried her to the deck steps. On, off, on, off, as fast as she could press the button, pointing the beam into the trees, into the grass, into the bushes and the sky.

11
BUGFIRE

IT WAS PAST nine-thirty when Owen decided he was ready to take his quiz online. Piper and I were playing our usual ball game in the family room, and Harriet had been text-tutoring him from my backyard, still taking in data. His parents were due home in an hour, he said, so I stopped the ball in my lap and signaled to Piper *time to sleep* by putting my palms together, laying my head on them, and closing my eyes.

Upstairs, while I arranged a small herd of stuffed animal friends at the end of her bed, Piper flicked her wall light switch on and off, like the little flashlight I'd stowed safely in my back pocket.

I covered Piper's hand with mine. "Leaving it off is a way for us to say good night in light language, okay?"

Her fingers wiggled underneath, trying to move the switch, but I held firm. "Now *you're* the firefly," I said, and she gave only a single protest kick as I lifted her away and sailed her to the pillow end of her bed. Either I got lucky or she was tired, and she let me tuck her in.

Outside her bedroom door, I waited on the floor of the narrow landing at the top of the stairs, listening for any sounds of her waking back up. After ten minutes, I knocked gently on the door of Owen's room, next to hers. "Don't stop the quiz," I whispered through the door. I wished I could see him before I left, but even more I wanted him to pass. "Just wanted to tell you I think Piper's asleep, so I'm going."

The door opened. Light from Owen's desk lamp shone from behind him in the doorway like a rising sun. I had a ridiculous sensation that I was standing in front of another human being for the first time in my life. We weren't touching, but I could feel the outline of his shape with my mind, and what that was, was strange. I took two steps backward, toward the stair-case, and, out of nervousness, asked a question I knew the answer to.

"Where is it you're going tomorrow, North Caro-lina? You sure travel a lot." He'd told me it was a trip to visit more of his relatives.

"Yeah, that's right, same old same old." Owen shook his head as if there was no help for it. "But listen, Alice, thank you. You're a babysitting genius. If you hadn't come over, right now I'd be screwed. My dad just texted, they're on their way."

"Harriet's the genius," I said. "I better run! Go back to your quiz!"

He raised a hand goodbye. "She is unusual," he agreed. "And thanks to that, I believe I'm in the process of redeeming myself for another week."

The unusual genius was sitting in the middle of the lawn when I returned, with her head in her hands. I lay down on the grass a few feet away. The unmowed stems poked me like pins. I asked, "Is something wrong?"

Harriet pointed at the treetops, which had turned into a black maze of crisscrossing lines and leaves against the night sky. "Those fireflies are too high to catch."

I saw what she was talking about: a kind that blinked several times in a row, zoomed a couple of seconds unlit, then rapid-fire blink-blink-blinked.

"At first I thought they must be a different species, because they flash differently from the others we caught," she said. "But our heated jar proved changing the air temperature can change the interval between the flashes. I think that means I can't use flash patterns to identify a species. So how does a person figure out the difference between all these fireflies, when they're up there and we're forty feet below?"

To my surprise, Harriet sounded genuinely puzzled. But of course I had no answer for her and was still feeling annoyed. "I wish you'd come and helped me at Owen's." It occurred to me that Harriet talked about species and experiments the way my old friends talked about going to the mall to buy jeans. "Is this what you did with friends in Minnesota?" I said. "Refuse when they ask a simple favor and then act like it never happened?"

Harriet didn't answer.

"Did you even have any friends in Minnesota?" That was mean. "Sorry, Harriet," I said. "Listen, if we're done with those warm-up activities, or whatever you call them, I'm going to sleep."

After a pause she said, "Sounds good, Alice," in a strangely artificial chummy way. "I need to sit here a while to figure things out."

Harriet, I saw, had what my dad had accused my mom all last spring of *not* having. Perseverance, a tendency to stick with people, things, or any subject, once she started thinking about it. When Harriet got stuck on something, she stayed with it as determinedly as she pushed her breaststroke down the pool, refusing to be distracted. It was turning out to be one of the things about Harriet I sometimes hated and other times admired the most. Or both at once, like now.

The air had cooled when I woke at 4:23 a.m. I knew the exact time because, without a cell phone, I'd started wearing a watch with an alarm to get to morning practice. I'd woken myself out of a family camping dream, because as I was dreaming I knew it wasn't true that the five of us had trips like that together. Harriet's sleeping bag was empty. I pulled on my fleece shirt and went outside.

She was watching the sky from the lawn, like before. I assumed she must have heard the tent zipper and knew I was there, but we sat in the dark without speaking, one behind the other. The stars overhead, visible between tree branches, beamed from whatever distant worlds they were busy illuminating, while the few fireflies still roaming the yard seemed to twinkle *we're down here, like you.*

Finally I stated the obvious out loud: "You're still watching."

"Yes," she replied.

As irritated as I'd felt before, I was impressed by Harriet tracking fireflies all night. Far fewer were flashing, mostly low to the ground. Every couple of minutes a burst appeared, then nothing, then another sparkling.

"There's something I've been meaning to tell you," I said. "You know how you say digits of pi before you dive? At the end of school, during exams, to stay calm I used to do this meditation thing we learned in P.E., repeating the freestyle record time in my head, as my mantra. Isn't that a weird coincidence?"

"How is that a coincidence?" Harriet said without turning.

"About repeating numbers," I said.

"Try thirty-two point eight-seven," she suggested, still faced away, in a light tone like she was offering to share her curly fries at the pool. I laughed. Of course Harriet knew the record time for Girls 13–14 backstroke, a stroke she didn't compete in, on a team she'd just joined.

"Thanks, Harriet." I knew she'd learned it for me.

Even the grass was going dark now, and an edge of dawn had begun to lighten the deep shade. I told Harriet I was going back to sleep. After all, it was Sunday. There was no meet or practice to get up early for, no reason not to sleep long into the morning. She nodded in acknowledgement. "One hour and twenty-two minutes until sunrise."

On Monday, at the end of my three hours next door, Joanna asked me a favor. "Eric and I went to a party at a neighbor's over the weekend. Owen babysat," she said. "It was the first time in months we'd tried going out for the evening, and it worked out so well, I'm thinking we might get away with it for our wedding anniversary, which is this Friday."

Clearly that was not a lead-in to thanking me for helping out with Piper and Timmy that night. Owen had kept things in the Ignorance Is Bliss category where babysitting was concerned. So I left them there. "Happy anniversary," I said.

"Thank you. Yes, well, you see, Owen is away now, and Friday is the Fourth of July," she went on. "We got married on the holiday. I realize you're likely to have plans with your family, Alice, but is there any chance you'd be free to babysit any part of that evening? Of course, since it is a holiday, if you could, I'd pay extra."

"Extra" was an opportunity to bump my cell phone savings fund that I was not going to refuse. I figured a little hesitation would be smart this time, however, so she wouldn't be suspicious. "I think that might work. I can let you know tomorrow."

"Wonderful! We could start late, eight o'clock, so if you had a late-afternoon barbecue to attend, it wouldn't overlap." Joanna's face showed feelings like some people wear bright colors. Every part, even her nose, smiled. "You know that French restaurant, a few blocks from here? It has a rooftop terrace where people said we'll be able to watch fireworks from the country club."

I knew all about the fireworks at Cherrywood Country Club. Every year, except when it rained and the show was cancelled, my family and hundreds of people from our neighborhood carried blankets, picnics, and chairs to the front lawn of the public library to watch those fireworks from across the road.

But if this year wasn't going to be like the others, I didn't want to go. Harriet and her family had been invited to the party at the club, so that's where she'd be, and it would be weird asking Georgia, Charlotte, or Malini after not hanging out for so long. Even if Dad made his usual blueberry pie and met me at the library with the twins, or Aunt Ruthie did, it wouldn't be the same without Mom and her fried chicken. The only time she made it was for our Fourth of July fireworks picnic.

On that Friday evening, Mr. Phoebe let me in the front door. He'd continued to be downtown most days I babysat, and we'd seen each other only a couple of times since that first afternoon. He greeted me with a dip of his head that seemed to say hello and goodbye in the same motion, like a busy teacher acknowledging a student in the hallway on the way to class.

"Ow-iss! Ow-iss!" Timmy's voice called from upstairs, and Joanna appeared on the second-floor landing.

"I made the mistake of mentioning you'd be here tonight, Alice, in case he woke up and found us gone. I'm afraid there's no way he'll go to sleep until you read him a book. Thank you again for doing this!" She laughed in that way I liked, a little at herself and half sad around the edges.

"Can we talk a minute, Jo?" Mr. Phoebe was frowning. I realized Joanna had invited me to call her by her first name, but Mr. Phoebe never had. I could think of him only as Mr. Phoebe anyway. A funny picture entered my head, of him and Joanna in combat. Their weapons were his nod and her laugh.

I waited for the sound of quarreling but it didn't come. When their bedroom door opened, Joanna was kissing Mr. Phoebe's cheek, and he smiled and patted her shoulder.

"Phone numbers are on the refrigerator," she said, coming downstairs, "and you know where the micro-wave popcorn is. Help yourself, and I made chocolate chip cookies. We'll be home by ten-thirty."

Timmy and I had a routine with *Where the Wild Things Are*. I'd start the final line, ". . . and it was still . . ." and then I'd pause.

Timmy liked to shoot his arms straight in the air like a football ref signaling a touchdown as he shouted, "Hot!"

That night, with him on my lap, I patted the space next to me on his bedroom floor for Piper to follow the pictures. When Timmy's arms zoomed up, she smiled and swayed from side to side.

We read the book four times before I lifted Timmy into his crib. In the time it took to tuck him under his basketball quilt, wind up the lullaby mobile, close the blinds, switch off the lights, and turn on the nightlight, he fell asleep.

"Let's go on the deck," I whispered, and tapped Piper's shoulder and picked up the baby monitor.

The sun still lit the sky from below the horizon, but close around us, darkness had started to blur the edges of everything. Fireflies blinked in the bushes and the grass. They flashed in the tulip tree across the fence. We had at least thirty minutes until night would settle in enough for fireworks. The notes of the lullaby plunked like a toy piano through the monitor's static.

Piper and I slid wood beads along colored wires that looped out of a maze toy. I pointed my index finger at a bead and moved it, and she imitated me. I tried pointing straight ahead, at nothing, to see if she'd do the same, like our ball game, and she did.

"Let me show you something," I said. I lifted her down the deck steps to the yard and set the nearest firefly on the back of her right hand. She stopped moving, and watched, like the other time.

"Remember? It speaks light language!" The bug flew off and flashed. I re-caught it, and Piper let me set it in her palm. When it didn't glow, she shook it off.

"There goes your bug," I said, as the firefly fell into the air and blinked, a dozen feet from us. "Now it's saying, 'Here I am—where are you?'"

It was time, I thought, to show her Harriet's stash.

Harriet had captured dozens of fireflies the other night and set them free in the tent. I hadn't noticed this until the next morning. She wanted them for a second night of experiments, she said. I worried about them crawling on me in the meantime, but that hadn't been a problem. Mostly, they crept along the canvas, the wood poles, or across the floor, without blinking much. Our second round of experiments was supposed to be tomorrow. But then we realized Harriet's grandparents would still be visiting for the holiday weekend, so we put the experiments off for a week. Meanwhile, I had a tent full of fireflies.

Piper allowed me to carry her through the dimming twilight around to my yard. It was only when we got there that I realized I'd left the baby monitor on the Phoebes' deck. I could hear the static clearly, though, so I decided not to go back; Timmy slept so soundly that I doubted even the fireworks from the country club would wake him up, although I planned to be back at his house long before they started.

Did Piper understand what a tent was? There was no way to know. If she tried to bang her head on the walls or grab poles, the whole thing might come down on us. We were lucky it hadn't the first time she snuck in. I unzipped and folded the door flaps around the entry so she could see the yard and run out if she needed to. If fireflies escaped, I figured I could make up the difference later.

I set two flashlights on Harriet's crates, a third on my sleeping bag, and a fourth in Piper's hand. She ping-ponged the beam all over. "Not like that!" I said, and held up my hands to mean *stop,* and she did, which seemed like a good sign.

"A firefly is a boring beetle until it lights up," I said. "I'm going to teach you to catch one."

Covering Piper's hand with mine, I pointed her flashlight toward a firefly clinging to the canvas. I pried its weak grip from the material and held it in front of her face. For who knows what reason, this firefly decided to glow just then. "That's perfect, Piper! When a firefly lights up, it's looking for friends. Put your hand like this," I said.

Each time I spoke, I moved my hands, and motioned, and pointed. I turned her palm up and slid the firefly into it. She allowed me to take her flashlight, which I set between my feet so it shined up, between us. I scooped four fireflies from the center pole and the floor, added them to Piper's hand, and cupped her other hand on top.

"Keep your fireflies like that." I put my hands over hers to show her. "Now wait—see if they glow." I gathered several between my own palms. In the middle of the tent the two of us stood, holding our fireflies, watching.

And then it came to me: the procedure for what was turning into my own, unscientific firefly experiment. Now that we'd done the basics of capturing one—flicking on the light, waiting till one landed, cupping the hand—I wanted to see if she had learned how to do it by herself— if she'd imitate me on the reaching and capturing.

And as that idea came into my head, something extraordinary happened. Maybe our fingers warmed the air around the fireflies by several degrees, like Harriet's accelerator jars in warm water. Or maybe it was the extra females I'd added earlier that evening—Harriet theorized her collection would blink more if we upped the number of females. Whatever it was, the fireflies in my hands began to glow, one after the other. I moved them under Piper's chin, like a shining buttercup. She looked me in the eye for a teeny tiny fraction of a second and opened her hands, too. Of the five bugs she held, first one glowed, then another.

Piper looked amazed. I had never seen this expression on her face—on anyone's face. It was nothing like the way she stared at the carpet or the skirt of the couch, or even how she'd watched the grass, almost as if she were in a trance, the first time I saw her. She seemed even more alert than when we played our ball game, as though the bugs fascinated her as much as Timmy's blue basketball fascinated him.

Slowly, carefully, she rotated her hand, as if it might be a sculpture, not connected to her body. Together, we stared at the fireflies. So I did not see her lips move.

"Bugfire," she said.

12
I AM SURE I HEARD IT RIGHT

TWO FUZZY SYLLABLES. Soft, high-pitched. The hard *B* was unmistakable; the *G* floated between *guh* and *uh*. *Fire* came out *fay-ah*.

I knew Piper meant to say *bug*.

I knew she meant to say *fire*.

Like I knew, by now, when she was tired or about to get upset. We'd spent enough time together for that.

I knew *bugfire* meant *firefly*.

One, two, three times I replayed the moment in my head. It was no dream, not imagined, nothing supernatural—it was like "terrible joy": an oxymoron, an impossible possible. Real magic.

Piper's blond-white curls shone in the flashlight beam. Our eyes met; she smiled. I was sure the smile was her way to tell me she knew she'd said a word. Had *she* heard the word she said? Did she know she'd made sounds? That, I wasn't sure of.

"Bugfire, bugfire, bugfire," I repeated, and held out the fireflies in my hands as I lowered them to the ground cloth and freed them. "Your bugfire is crawling, Piper. You're right. Fireflies are bugs that look like sparks of fire. Bugfire."

Not even a crack appeared between her lips. She couldn't or wouldn't say it again, as if someone had switched her off. She shook the fireflies from her hands. I turned a flashlight on and off and waved it around like she had, in case that was part of "bugfire." But she just lay down on my sleeping bag and appeared to be watching the ceiling.

Still, I couldn't wait to see Joanna's face when I told her. She'd want a moment-by-moment description. I'd have to be vague about "where."

To be honest, I'd forgotten Timmy's monitor. Its static had blurred into the night sounds of the neighborhood. Blood rushed to my head, as if I'd been caught. We'd been away from the Phoebes' about twenty minutes, and the circumstances could not be explained in a way that made me look responsible.

"Dad, I need to ask you a question." I called him from the Phoebes' kitchen phone. I'd set out farm fences, tractors, and animals on the family room carpet for

Piper after I'd carried her upstairs with me to check on Timmy, who, thank goodness, was just fine and asleep.

"Sure, sweetie." In the background, music played from my brothers' favorite video game. "What's up? The boys and I decided to stay in this year and watch fireworks on TV—I think they're about to start. We're at my apartment." I remembered the last time I'd sat between them on the couch in the living room in our house while they battled those same 3-D giants.

"I can tell. What kind of pie did you make?"

"Pie is in the category of Traditions That Fell by the Wayside This Year." He laughed. "We'll pick it up again, in the future. But I'm guessing that's not the question you called about. How are you?"

"I'm fine, I'm still babysitting. I took the girl, Piper, outside to play, and I wasn't supposed to, and now I think I should tell Mr. Phoebe and Joanna when they come home. . . ." I stopped. I felt sick on top of jittery that Piper had spoken a word.

Dad waited. I was hoping he'd say something, so I waited too. After a couple of seconds he said, "I'm not sure what you're asking. You want to know if you should tell the parents of the girl you're babysitting that you took her outside the house, which you weren't supposed to do? The girl is safe? Nothing is wrong, nothing happened?"

"Nothing bad happened," I said.

"Your conscience is tugging at you, am I right?"

"I guess that's it," I said.

"Hang on." I heard him tell Mike and Josh they had three minutes left before it would be time to pause the game. "Okay, I'm back, Triple A. You called me, although I'd wager you're certain what I'll say. Which means you called to hear me say it: There are few times in life when the truth is inappropriate. Or at least a version of the truth that takes kindness into consideration. However," he added, "there can be a fine line between a lie and an *inexact* version of the truth."

"Yessss—go!" Mike said in the background.

"No, you hit it," said Josh.

"Boys, time's up, please! Triple A?" my dad said. "Am I being helpful?"

"Yes. Thanks, Dad."

"Would you like me to swing by for you after the parents get home? You know I've got room," he said. "I have a new pullout couch, though your brothers are bouncing it to death at the moment."

Suddenly, I wanted to hang up. I didn't want to hear about the couch or apartment or them watching fireworks on TV. I said, "I have to go now."

"All right. I'm glad you called. If you have more questions call back, Triple A. Any hour, day or night, you know that. Never hesitate. I'm ten minutes away," he said. "Well, twenty."

I dialed Joanna. I wanted to tell her the thing she wanted most in the world to happen had happened. But where was the line between the truth, and what I could leave out and not be lying? Her phone was ringing. I'd have to figure it out as we talked. If I hung up now, she'd see the home number on her screen and call back.

"Yes?" Mr. Phoebe. *Oh no.*

"May I speak to Joanna, please?"

"Is this Alice? She's not available at the moment. Is everything OK?"

"I can call back . . . ," I began.

"If anything's the matter I think you better tell me," he said.

"Well, I was teaching Piper how to catch fireflies." I didn't know how to get out of it. "I'm not sure if we were supposed to go outside," I added, to fuzz over the "where" part. "Is Joanna there yet?" This wasn't at all how I imagined sharing the news.

"She's in the ladies' room. What happened?"

"And, um, while we were, I heard her say a made-up word."

"What?" Mr. Phoebe said. "Are you in our house now? Where's Timmy?"

"We're in the family room," I said. "Timmy's in his crib. . . ."

"Is there an emergency?"

"Not exactly, but she got so excited by the fireflies that she started talking to me and I thought Joanna would want to know right away because . . ."

"All right, you can stop there," he interrupted. "Please stay indoors. We'll be home in ten minutes." He hung up.

I didn't understand. I felt worse than before calling Dad and wasn't sure what to do. Ten minutes was how long it would take the Phoebes to walk back from C'est la Vie.

The first fireworks boomed from the country club. Piper raised her head from the block tower she was building. I wondered again about vibrations. I hadn't felt anything.

"What do you hear?" I asked. No answer. "Can you say 'bugfire'?" I tried, hopefully.

Without responding to me in any way, she swiped the tower over. The fireworks rained crackling explosions. They jumped the static in the baby monitor, which I'd set on the kitchen counter near the sink. The monitor had the effect of making each explosion seem to blast twice, from upstairs and downstairs. Amazingly, there was nothing from Timmy. He slept right through.

With my family, on the library lawn, we'd raise our gaze above cars passing along the avenue in front of us, and above the two-story nets enclosing the club's tennis courts, for our view of the colored rockets spiraling up, and the lacy lights raining down. From the Phoebes' deck, the tops of the color bursts would be visible through the surrounding trees. But I decided against trying to connect the sounds to the lights for Piper. I didn't want to confuse her, or even start a tantrum—or risk being outside when the Phoebes walked in.

To make it look as though we'd spent most of the last hour in the family room, I scattered Legos, balls, and more blocks and books around the carpet. When the key turned in the Phoebes' front-door lock, Piper and I were on the couch, and I was pointing at pictures in a book.

"What a disaster," said Mr. Phoebe. He switched off the monitor. The house grew as quiet as if an audience was waiting for us to recite the next lines of a play.

Joanna knelt on the floor by the couch and pulled Piper into her arms and stroked her hair. "It's my mistake, Alice," she said. "I'm sorry."

I had no clue what she meant. The only part I got so far was that Mr. Phoebe thought me babysitting was a disaster.

"I was planning to clean up before you got home." I decided to misunderstand on purpose and slid off the couch to collect the books I'd tossed on the floor.

"My wife says she filled you in on Piper's condition, so it's difficult to imagine what you could possibly have heard." Mr. Phoebe placed both palms flat on the kitchen counter and appeared to be examining his fingernails. "Let's see. You left our son alone in his crib in the house while taking our daughter outside for some reason of your own. For how long?" He looked up at me with a hard stare.

"Only a couple of minutes, to catch a firefly on your deck," I answered. Making the lie worse felt like my only choice.

"Where our daughter, who has been mute since the age of two, carried on a conversation with you?" he said, like he couldn't believe how stupid I was.

"I really did hear it," I tried to insist. "She said—"

Outdoors, loud, continuous crackling signaled the grand finale of the country club's display.

"Jo, what did I tell you?" Mr. Phoebe interrupted, and they looked at each other and not at me. For a moment the three of us listened, and although it was the kind of noise Piper could supposedly hear, she didn't seem to. The sound let loose something in me—I was mad Mr. Phoebe automatically disbelieved me—and I faced him from across the room. "Mr. Phoebe—"

"Don't," he said, raising his hand to stop me. The fireworks' final pop sputtered. In another minute, I knew, people would be folding up blankets and chairs, collecting their picnic trash, walking home. My nerve seemed to fold up, too. Partly because Joanna remained silent, partly because it was harder than I expected to sort out what I wanted to tell the Phoebes that was true, from the details I didn't.

Hot tears puddled my eyes, so I turned my back to put the books away on the deep built-in shelves. I couldn't help remembering Super Bowls here on Mr. Salgado's TV, eating cornbread and his secret-recipe chili while he and Dad made jokes about the ads. If only Mr. Salgado hadn't moved. If only my dad hadn't. In more ways than one, I realized, I'd crossed that line he talked about, between an inexact version of the truth and a lie.

"Eric, all right, but I think Alice meant well, and the kids are fine. Let's call it a night," Joanna said from the rug behind me, and tapped my shin. I wiped my eyes on my arm before turning around. She was trying to pay me. At least she smiled when I refused the money.

Later, as I lay in my sleeping bag, I kept repeating the words I wished I'd said: *Piper and I walked off your property to the tent in my backyard. I left Timmy and his monitor behind. It was wrong, I'm sorry. . . .* And the answer I wished I had heard: *A great thing happened because you broke those rules, Alice, so we thank you.* Pictures, too, I saw over and over: Piper and me rolling a ball, playing with felt boards, blocks, on the deck, in the tent . . . until I must have fallen asleep, because angry voices from inside the Phoebes' house woke me.

My watch said 1 a.m. It was not good to lose sleep before an A meet, and that made me worry about my race. Next door, the conversation was impossible to make out. The Phoebes were used to closed windows and air-conditioning, Joanna had once said, being from Arizona. I knew what it was about, though. Mr. Phoebe was mad at her because of me.

I didn't remember falling asleep again, but I must have, because my watch alarm woke me for the Saturday A meet.

Without going into the house, I left for the pool. The snack bar cooked great breakfasts for Saturday A meets, and the thought of their egg sandwiches distracted me from last night. So did the swim meet, which the Sharks won easily. Again I raced backstroke, but finished last, three-tenths of a second slower than my seed time.

"No hope for thirty-two point eight-seven now," I grumbled to Harriet afterward.

"My calculations aren't altered by one outlier result," she insisted, and pointed out we had two B meets and three A meets left in the season. This was Harriet's way of being nice, I knew.

I'd been waiting to tell her my "bugfire" story until after the meet, when we could talk in the snack bar. It turned out Harriet had to leave right away to go to a holiday barbecue with her parents. Lydia was picking her up and could give me a ride home, if I wanted.

"Yes," I said, thinking I could tell her about Piper on the way. "I wish I had a big sister to drive me anyplace I wanted to go."

"That never happens," said Harriet as we walked out of the locker room. "Swim-team rides are part of her deal to get the car."

Coach B was posting the final lineup for Relay Carnival by the front desk. Relay Carnival was my favorite summer meet. I'd swum it every year since first grade, but nearly all the relays were for freestyle. My only chance of making the lineup was if she'd given slots to swimmers with lower times, so more people could participate. The coach had never changed her winning strategy before, though.

I read over her shoulder as she tacked the sheet to the team bulletin board. My name, which used to be there three times, five times, did not appear once. Harriet made it onto one of the few relays where you could swim breaststroke.

"Sorry, Alice," Coach B said.

"I wasn't expecting anything," I answered, trying to sound like *hey-no-big-deal*. But I felt as disappointed as if I'd been left out on purpose. It was like another piece of my summer had been deleted. "If you want," I continued, in my attempt to seem just fine, "I could come along to help with the Eight-and-Unders."

"I was about to ask you that," said Coach B, who, if she heard the wobble in my voice, ignored it. "You're a good sport, Alice."

"Why does it have to be on Thursday?" complained Harriet as we continued to the parking lot. "I wanted to spend that night in your back yard."

"Aren't you excited you get to swim?" I asked.

"I'm meeting people at Jollibean in twenty minutes. Come on!" Lydia shouted from the Barclays' car.

Harriet, yelling *UGHHHHHH,* sprinted the final distance to the passenger door, where she tripped, spilling her goggles, cap, towel, shampoo, notebook, and pencils out of her swim bag onto the asphalt.

I stooped to help. "Harriet, I don't need a ride, it'll save time."

"No worries, Alice, get in. It's on the way," Lydia said. She was texting as we pulled out of the lot. According to Harriet, Lydia already had a hundred friends at

Cherrywood High, even though she didn't start school there until August.

"Hey, that's illegal and unsafe," Harriet said, *"and Mom said not to."* She took her notebook from her bag and started scribbling in it. I was too nervous watching other cars to bring up Piper.

Ignoring her sister, Lydia answered a call on her phone and kept it wedged between her ear and shoulder all the way to my house.

"Bye, Alice," Harriet said. "If I'm still alive, see you at Relay Carnival."

"I love Sophie's green one," Lydia said into the phone, waving to me, and crunched the speed bump.

I made a PBJ in the kitchen and brought it outside to eat on top of the picnic table. As soon as I had settled into position, I replayed that moment from the tent in my mind a few more times—I was *sure* I'd heard Piper say "bugfire"—until the screen door wheezed behind me.

"Please get off there and turn around." Mom sounded like she'd caught a trespasser on our property. As far as I knew, it was her first visit to the backyard since her accident. I climbed off the table.

"The neighbors called." She wore her pajamas and robe and leaned on her cane for balance. "Apparently, last night they had to cut short their evening out because you claimed there was an emergency, which turned out to be some sort of fantasy—or possibly a cruel joke?" she said. "You also left one of their children upstairs alone while taking the other outside, out of earshot?"

"No, that isn't what happened," I protested. Although I knew what probably had: Mr. Phoebe had called, not Joanna.

"I have to sit down." She walked carefully to the picnic table, swung her legs across the end of the bench, and fit them underneath. It was strange seeing her there.

"This is so unlike you, Alice," she continued. "Frankly, I'm worried about you. Did you *ask* my permission to babysit next door? No. Did you *tell me* you were going somewhere last night? No. Now you've embarrassed our family for the second time this summer. You may recall the night before Dad moved, when you took it in your head to run away and we had half the county police department looking for you."

"Mom, I'm sorry about that night," I said. "I said I was sorry, and it wasn't running away. I fell asleep at the pool and came home when I woke up." Let the ants eat the sandwich, I thought, tossing it into the bushes.

"Alice, that's wasteful."

I began pacing up and down the patio, feeling like a zoo animal.

"I want you living at your aunt's, starting tonight, and, next week, you can begin volunteering at her camp, where you'll have supervision and be doing something useful," she said.

"Mom, no," I protested, thinking fast. "I have Relay Carnival on Thursday night. The coach is counting on me." Mom would assume I was swimming, since I had every other year. She knew it was an honor to get into the Relay Carnival and wrong to let the team down. Plus, Coach B really was counting on me to be there.

"I don't know what to think about that, except I've never heard of anybody so full of excuses," she sighed. "You may like to sugar over problems, Alice, but pretending they're gone doesn't erase them. I'm worried about how impulsive you've become. As much as you want to help, it's not helpful—in fact it's cruel—to call people home from the middle of dinner, on their anniversary of all things, to say their disabled child has miraculously overcome a problem they need all their strength to face."

I stopped pacing. "But I did hear her, I swear."

"Oh, Alice," she said, as if we both knew that was impossible. "Here's a couple bravely coming to terms with the fact that their lives are changed forever. They're still trying to adjust to the idea that so many of their dreams have died. And you try reigniting that hope anyway, it's just thoughtless." The way she started to cry, you would have thought Piper was her daughter.

Mom lowered her head into her hands. "On top of everything else, I'm a failure as a parent. I feel like I've failed at absolutely everything."

Code Mud. I should have seen it coming. Maybe I hadn't because I was busy feeling like a failure, too: I'd broken babysitting rules, told the Phoebes less than the truth, hadn't convinced Dad to move home, and while I'd gotten into two A meets for backstroke, was nowhere near fast enough to get my name on the record board. Plus, Mom was practically out-and-out wailing.

Our voices weren't muffled, and the roof of the Phoebes' house was visible above the evergreens. I felt exposed, and spoke in a half whisper. "Mom, of course you haven't. I'm sorry I upset the Phoebes, I shouldn't have called them. Maybe I got it wrong when I thought I heard the girl speak," I added, even though I didn't believe that. "When they got home, their kids were fine," I threw in, echoing Joanna. "Piper, the girl, really likes me, thanks to everything I learned taking care of the twins."

Mom stretched her shoulders and extended her arms, as though she were performing one of her physical therapy exercises. She appeared to be reconsidering. "Well, perhaps that Mr. Phoebe got a little worked up," she conceded. "Maybe I'd overreact in his situation, too. It wasn't clear what he wanted, other than to complain and tell me I ought to reassess your ability to distinguish between fantasy and reality. On the other hand, he said his wife and kids were visiting family in North Carolina the rest of this week, but she'd be in touch about the following week. So what does that say?" She rested her arms. "Why must every single thing be so difficult? I don't know what I've done to deserve any of it." She held the tabletop for balance as she stood up. "I guess there's no need to drag this out, Alice, since we've got enough going on as it is. I suppose, if they're counting on you for Relay Carnival, I know how those meets are. But after that, I think it would be best if you moved to your aunt's."

"Thanks, Mom," I said, to sound agreeable without agreeing.

"All right, I've got to go in." She glanced at the branches of the tulip tree, overhanging the table, as if she doubted their ability to stay in place. "No more of those phone calls!"

13
THE RELAY CARNIVAL

THE AFTERNOON of Relay Carnival, I found a message on the kitchen phone from Georgia. I hadn't replied to texts she sent when she returned from camp, so she wanted to let me know she'd emailed, and other people had, too, and bye again, she was leaving for a trip with her parents.

A visit to the library would be an easy detour on my way to the pool, I decided. I rarely checked email—mine was mainly ads and spam. With an hour to go before Relay Carnival, I got on a computer in the glass-enclosed study room. Georgia, Malini, and Charlotte had wished me happy birthday, weeks ago, and sent links to YouTube clips from their shows at camp. Malini forwarded a picture of a guy she was really into, who she'd met there, plus announced she was on Instagram now. Dad, who loved the internet so much, said I wasn't allowed on anything that fell into the category of what he called Snooping Media until high school, although he had a Facebook page.

Yes, I was surprised they'd written, and surprised I was glad, and embarrassed all over again that, without explaining much, I'd quit spending time with them. I still didn't want to. They'd known me my whole life, so it seemed like giving them details that changed everything they knew about me was sort of like ripping up that whole life. Maybe that didn't make much sense, but that's how it was.

I wrote back thanking them, saying that I'd missed their texts because my phone was broken and so was our internet, and I'd just seen their emails. It was great they were having a great summer, I said, and my summer was great, and if they were ever at the pool it would be great to hang out.

Hopefully, I added to myself, when Harriet wasn't around.

Then I googled *crush feels like a rubber band or gravity* to find out if anybody else thought that. Also because I had no email address for Owen and wished I could be writing him. It was really kind of outrageous I didn't have a phone.

Science articles popped up, explaining gravity, and medical articles describing breathing problems that made you feel like you were being squished by rubber bands. After that came the articles about crushes.

The ones aimed at parents said, "Aren't our kids cute but keep your sixth grader from pairing off too soon on dates," which made me feel old. The articles giving advice to kids said, "Oh don't worry, whatever strange feeling you're feeling, with your cheeks flushing or finding yourself speechless, that's all normal." No one mentioned rubber bands. In my head I could hear my dad saying, "That falls into the category of Some Answers Aren't Online."

By now I was cutting it close to the time I'd promised Coach B to show up to help with the Eight-and-Unders, so I hustled to the pool. The Sharks were hosting the five other teams in our division for twenty-two relay races. The upper and lower parking lots and neighborhood streets were already packed with cars. Hundreds of people filled the pool grounds. The lawn had disappeared under chairs and bags, coolers and towels, and officials loaded the air with sound system tests and repeated announcements. I showed my group and their parents where to go and what to do. This included fishing three girls out of a towel fort and rounding up two boys from the snack bar. "Even if you're only in one relay," I said, "it's better to eat after your race."

Relay Carnival is crazy, which is why I liked it. "What's my blood type?" Coach B prompted several times through the roar. "B Positive!" we shouted back.

Dressed in a lobster suit, a coach from the Fairmead Lobsters did silly dives off the high board synced to Fairmead team cheers. On his third jump, with Lobsters screaming at the top of their lungs, I heard Harriet's voice: "Alice T. Spaniel! Here, girl!"

Again? She totally knew that story was private. I was in the Sharks team area with my crew of the youngest swimmers. All I needed was for that name to spread—I'd be laughed at forever. Then I saw that, along with Harriet, Coach B was waving furiously at me from the officials' table.

"You guys hang out with Mario, okay?" I said to my group. Mario, a senior in high school, was a junior coach, like I wanted to be someday.

Harriet dodged toward me through an obstacle course of tote bags, chairs, swimmers, toddlers, parents, and grandparents. "You're swimming!" she shouted, motioning that I should follow her.

"Someone scratched?" I called, but she was already darting back to the coach. Kids almost never dropped out of Relay Carnival. If they did, coaches could register a max of three substitutes at the referee's Scratch Meeting.

When I caught up to Harriet, she hugged me. "Elise Eggers didn't show up, so Coach B called her house. She has a fever, she vomited, she's in bed."

My blood felt like it was speeding down a highway express lane, and an unexpected tollbooth popped up— my heart—which forced the blood to pound it so hard that for a second I couldn't move. I'd resigned myself the day Coach B posted the lineup. If this news was true, one piece of my summer could be the same as every other year. On the other hand, Elise was our best 13–14 girl swimmer. If this news was true, it was terrible news. Chances for a Sharks win at Relay Carnival had dropped. Way down.

"What am I swimming?"

"All I know is Elise was doing Girls Thirteen– Fourteen Medley Relay with me."

At the officials' table, the ref appeared to be waiting impatiently for Coach B.

"I don't think I need to ask if you want to swim, Alice," Coach B said, "or if you're ready. But do you have your suit by any chance?"

I mean, how could a person go to a meet and not wear the team suit? I lifted up my Sharks T-shirt to show her.

"Excellent." She waved at the ref. "I'll ask the Marlins' coach if you can warm up with them."

"What am I swimming?" I prayed for freestyle. What I'd done seven carnivals in a row.

"Event twenty—back. Sinjin is doing Elise's other races."

Okay, all that matters is I'm swimming, I thought, while Harriet nodded at me, a big grin, like she'd predicted this.

Coach B smiled at my happy face. "I still need you to help with the little guys. Make sure they get to the clerk on time, okay?"

"Yes!" I said. "Thank you so much!"

"Thank *you*, Alice," she said. "You've made yourself indispensable."

"Take this—" Harriet undid one of her pigtails and handed me the scrunchie. It was only then I saw she'd changed from loons to sharks. "For good luck. Put it on under your cap."

I was the single blue suit in the water warming up with Marlin reds. I double-checked my stroke count from the flags to the wall in this pool: five again. There were only a few minutes to swim before they told everybody to get out for the national anthem.

"Looking good, Alice," Coach B said.

I was too nervous to tell if I did or not. Plus, I had to get Joey to the Clerk of Course table to check in and show him to his lane. It was his first-ever relay, and the final lap. Joey was a friend of my brothers' at school. He looked as nervous and pale as I remembered feeling before my first relay race, surrounded by bigger kids who all seemed to know what to do when I didn't.

"What's your favorite game you wish you owned?" I asked him.

He looked surprised. "Space Raiders Five."

I leaned down and said into his ear, "Swim your lap like Space Raiders Five is right there at the end, and you get to play it ahead of anybody you beat. And there's pizza."

He nodded, serious.

"Swimmers, take your mark," called out the parent working as the starter.

The buzzer sounded, light flashed, six kids dove, eighteen thumbs pressed stopwatches, and Joey, when it was his turn, took first.

It was one of those rare, hot, late afternoons that melted into early evening without even a threat of a thunderstorm. Rain so often rolled in as summer evening meets got underway that we were all used to delays and cancellations. But tonight, wisps of cloud floated by; a few white jet streaks fluffed into thicker ripples. I hadn't eaten my traditional pre-meet pasta and now it was dinnertime. I was hungry. I decided to take my own advice and survive on Gatorade until after my race.

Medley order is back, breast, fly, free. That meant me, Harriet, Sinjin, April.

Harriet offered to give me legs for my push-off. From the water I reached up and grabbed hold of her ankles. "Do me a favor," I said.

"What? I am doing you a favor."

"No calling out T. Spaniel!"

"Swimmers, take your mark," announced the starter.

Here I was, facing the wall, pulled-up ready for my backward leap. All seven Relay Carnivals I'd swum before, I'd been above where I was now, on the deck, where every freestyle race began: standing, looking straight ahead into the pool, bending forward to take my mark, one foot in front of the other, in the track-start slingshot position, to spring and streamline in.

This was all wrong, being down below and in the water, looking at the starting wall and the back of Harriet's legs. I felt like a plant torn out from the place it had been growing happily and stuck in a new garden. Never mind Harriet's predictions, because, for one thing, my pathetic losing finish last Saturday. Why had I agreed to this?

EHHHH—the flash of light—I arced backward, seeing nothing of where I was going, only feeling my hands and head and body break the surface, to re-enter the water. Underneath I dolphin-kicked a few yards and expected to come up stiff and awkward. But to my surprise my arms felt loose as I reached, and strong, as I pulled and watched the sky. I was liking this, facing the wrong way, not seeing the end of the pool. I knew exactly that it was: flags . . . five strokes . . . the wall . . .

Flip-turn, yes—and the voices of the crowd inflated the air with a cushion of energy—and I pulled the second twenty-five meters like I was ripping into wrapping paper on a huge, happy gift . . . flags, five strokes, the wall . . .

Harriet dove over me.

Panting hard, I climbed out in time to watch her surface from her tremendous pullout.

"Did you see what you did?" cried April, who was two years older than me, turning fifteen, one of those kids with the good swimming birthdays.

How badly had I slowed the relay, as the sub? April wasn't rude enough to get mad at me, was she, right before she swam? I was confused: she was grinning.

"Look! You finished first!" she said, and I climbed out of the water to see the pool.

Somehow I had. It took another moment for my relief that I hadn't screwed up to turn into excitement, like Sinjin's and April's. The three of us focused on Harriet, who, on paper at least, was capable of holding a lead against every breaststroker in the division except one: her current opponent, the Stingray she'd beaten at our first A meet who still had faster times. And Harriet did hold it, barely, even against the faster swimmer—who either had another bad day or wasn't quite able to make up the difference from my surprising lead.

And Sinjin held it.

By the time April dove, we had half a length's lead over the other five teams. When she touched the wall for the win, loud cheering erupted from every Shark swimmer and parent. Coach B threw her baseball cap in the air.

In each event, the winning relay team qualified to swim the same race at the All-Star meet at the end of the season. From nothing, from a fluke, I'd won a gold medal and was headed to All-Stars. I barely knew April or Sinjin before today. The four of us hugged like crazy.

The Sharks placed second overall at the Carnival, and would have been fourth without our relay win. At the end, as Harriet and I were collecting our towels and swim bags in our team area, she startled me by saying, "Alice, I'm sorry I didn't help you with Owen's brother."

I was still so up from the relay, I laughed. "You pick such strange times to say things."

"Girls, more good news!" called Coach B, to gather the four of us together again. "First things first." She handed around matching glow-in-the-dark shark key chains.

"What's the news?" asked Sinjin.

"Your relay broke the Sharks record for your event by more than three seconds," she said. "No one had beaten it in ten years. It's going to be a long time before that gets knocked off the board."

14
LUCIFERIN AND LUCIFERASE

OUR RELAY CARNIVAL medals came in clear sealed minibags, with white stickers listing our four names, winning time, team, and event number. The round piece was the size of a dollar coin, and the first-place gold hung from a triangle of blue ribbon, with a safety pin on the back, so you could wear it or mount it to display. On the gold was a map of the state of Maryland and the name of the league.

Here was proof, I thought, when Coach B handed me mine, that I hadn't lied to Mom about the meet after all. Plus, I'd swum straight into a perfect reason to go on living in the tent, until the All-Star meet.

I used Harriet's phone to call Dad from the pool. "Wow, Triple A," he said, "I can't believe I missed it. You didn't tell me you were swimming!" No, I hadn't, because he would have come to watch and discovered

I wasn't scheduled to swim, just got lucky about Elise. He didn't object when I said I needed to attend every workout for three more weeks.

"The record is the best part. Coach Bowling thinks it'll hold a few years," I said.

"I bet it's going to be hard waiting for them to switch out the old names and put your relay up there," said Dad. He knew exactly how I felt. It could take weeks for the parent volunteer to update the white plastic letters in the slots on the board.

"Oh, I won't be checking more than ten times each practice," I joked. "So it's okay with you if I stay with Mom until All-Stars?"

"Yes, it's great you're working so hard this summer on your swimming," Dad said. "I'm proud of you, sweetie."

The county All-Stars for relays and individual events were the final meets of our summer-league season. Unlike the rule that allowed me to swim at the last minute during Relay Carnival, no substitutions were permitted for All-Stars. The same four members of our winning team had to swim, or we would forfeit. It was all of us—or none.

I reminded Mom of this the next morning, when she started lobbying for me to move to Aunt Ruthie's now that Relay Carnival was over. Twice before, I'd qualified for All-Star relays that fell apart because one of the four kids was going to be away on vacation the day of the meet. Remember, I said, how disappointed the other kids and parents had been, us included. I wondered if she did remember. It was almost like I'd had a different mom back then.

"My teammates and their families expect me to swim," I went on while she sipped the coffee I'd brought her in bed. "How embarrassing would that be, if I pulled out and let them all down? I have to be at every practice."

She sighed. "You *have* to be at practice. You *have* to help with babysitting. You *have to be* as difficult as your father, don't you?" She was shaking her head, but she didn't say no. "He actually called me about this. Let me just say, while I don't agree it's the best use of your time, Alice, for now I'll go along."

"Thanks, Mom!" My heart thudded hopefully at the news of Dad calling and her taking his advice. Maybe they were starting to be friendly again, I thought, and, encouraged, I took the medal from my pocket. "Look," I said. "We broke a Sharks record."

She peered at the little bag. "So," she said, "if you're going to be here, how about sleeping in the house?"

"Is Dad moving home?"

"No, Alice." Mom sighed as if I'd asked a tiresome question and relaxed against her pillows. "I don't see what that has to do with it."

I felt afraid suddenly, reminded of everything in my family that had gone wrong. "When he does, I will," I said.

"You're turning into a difficult teenager, Alice. I don't like it," Mom said. "I don't have the stamina to take down that tent myself, and your father goes on saying it's fine."

"Sorry," I answered, so it sounded like *sorry-not-sorry*. "Can I refill your coffee?" I added, to remind her that I helped her, and also that I wasn't budging from how we'd been living so far this summer.

"No thanks." She smiled faintly, as if she understood, and in spite of her irritation appreciated the offer. "Let me rest now," she said, and I regained my feeling of victory and possibility.

The win at Relay Carnival floated me through the rest of that day and also the Saturday meet, where in my charged-up state of mind I won third place in backstroke. Another sign, Harriet said, that her prediction was coming true. I had not moved up from my rank as the third backstroker in our age group, though, behind Elise and April. My best time remained more than four seconds slower than the elusive 32.87. But I realized I didn't quite care that I probably wasn't going to stand out in an individual race this summer. Now that my name was going on the record board, it seemed to matter less to me what for.

At the end of the Saturday meet, Harriet wanted to come over to use Mom's darkroom for more firefly experiments. I needed a while to give Mom advance notice, since we'd be indoors, in the room with her cameras, and I told Harriet to wait a few hours.

Mom was sitting at the kitchen table, drinking coffee and peeling a hard-boiled egg, when I came inside to make a post-meet PBJ.

"My friend Harriet will be here later." I tried to sound super casual, to keep Mom from freaking out. "She needs a room with no light and a sink for a science experiment, for school. So I told her we could try our darkroom."

"And of course you didn't ask me first, Alice!" Mom laid the egg on her plate with the debris of shell and sighed. "Not that I'll ever again in this life use a film camera. But don't touch my photo things, please. I think your father broke my enlarger."

"We'll only be using the sink and the counter," I assured her.

"You'll do what you'll do, Alice, won't you?" She bit into the egg and chewed and added, more to herself, it sounded, than to me, "Well, pick your battles, as they say. I have enough other things to worry about."

Like what? I could have asked. Her problems seemed fixable to me, starting with why not invite Dad home. But to avoid trouble I said, "It'll be fine, Mom," and I went upstairs to collect her laundry and put in a load for us both.

The cherry blossoms were long gone and the old trees had leafed out in a green shade from the warm afternoon sun over Summit Avenue as I walked to the pharmacy, where Harriet and I had agreed to meet. She needed last-minute supplies and wanted my help carrying them to the tent.

Cherrywood's commercial strip squeezes into two blocks along Brookville. In the first, a pharmacy, grocery store, café, dry cleaners, and barber shop. The fancy French restaurant, C'est la Vie, takes up the second block. My dad had taught me to ride a bike in the parking lot on Saturday mornings and Monday evenings, when C'est la Vie was closed.

The grocery and pharmacy let Cherrywood families put purchases on store accounts, using phone numbers to keep track. Officially, kids weren't allowed to charge candy to phone numbers. One clerk at the pharmacy, however, who seemed to know my mom was confined to her bed, never took my cash when I set a pack of M&Ms or Skittles on the counter. This had started during the winter, when Mom was trying out medications to find one that worked.

When I caught up with Harriet, she was setting a jug of distilled water and two eyedroppers on the checkout counter in front of my favorite clerk.

"Two syringes, please," Harriet said.

"Syringes?" The clerk, whose name was Angela, glanced with surprise from Harriet to me—I was standing a little behind her—and back to Harriet. "Have you brought a prescription?"

Harriet shook her head. "They're for a science experiment, although I'm not sure why that matters."

"Syringes come with needles. You need a prescription." Angela was not unkind, but she was firm. I could tell she disliked the professor-ish twinge in Harriet's voice, which I had to agree came across as snooty, especially if you'd never met Harriet. If she'd been attempting to charge candy, Angela would have said no way.

"Well, I was hoping to use the needles for measuring," Harriet said more normally. "I could try without needles, I guess. Do you sell syringes without needles?"

"I can't sell you those."

One thing I'd noticed from waiting in line to pick up my mother's medicine: if people spoke to her impatiently, or too insistently, Angela could be stubborn. She set her mouth as if she'd finished with Harriet, and said something we couldn't hear to the other clerk helping the pharmacists. This second woman moved around from the high rear counter, where the medications were stored, to have a look at Harriet. She shrugged at Angela.

"Excuse me." I stepped forward, smiling like they and I were old friends. "All we want is two empty syringes, without any needles." Something told me they hadn't figured out Harriet and I were here together.

"These are for your mother?" Angela asked with some hesitation. "Your mother is not diabetic, is she?"

I had no idea why she asked that until I remembered, if you were diabetic, you had to give yourself shots.

"Yes, they're for my mother's account," I answered vaguely.

"Let me ask the pharmacist," she said.

Harriet hadn't told me in advance what she'd be buying. It hadn't seemed a big deal, but now we both wanted to be given what we'd asked for. I was losing track of how many times I'd crossed that line my dad talked about, between an inexact version of the truth and a lie; there were certain advantages to blurring it, I was finding. I wondered if Harriet thought this line was the same as the one between warm and cool? She was smart enough to keep her mouth shut.

The line behind us had grown to five people.

"Okay, we can give your mother two syringes without needles."

I slid two packages of M&Ms onto the counter with the other items, and Angela's face softened. She smiled. "Now tell me your phone number again," she said.

"What *do* you need syringes for?" I asked as we walked by a bride and groom posing with their guests at the entrance to C'est la Vie. The doorway had been decorated with garlands of white flowers. "My dad taught me to ride a bike there." I pointed to the parking lot where three black limos waited.

"I never learned how," Harriet said. "The syringes are for adding tiny drops of water to a beaker."

"You can't ride a bike?" I was surprised.

Before we'd entirely passed the wedding group, Harriet stopped short, ripped a hole in her bag of M&Ms, and shook three into her hand. "There's a substance that carries energy between living cells, like this—see?" She rolled a blue M&M back and forth between two yellows in her palm. "The blue one is that substance, ATP, adenosine triphosphate."

"Harriet, keep walking. These people are taking pictures," I said.

"I'm showing you my experiment in M&Ms!" she went on, as if it bothered her that I was changing the subject. It was hard to tell, from where we stood on the sidewalk, how much we were in the way. Harriet said, "The blue one helps fireflies make light. It has to mix with two other key ingredients, luciferin and luciferase. Those are the yellows."

The wedding photographer lowered his camera and glared. "Harriet," I said, "you are in a galaxy far, far away." I began walking quickly to put distance between us and C'est La Vie. "Sorry!" I called. "Congratulations!"

"You know, Alice," Harriet said, finally looking up from her M&Ms and seeing what I was apologizing for. "You're a good person. You try to do what's right."

This was uncharacteristically corny for Harriet. "We were in their way." I crumpled the M&M bag for trash in my pocket.

"I bet you pick up other people's litter, too, and carry it until you find the appropriate trash receptacle." Harriet was sincere and not making fun of me.

"Well, sometimes."

"C'mon, race you!" she shouted.

I let her go ahead. The midafternoon air was hot. The thick, gnarled cherry trees lining the street were unimpressed by the weak breeze; walking stirred it up a little. I was glad Harriet was coming over, but I did worry about what I'd promised to help her do that night. When she had first asked to keep fireflies in my tent, she wanted to catch two hundred. More than she needed, she said, "but I figure we'll make mistakes when we dissect them."

"*We'll* make mistakes?" Killing fourteen by accident on my birthday had been enough firefly killing for me. "I'm joining the Society for the Prevention of Cruelty to Insects."

"I meant me," she said. "But I hope you know that fireflies are making valuable contributions to medical research. Scientists have used firefly light to mark cancer cells in order to kill the bad cells with lasers."

"Fireflies can't sign a consent form," I said. "They don't know they're sacrificing themselves for science. And I didn't hear you say *your* experiment will make the world a better place for humans or fireflies."

"Like you said, Alice, it's only middle school. I'm not out to win a Nobel Prize. Just the county science fair."

So we made a deal: if she agreed to reduce the number of fireflies by half, I'd become her assistant assassin. That way, I'd save the lives of a hundred fireflies, and, indirectly, thousands of their descendants.

But Harriet sprang another surprise back on top of the picnic table. She wanted us to catch a fresh hundred in jars that evening.

"Please don't be mad, Alice. I reread the instructions: for optimal results, you're supposed to catch them the night you use them. The fireflies in the tent can be backups. We'll let them go when we finish."

At that moment Owen appeared in the yard, math homework in hand. "Hey," I said, feeling a blush bloom across my face. "When did you get back?"

"Hey, Alice. An hour ago," he said.

"He texted at the pharmacy, I forgot to tell you," Harriet said. "What's so funny?"

"Nothing! I don't know." I was laughing for some reason.

The two of them went over his latest assignment until sundown while I read *David Copperfield*. Then Harriet had us help her jar thirty fresh victims. She set their container in the freezer along with a mortar and pestle, and killed an equal number of fireflies by the same method in a second jar. Then Owen said he'd have to leave in an hour, so Harriet decided we could try her experiment with sixty.

"Do we *have* to cut up all sixty?" I said. The three of us were sitting on top of the picnic table. Dusk was collecting in dark patches in corners of the yard.

"I'll do it! I've had knife training," said Owen. Last spring, he said, he'd worked at a Japanese restaurant where the chef had taught him how to slice raw fish for sushi.

Every time I learned more facts from Owen's life, the less I felt I knew about him. You'd think that would shrink my crush. But no, the opposite. I'd only felt it grow until it had become like an invisible friend that kept me company.

Harriet went and got a second mortar and pestle set, a hot plate, another cutting board, X-Acto knives, digital thermometers, beakers in bubble wrap, and a bundle of test tubes. "Jeez, you guys are prepared," Owen said. I wondered if she'd brought over more supplies tonight. I didn't remember most of that from when we'd first unpacked her suitcases.

Mom could *not* see us bringing in so much stuff to the darkroom. "We have to be super quiet in the house until we get downstairs," I cautioned. "My mom sleeps at odd hours because of her . . . current schedule."

We moved silently through the kitchen, stopping to collect everything from the freezer, and went down to the bathroom in the basement.

"It's a *yanagiba*, a mini willow blade," Owen said as Harriet handed him an X-Acto knife. "We use those for sushi."

The knife was for separating a firefly's abdomen from the rest of its body. That lower belly part contained the light-producing chemicals.

Mom had mounted an amber darkroom light in the bathroom, which my dad had left up. By this dim glow, Harriet showed Owen where to insert the tip of the blade between the dark and light-colored sections of the abdomen. She made her incisions with so much confidence, I wondered how many other victims she had practiced on before tonight.

"I'll process five, and you do five, Owen," she said.

"Why 'process'?" I said, "when you mean 'slaughter,' 'dismember,' 'slice and dice'?" I was avoiding looking at the contents of the jars—more than four times the number of fireflies who'd perished being my birthday cake. I felt like apologizing to them.

"Alice, they're dead already. The freezer did that," she said. "When you eat a hamburger, meat comes from the meat-processing plant, right? People don't say, 'Here's ground beef from the cow-dismembering factory.'"

"Done," said Owen. Little piles of insect parts were arranged neatly on the white plastic cutting board.

Harriet gave him the rest of the job.

"What's with the cold board, by the way?" Owen shook out his wrists to warm them and resumed his precision cutting.

"Inside the abdomen parts you're *harvesting*," she looked at me, "are two chemicals. Luciferin and luciferase. When they combine, they glow.

"Heat wrecks luciferase. It changes the structure of the molecule," she went on. "When that happens, the luciferase can no longer combine with luciferin. So there's no light. If we keep the luciferase cold, its power will last longer."

"Like storing milk in a refrigerator," I said, explaining to myself out loud, "so it stays fresh."

"Correct," Harriet said.

"Whoa, we're in school," said Owen.

"This is exceedingly better than school," declared Harriet.

I asked, "Is there something I can do that doesn't involve dead bodies?"

Owen looked up at me from his surgery and grinned.

"I know." Harriet put me in charge of prepping the water, mortars, and pestles. Boxes of my mom's old supplies and cameras cramped the floors and filled the shower stall. I made room for the hot plate on top of the toilet lid, and Owen shared the sink space.

"Now comes the tricky part," Harriet said.

"We weren't doing that already?!" said Owen.

The next step, she explained, was to make two mixtures. She asked me for the cold items and turned off the amber lamp. The only hint of light slid under the door from a nightlight in the basement. We waited several minutes while our eyes adjusted to the near-black shadows.

Then Harriet counted ten abdomens into the chilled mortar, ground them with the pestle, and added a few drops of cold water through a syringe. A yellowish glow hovered in the mortar bowl.

"It worked!" I exclaimed. It *was* amazing to see light come from nothing.

"That bowl contains luciferase and luciferin," Harriet said. "A firefly keeps them separate until it blinks. We mixed the chemicals together by grinding the abdomens. That's why it glows."

Piper wouldn't have understood it was firefly light, but I wished she could see this. The surprise might have shaken through her, like in the tent, and then, who knows? Maybe I could have proved I was right.

As the light in the bowl faded, Harriet announced, "The luciferase is still there. But the luciferin is used up." She poured the small mixture into a test tube and set the tube in a beaker.

"Do you want ice for that?" I asked, remembering my job.

"No, now we need it to come to room temperature, the way it is inside a firefly." Harriet turned on the darkroom light. "Where's the thermometer?"

Owen passed it to her and shot me a look. Wasn't it amusing, his face seemed to want me to agree, that he and I were along for this ride on übernerd Harriet's odd adventure? I was glad it was so dark that, when I nodded, there was no way to see my face go red again.

Following her instructions, I boiled water on the hotplate and heated the second mortar and pestle under the tap in the sink. She repeated the same steps as before, this time grinding abdomens with the warm pestle, and adding drops of hot water.

"Doesn't that ruin the luciferase?" I said, worried that even Harriet could make a mistake.

"Exactly," she agreed. "We want it ruined. We're creating a mixture in which only one chemical works. The luciferin."

This one also glowed faintly until Harriet poured it into a test tube and set the tube in the beaker of heated water. When the light died she declared, "Okay, now the luciferase is kaput. Only the luciferin works. And it can't make light by itself." She made more notes as we waited for that tube to cool to room temperature.

"Now both mixtures are close to the temperature they'd be inside a firefly," she said. "Time for the grand finale." Harriet held up the two tubes, neither of which contained light.

"Witness what happens inside a firefly," she said. "I am pouring the tube of luciferin into the tube that still contains luciferase."

Like a witch's potion, the yellowish glow returned.

"Ta-da!" said Owen.

"It's like magic," I said.

"It's exceedingly efficient is what it is," said Harriet. "Old-fashioned incandescent light bulbs emit 10 percent of their energy in the form of light, or less. The rest is heat—wasted, if you're looking for a light source. Whereas"—she paused—"I mean, by comparison, firefly light gives off no heat. Almost 100 percent of the energy produced by fireflies is light."

I'd been following Harriet's explanations well enough to understand that the goal of her experiment was to recreate firefly light, and that she had succeeded. So it was confusing when she shouted, angrily all of a sudden, "Ohmygodohmygod! I'm an idiot, full of sound and fury, and it all signifies nothing!"

"Huh?" said Owen.

"I thought the experiment worked. All I get is that you're quoting something," I said.

"*Macbeth* act five near the end. I am so dumb." Harriet turned on the overhead light, sank to the floor, and stared into a pile of old camera boxes. I leaned against one of my mother's portfolio cases.

"What a waste of time," she said.

"Did I cut something wrong?" asked Owen.

"Not at all." She crossed her arms and rocked back and forth on her heels. "Dumb, dumb, dumb."

"Is this a way of telling us you killed sixty fireflies for nothing?" I asked.

"Everyone makes mistakes," Owen said, with a shrug to suggest I should go easy on Harriet.

She spread her fingers, palms up, and repeated those words, as if he'd uttered the solution to a hard riddle. "Everyone makes mistakes!"

"What?" Owen and I said together.

She rose to her feet. "Your basic stale proverb. Maybe you've heard this one: 'No two persons looking at the sky see the same shade of blue'? Well, that's my problem. I wanted to find out if mixing firefly chemicals at different temperatures creates different colors of light," she said. "But I have no instrument to measure color or brightness. Only my eyeballs or yours. I need an accurate, objective tool. Since I don't have one, the most I could do tonight was show that, when you remove two substances from a firefly and recombine them, they glow. There were no variables to measure. That means I performed a demonstration, but not an experiment."

"You're making it too hard," I told her. Harriet had no clue how far she was overdoing things, by the standards of most kids at Cherrywood Middle School. "Your experiment could be a lot simpler and still win a prize at the science fair."

"That's true," Owen said.

"That's not true," she snapped. "Neither of you knows what you're talking about."

I was just thinking how much I disliked Harriet's condescending tone, and wondering if the reason she'd been wanting to hang out had mostly to do with my backyard and her geeky interest in fireflies, and not a lot with being friends—when I heard Mom from the top of the basement stairs: "Alice—Alice Amary Allyn—I know you and your friend are down there. Come up here now—immediately!"

15
TAKE ANOTHER PILL

"WHAT ARE YOU doing in the basement!" It was more of an accusation than a question.

"Harriet's experiment," I said from halfway up the stairs. "I told you we'd be using the darkroom, remember?" It seemed best not to mention I had a second friend over, a boy. Besides killing too many fireflies, we were doing nothing wrong.

Mom stood in her bathrobe in the open doorway and spoke in a low, quiet, controlled voice, full of scorn, a voice I heard only during her most terrible fights with Dad. "I have just gotten off the phone with Kathleen Rubio, the head pharmacist at Cherrywood Pharmacy." My stomach dropped. "As a courtesy, a community service, she said she was calling to be sure I indeed needed the syringes you purchased for me today! She said her staff agreed to give them to you because they know our family. However, after you left she thought she had better double-check our family pharmacy files, and she correctly realized that none of us uses medication requiring injections. That's twice in one week I've received complaints about your egregious behavior, Alice. Granted the man next door sounded a bit full of himself. But this is beyond embarrassment. You are further gone than I ever dreamed."

"I can explain—"

"And what is it this time?" She had been leaning on her cane, and now she pounded it on the floor. "You and your friend, who by the way I have never met, are doing drugs? Her mother sounded nice on the phone, after you had lunch there one day. She probably has no idea, either. Don't think I won't call her."

"Calm down," I said, stepping back to a lower stair and thinking: Code Mud. Code Mud had never happened when anybody besides my family was in the house.

"Injectable syringes are used by people abusing illegal drugs," my mother declared.

"The syringes are for Harriet's science experiment," I explained.

"Then why did you lie and say they were for me?" she went on, hard and hateful.

"Harriet needed them to measure water," I said. It wasn't going to work this time, to offer to bring herbal tea up to the bedroom if she would agree to go lie down. That's what I wanted, words to persuade her to grab the banister behind her and go away. "I thought the pharmacy wouldn't give syringes to us unless the clerk thought they were for you. I don't see why she called, since we bought them without needles. They're no good for drugs without needles, right?"

"According to Mrs. Rubio, needles are easy to come by—for junkies. If I find they've been used, I'm sorry, but it's going to be tough love: they are going to be analyzed in a lab before I'm going to believe you." Her voice was so cold. I thought of the jars Harriet had stuck in the freezer.

"Mom—that's crazy. You're being ridiculous."

Her frown creased lines into her face so deep, she looked like an angry emoticon. If she hadn't been so mad, with her bathrobe tied messy and uneven and her knuckles white from gripping hard on top of the cane, I could have almost laughed.

"Am I?" she said. "You're the liar. You just admitted you purchased syringes, saying they were for me, which is a lie."

"Mom, I am way too young to do what you're talking about."

"After this last year, I'll believe anything and trust no one."

She was talking like I was a stranger. "The person in the family who takes drugs is *you*, Mom," I said. There were so many things I was tired of, they all came out at once. "I don't even know what they are. You take drugs to make you sleep. You take them to make the pain in your back go away. You take them not to be depressed. If anyone's addicted to taking drugs, it's you. *I* am not taking drugs. I'm the one who picks them up for you at the pharmacy. All I'm doing is helping my friend do a stupid science experiment that's not even working!" I spun around.

"Don't you turn your back on me."

"Maybe Mrs. Rubio was calling to make sure *you're* not the junkie!" I was let-loose shouting now.

"Do not speak to me that way!" Mom ordered. "I should have sent you to your aunt's the day your father moved out."

I closed my eyes and tried to see sky like I was swimming backstroke. I felt the cool, sure water, even my arms pulling to the blue-and-white flags—and it all came clear. "I'm sick of being suspected I'm doing something wrong and yelled at when I try to help people!" I said. "I hate how everything you remember about our family is bad. I'm tired of trying to keep you from crying and taking care of you and it does nothing and all you do is complain. None of my friends make their moms lunch!"

"Alice! Alice, stop!"

But I couldn't. I felt as fierce as when I was trying to win a race. I opened my eyes and walked back up the stairs toward her. "*You* drove Dad away. *You* got rid of Mike and Josh, and now you want to get rid of me, when everything is fine. You've ruined *everything* for *all* of us."

Mom moaned in low gasps, the start of her *eh-eh-eh* cry. "Why is this happening to me?"

But now I felt as cold as she'd sounded. "Just take another pill," I spat at her. "And go back to bed."

16

TELLING OWEN

FOR ONCE I hoped Harriet was so interested in her science details in the darkroom that she hadn't paid attention. I couldn't imagine her ever talking like that to her parents, or even to Lydia. I couldn't stand the idea of Owen telling Mr. Phoebe and Joanna, which would confirm I was as bad as they thought.

Something had broken, something was finished with Mom and me. I didn't know what. I couldn't describe it. I hated me, her, pretty much the whole situation. There was no way I was going to do what she wanted.

I wished I'd never agreed to help Harriet kill fireflies that were now dead for no reason. She was probably going to tell me we needed to kill hundreds more for some new experiment. And when I refused to help, she'd stop hanging out with me and spend all her time with Owen, they would do math and he'd cut up two hundred fireflies in two seconds and become her boyfriend—though it was hard to imagine Harriet having a boyfriend, so not that part.

I hated that Mom accused me of lying when the trouble started because of her, and I hated, on top of that, that the Phoebes thought I was a liar, too.

I felt like I was a liar.

I was a liar.

"Excuse me, Mrs. Allyn!" Harriet nudged me out of the way and climbed to the top of the stairs. Mom backed off from the doorway, into the kitchen. "Here are the syringes."

At the sight of Harriet, *exceedingly* short Harriet, with her glasses, her Sharks hair scrunchies, her swim shorts and team T-shirt, my mom looked puzzled. She seemed stuck for something to say and kind of sank down at the kitchen table.

In a flat, stiff voice on purpose, I said, "This is my friend Harriet Barclay."

"Hello." Mom nodded almost formally. "I had a nice talk with your mother the other day."

Out of the corner of my eye, I saw Harriet look at me out of the corner of hers. Owen, wisely, had stayed in the basement.

"Well, how do you do," Harriet said. She held out the syringes to Mom, who took them and rolled the little tubes between her fingers.

"Tell me what this experiment is all about," Mom said in the same relatively normal tone. She was looking at the kitchen wall, as if, in fact, she'd prefer not to hear the answer.

"Of course," Harriet said. "Well, for Lampyridae of the species *Photinus pyralis* and *Photuris pennsylvanicus*—that is, assuming the Lampyridae we collected do fall into these two most common species, which Alice helped me out so much with confirming by visual inspection . . ."

Here Mom glanced suspiciously at me. The idea of me assisting with a serious biology experiment must have sounded like a stretch. Harriet continued as if she were speaking to the science fair judges: ". . . there exist color variations in the light produced by the ordinary chemical reaction of luciferin with luciferase, variations I hoped to alter by controlling the temperature at which these two substances, when isolated, interact. However, tonight I encountered substantial obstacles to taking accurate readings. . . ."

The wrinkles on my mother's forehead relaxed completely. I knew those syringes weren't going anywhere.

In fact, she set them on the kitchen table. I also knew she was wondering why on earth I was suddenly hanging out with a girl like this, a rocket scientist way out of my orbit.

"Well, that's very interesting. You girls have fun," Mom said, pronouncing each word slowly, as if I had brought home a friend whose first language was not English and whose native culture was also foreign. "Have a snack if you get hungry." She didn't look at me again, and I stared at the floor. "Good night," she said. She climbed the stairs one at a time with her cane. It felt like the slowest ascent in the world.

Until we heard her bedroom door shut, I didn't look at Harriet either, and she didn't look at me. "So," I said, "is it time to clean up? Or are we doing the experiment over?"

"Alice, I'm sorry, I didn't realize . . ."

She left the sentence unfinished.

"How awful I am?" I half joked, embarrassed.

"You know that's not what I mean." Harriet's head, eyes on her toes, shook short and fast like a bobblehead.

Whether it was my mom or the failed experiment, Harriet decided we were through for the night. After speed-cleaning the darkroom, the three of us snuck out the back kitchen door. Harriet wanted to do more research at home instead of sleeping over, or so she said, and texted Lydia for a ride.

"What about the fireflies in the tent?" I asked. "You said we were going to let them go when we finished." The fate of those fireflies was irritatingly of less concern to Harriet than her experiments.

"Can it wait until tomorrow?" she said.

"I'll help with the fireflies," offered Owen, and Harriet left to wait for Lydia in the front yard.

In the tulip tree, up high, and in the oaks, maples, and pines in surrounding yards, it looked as though someone had strung up beaded lights, and each tiny bulb was blinking on its own circuit, at a different time. I told Owen those fireflies probably belonged to different species from the ones lower down, in case that kind of thing interested him, and pointed out a few blinking greenish lights flying in the *J*-swoop pattern near the grass.

"I didn't see fireflies where I grew up," Owen said.

"Because you lived west of the Mississippi," I told him. "In the U.S., most fireflies are east of the river." More Harriet facts.

"Why do you think flying insects with lighted butts exist?" he said.

"I don't know." I shook my head. "You could ask the same question about a blade of grass or a picnic table."

"Except the grass and the table don't illuminate with chemicals only Harriet understands. She's the

scientist," he said, laughing. "And you're the philos-
opher." He pulled out his phone to check the time. "I
have fifteen minutes to liberate fireflies."

I felt my heart pound as he followed me into the tent.

"You've got furniture!" he said.

I explained that the shelves and equipment belonged
to Harriet, and showed him my setup of pillows and
sleeping bags. Now that we were here, it was obvious
it was going to take longer than fifteen minutes to find
the fireflies in the folds of the canvas. I'd need a ladder
for the ones on the ceiling. "Never mind," I told Owen.
"I'll just do it tomorrow when it's light." I kind of liked
having them in there with me anyway, by now.

He made no motion to leave, so I set a flashlight on
the floor, pointed away from us at Harriet's shelves, and
sat down on the sleeping bags. He snapped a picture of
a firefly on the center pole and took a seat near me.

"Nice phone," I said. It looked new.

"My dad gave it to me." Owen paused. "He and
Joanna told me what happened, by the way."

"That's embarrassing." I felt my face grow hot.

"You don't seem like a person who would make that
up," Owen said.

"Your dad said I did. At least Joanna said I might
have just imagined it."

"Isn't that the same?" he asked.

"No. It's like the difference between a lie and a good intention," I told him. "But I didn't make it up, and I didn't imagine it, either."

"Alice, if you say you heard Piper talk, I believe you. It's strange no one else has," he conceded, "but that doesn't mean you didn't. She hasn't talked once since I've been here, but Joanna says you two do have something special going. Maybe she only does it for you."

"It was the fireflies," I said.

Then neither of us spoke, and neither of us moved. Out of nowhere I hoped Owen wanted to kiss me. It was a thought I'd never had about a boy. Scary, but I didn't stop having it. I could feel how close to me he was sitting, even though I was looking in another direction. The air was stuffy, and I whiffed sweat from my Sharks T-shirt and remembered Coach B's voice saying, *Relax those shoulders,* so I did.

Owen reached out and touched my wrist. "Alice, I know what you're thinking. I mean, I guess I don't *know*."

My heart bounced, or flipped, whatever that is, since you can't see it move. I kept my eyes on the plastic crates.

He touched my cheek with the back of his fingers. The rest of my body couldn't move, which was dumb, and yet I let it be that way, to capture the feeling of his fingers as long as possible.

"I should tell you," he said, "I have a girlfriend, in Denver." He paused, and laughed a little more. "I like you, Alice, but I promised . . ."

"Oh, that's fine!" I interrupted, as though I were in a big hurry, and I shook my legs out like we did after stretching exercises at swim workouts. "What's her name?"

"Riko. We met at her family's restaurant."

I felt like a ladder had been pulled off from a place I wanted to climb to. I felt surrounded by a much bigger empty space than actually lay between us. Thank goodness the light was pointing away from my face.

"I worked there after school and on weekends," he continued, "more hours than work permits let you when you're fifteen."

"Because of her?" I settled cross-legged, like on top of the picnic table. Maybe if I asked questions like I was interested in his girlfriend, I would trick myself into not caring that he had one.

He nodded. "I liked working there, too, much more than homework, which sort of dropped off, which is why I ended up retaking math in summer school."

"Didn't your mom notice about your homework?" I asked, getting genuinely interested in Owen's other life for the first time.

"No. She doesn't pay attention to stuff like that. She has two jobs and school at night. Whether I do homework is up to me, she says. I think I want to be a chef. I could have shown you guys how to make firefly sushi out of Harriet's well-stocked personal collection. . . ."

"They're not hers!" I protested, louder than I expected. "They're bugs, they belong to the air!"

"I was just kidding, Alice." He knocked his knee against mine. "What's wrong?"

"I'm sorry." I felt a little stupid, when I knew he wasn't being serious. Or sort of knew. "It's just that nothing ever works out. I hate—everything." Which wasn't true; Relay Carnival worked out. I didn't hate everything. I liked fireflies, Piper, Harriet. I liked Owen. I could think of dozens of things I liked. M&Ms. And suddenly I was crying.

Owen put his arm around me. "Aw, Alice . . . Alice, it's okay. I wondered why you were sleeping out here so long. Is it because of your mom? That was . . . intense."

"It's because she went to the grocery store to buy hot dog buns," I said, and I laughed, because his arm made me nervous, and because I wanted it to seem like I was making a joke, because I was wiping tears from my face, and because it all came down to something that sounded so silly, a small bag of bread.

Then I told Owen what I hadn't told Harriet. How, after my mom ended up in the hospital for three months and had six operations, by the time she came home, the rest of us had practically gotten used to her being gone. How my parents fought all the time, she kept crying, my brothers cried when they heard her, and she never wanted them in her room. How she stayed in there except if she had a doctor's appointment, and I had to take care of Mike and Josh if my dad wasn't home. "And then she asked him to leave, so my aunt took Mike and Josh, and everybody wanted me to go there, too," I said. "I love Aunt Ruthie, but she lives too far from the pool. If I couldn't at least swim on the team this summer, it seemed like everything would be gone. But if Mom had just been willing to eat those stupid hot dog buns that we already had, that the rest of us were perfectly fine with, I bet none of this would have happened."

"Alice, wow," Owen said. "That is a lot to carry around." He was silent a minute. "So this is the escape tent?" he added. "What will you do when it gets cold?"

My left foot was starting to tingle. When I moved it, he took his arm away to press his watch button. I had to admit I felt relieved when he did that. "I don't know. But . . . I did lie to your dad and Joanna. Harriet had put all these fireflies in the tent, so when I thought of teaching Piper how to catch them, I brought her here. This tent is where I heard her talk. Not your deck. I left Timmy behind, and I forgot his baby monitor. If he'd woken up, or something had happened, I never would have known." I gulped. My body felt sticky with nervous sweat. "There's so much I screwed up that I can't undo. That's the real truth."

Owen was quiet. "That's funny," he said.

"It's actually not."

He laughed. "Well, what you said? Kinda sorta how I end up feeling a huge, huge, huge percentage of the time—pretty much only because I exist."

"What does *that* mean?" I said.

"For me? I don't know. For you, I think it means don't be too hard on yourself, Alice."

That reminded me of a saying of Dad's I'd forgotten: there's always a way to find something to put in the Silver Linings category. There must be a way to make something good come out of my mistakes. "Owen, let's prove it wasn't wishful thinking. *Or* imagination." I held up his phone. "We could use this."

"Video?" he asked.

I nodded.

"Right," he said. "Let's do it."

"One other thing," I said. "Do you ever wish your parents lived in the same place, and your dad had never met Joanna?"

"You are the girl with a thousand questions," Owen said. "No. I don't. That kind of wishful thinking wouldn't do anyone any good. What *would*, is your video. That could do a lot of people a lot of good. I'm late," he said, getting up. "Make a plan." And then he left.

17
FINALLY

THE EVENTS OF that night fell into so many different categories that, in the morning, when I climbed onto the picnic table, my legs wouldn't stay crossed. I had too much to think over. It was two hours too early for the pool, though, so I decided to cut the grass.

The front yard was done, the back was almost, when Dad strolled in through the side gate. He had on jeans and the heavy boots he wore for mowing. I switched off the mower. "Aren't you supposed to be at the library?"

"Hi, Triple A. I'm very well, thank you, how are you? Ordinarily, I don't work on weekend mornings," he said.

"Or live with your family, either."

"You're in a fine mood. Sit with me." He nodded at the grass. "Thank you very much for that."

"This is the fourth time, and today I used up the gas in the container," I said, "so we need more. I haven't been edging or trimming. . . ."

"Sweetie, no one's expecting you to do any of this, though you know I'm grateful to you for filling in."

We sat across the picnic table from each other. Here was the chance I'd been hoping for, since Relay Carnival. "Dad, don't you think it's a mistake, the five members of our family living four different places? It's like there is no family."

"Nothing's stopping you from living with Mike and Josh," he said mildly.

"That's not what I meant." I reminded him I had practice for All-Stars.

"Well, nothing's keeping you from sleeping in your bedroom, either, for that matter," he said, "though a tent does look more fun." He caught my eyes and smiled. "I did come here this morning to talk about exactly this, to tell you one important thing." He clasped his hands on the table and folded mine in between them. "If you prefer not to visit my apartment for now, that's okay, I understand, but I wanted to let you know I've taken out a year's lease. I had to decide last week and sign the papers. I'm working with your mom on how we'll arrange things for you and the boys when school starts." He raised a palm to stop me when I tried to interrupt. "I don't have news about the house yet, but I'll take it from here with cutting the lawn. No need for you to keep doing it."

"That's . . . six things," I said, water filling in around my eyes.

"Alice . . ."

"You said one thing. And I'm not living anywhere else besides this tent until you move home."

"Triple A . . ." He tried to pat my hands to comfort me but I pulled them off the table, into my lap, and turned my head. "Your mom doesn't want me to come back, and well, I've decided that, even though it makes things harder on our family, it's for the best. She's less upset, we've managed to fight less, and you kids need to stop hearing all that."

The hope I'd had drained out, like someone had emptied the water from Cherrywood Pool and told me to get in and swim laps anyhow. "If you hate it here so much, why did you come all the way over to tell me? You could have called!"

"I'm sorry," he said. "I'm very sorry for you and Mike and Josh. We have to try our best to make it all work."

"If you did your best, you'd put up with Mom and move back," I said. "If she did her best, she'd put up with you. You picked each other. Then you had us. And if you're thinking of marrying another person, I read online that second marriages end up in divorce even more than first marriages."

Dad seemed relieved, which was irritating. He smiled at me, which was more irritating. "Marrying someone else is the last thing on my mind. As a librarian, it's my job to remind you to verify your internet sources, although I've read that, too."

"That would fall into the category of Horrible."

"All right." He stood up from the table. "Thanks to you, there's no lawn to mow. I've said what I came to say. I hate making you sad. How about we make the best of this imperfect path we're on? I can give you a ride to the pool, if you like."

"It doesn't open for another hour."

"Well then." He clicked his tongue, like *What can you do.* "I am sorry that wasn't what you wanted to hear. We'll talk more soon." He came around and kissed the top of my head.

For a while, I read on the picnic table and peeked at the end of *David Copperfield*, which I'd decided to use for my summer book report. Just as I hoped, David married Agnes, and they sat together around a warm fireplace with their children and lived happily ever after.

"Alice? Do you have a minute?" It was Joanna on her side of the fence, at the rosebush.

Without my dad's attention this summer, the roses had grown in a hundred directions on our side. Up, in, out, down, over, straight, arcing, weaving. Dozens of pink-white blooms and rows of shark-fin thorns sprouted on every stem.

"It's about the other night," Joanna began, as I came over. "I'm afraid Eric was already upset with me for not hiring an adult sitter." She folded back two long stems of the bush to widen the view. "It's been a complicated move for us from Arizona. We've dropped the ball in so many ways with Piper. How did Owen put it this morning? 'A collision between your kindness and wishful thinking, and our falling hopes.'"

"I apologize for upsetting you," I told her dully. "I made a mistake." It was the right thing to say, so I said it, without specifying what I'd done wrong. Unless Owen had revealed I'd taken Piper to the tent, that remained my secret. But why, I wondered, after saying he believed me, had Owen told his stepmother that what I heard was "wishful thinking"?

We all knew Piper made grunts, squeals, and cries, Joanna was saying, "so it's understandable you could have wished a word from her sounds. You want her to get better, we all do. There's nothing we want more." She laughed at the obstacle of the rosebush between us and let go the stems she held. "Anyway, there's lots to do, from yardwork to our hunt for a permanent sitter," she went on. "And until I figure things out on that score, if you're still up for it I could use you as a playmate for Timmy in the mornings for a few weeks. If you no longer want to, I understand."

Of course I said yes, and Joanna and I agreed on the usual time for Monday.

It felt great to be back in the water at Monday's morning practice, getting ready for All-Stars with backstroke tips from Coach B. "Dolphin kick no more than fifteen meters or you'll be disqualified," she began. "Turn into the wall on your last pull, make it one continuous motion to avoid gliding." She assigned me arm-up drills with six-beat kicks, one-arm drills with a pull-buoy, and kickboard sets to strengthen my legs.

April, Sinjin, Harriet, and I also practiced our relay starts. There's a rhythm to relay starts, because there's no light or buzzer. You dive as your teammate finishes. She has to touch the wall to end her part of the race before your feet leave the pool deck to begin.

When I tried to discuss the night in my basement with Harriet, she cut me off. "Exceedingly regrettable, in more ways than one," she said, raising a hand to stop me. "No need to revisit." Immediately after practice, she rushed to the parking lot for her ride to another day camp, I forget what kind.

At the Phoebes', Joanna reverted to our old routine as soon as a mom from down the street invited her and Timmy for a playdate: I was left in charge of Piper. By now, she and I were communicating with nodding, shaking heads, pointing, touching, smiling, frowning, like she did with her mom. Not perfectly, not all the time. But I had the satisfaction of accomplishment when I understood correctly that she wanted a cookie or to play our ball game or to watch television. When we unpacked a tub of dolls on the family room carpet, I figured this was as good a time as any to practice for filming with Owen. Tapping Piper's shoulder, I asked out loud, "Can you say 'doll'?"

She giggled and stood. Her gaze abruptly fixed on something, I couldn't tell what, out the windows behind the couch. "Bugfire!" I said.

Piper's mesmerized expression, past me into the trees and sky, was like the day I first saw her in her backyard. I knelt to put us eye to eye and tried *"Piper,"* *"snack,"* *"dress."* No response. Until I held out my hand. Then Piper's eyes moved to me. She took mine, smiled, and didn't object to being led up the staircase. I knocked on Owen's door.

"Oh hey, Alice, I didn't know you were here yet." The crush rushed in, but my mission for Piper felt more important. He swiveled his desk chair to face us and lifted his phone in the air. "Should we give a try?"

"I did." I shook my head.

Piper pulled her hand from mine and climbed into a lumpy beanbag chair in the corner. "Owen, why did you tell Joanna what I heard was 'wishful thinking'?"

"Oh, that. I figured it was our best shot at sealing a deal for you to keep babysitting. To have chances like now. Want to sit?"

I molded a spot in the beanbag beside Piper, who promptly moved to my lap. "Also," I said, "why would Joanna ask me to, after the other night? I'm glad—it gives us plenty of opportunities. But why not ask you? They can't be making you study math twenty-four hours a day."

Owen looked at his calculator guiltily. "I asked not to, this summer. Last year, too. It's a jinx thing. Going back to when she was born, the first time I held her. She slid onto the floor on her head." He closed his eyes and reopened them. "When she was Timmy's age, before she got sick, one time I was in charge of her and we were going downstairs in the old house. She was in front, she tripped and bumped her head and lost consciousness."

He shrugged like he was a hopeless case. "We did the whole nine-one-one thing. They said she was fine, and my parents claim there's no connection to now. But I can't shake it. Or that my dad suspects it." He clasped his hands decisively on his knees. "I'm very up for this video. Tell me what we do."

I said we had to film at night, with fireflies. We made a plan for Owen to bring Piper outside to the lawn behind the Phoebes' deck between her dinnertime and bedtime. I'd prepare fireflies in heated accelerator jars, the kind Harriet had shown me how to make.

Early that evening, however, it rained. Without a way to text, we'd agreed in advance not to try in bad weather. Instead, I read *David Copperfield* by flashlight. It was comforting to know, from skipping ahead, at least David's troubles worked out by the end.

The air in the tent grew thick, and fast loud drops beat on the canvas. The sound reminded me of the time a music teacher at school had lifted the lid of a piano to reveal the hammers hitting the strings. She said the piano was a cousin of the drum.

I couldn't help thinking this rainstorm was a percussion instrument, too. Like maracas in the heavy downpour when it crackled. Like sandpaper blocks when it slowed to a soft, shushing drizzle. And in the middle of the night, it sounded like people who couldn't figure out where to put their furniture, so they kept rearranging it in different rooms of the sky. Lightning lit up the tent, and water dripped down the center pole and through the seams.

It had been days since I'd seen fireflies blink in the tent. The ones I'd found, I released into the grass. In the rain, I came across one or two more in the folds of the canvas. If there were other leftover bugs, perhaps they'd snuck out.

I covered Harriet's shelves with plastic garbage bags and spread two on top of my sleeping bag like a thin bedspread. I had no desire to go in the house. I wasn't afraid; I was listening for a message in the sounds to tell me how it was that Piper could hear these nature noises but was deaf to words. I remembered the yellow-striped firefly I'd set in her hand. Her outstretched palm allowing me to add four more. The look on her face when she said "bugfire." At that moment, a spark had crossed over from nature to language—why?

Unfortunately for our plans, the same weather held the next day. Rain starting in the late afternoon, ending by sunrise. Wednesday, when the final B meet was also cancelled due to rain, it felt like the rain must have been chatting with my parents. Together, they'd agreed to drown my summer, to keep so much from happening how I wanted.

Of course it had to be the day of Owen's next trip when the sun finally came out. Before Joanna drove him to the train station, we walked together to Cherrywood Pool, where he was meeting Noah Gaines for a quick game of tennis. My mood seemed to sink with each step, and Noah was already waiting for him out front by the courts.

"In ten days, when I'm back, we do the video," Owen said. "One hundred percent. It can't keep raining. Got it?" We'd have three weeks then to try, he said, before his flight back to Denver for the new school year. He patted my back and signaled goodbye with a twirl of his racket.

I waved, already missing him, yet glad about Riko, too, not that that made any sense.

Out of habit, my eyes skimmed the Sharks record board as I crossed the deck to the lap pool area to set my bag down before practice. And then I saw it, bang, like the loudest thunderclap from the rain, pots clanged, major drumroll: GIRLS 13–14 MEDLEY RELAY, 2:19.36, A. ALLYN, H. BARCLAY, S. REED, A. WANG

I've always loved Cherrywood Pool.

Now I belonged here forever.

Finally!

I slung my bag on a chair and—not caring if the guard blew a whistle at me for running—rushed back through the clubhouse out to the tennis court where Owen and Noah had started playing. "Owen!" I shouted. He lowered his racket from serving and came to the fence where I was standing. "Something good happened!" I said. "My name's on the board!"

"Nice!" he said.

Did anybody really get this, besides me? It felt bigger than I could explain.

When you've worked years for something that seemed like it would never happen, due to a crummy swimming birthday, anatomy, and who else was on the team—and then it did happen, by accident?

GIRLS 13–14 MEDLEY RELAY, 2:19.36, A. ALLYN, H. BARCLAY, S. REED, A. WANG

GIRLS 13–14 MEDLEY RELAY, 2:19.36, A. ALLYN

A. ALLYN

This may sound strange, but when I went back in and read my name there for the tenth time, I thought I knew why fireflies fascinated Piper. They were like a spark of possibility—a flash of magic—that at any moment life could give you what you most hoped for, even if it came by accident: *bugfire*.

18
FORTUNE COOKIES

"HARRIET, DID YOU SEE? Our relay time is up on the board."

I caught up with her at the snack bar window. We had branched out from curly fries to fruit smoothies and cheese quesadillas to be healthy. "I'll wait here if you want to go look," I offered.

"I saw." Our food slid onto the pick-up shelf and Harriet reached for hers.

"Aren't you excited?" I followed to a table with mine. "I've been wishing I could be on there since I was six."

"It's nice. But the Cherrywood Sharks record board isn't high on my list of top life goals," Harriet said.

She hadn't spent more than half her life on the Sharks like I had. Oh well. I was happy.

"Speaking of top life goals," I started out, "please tell me that whatever your next experiment is, it's not about chopping up the rest of the fireflies in my yard."

Harriet said, "I assume you know the story of Archimedes and the bathtub?"

"I do not." I ate a quesadilla triangle. A picture appeared in my head of us shaking fireflies out of a jar over a bathtub.

"One day the ancient Greek ruler of Syracuse orders herself a new crown," Harriet began. "The goldsmith delivers a crown she says is made of pure gold."

"Wait a sec," I interrupted. *"Herself? She?* Ancient Greece, you said. Wouldn't it be a *he?"*

Harriet shook her head to mean it didn't matter. "The story is most likely apocryphal." She saw I didn't know that word. "It probably is not true. He, she, they—gender is beside the point," she went on. "The ruler suspects she's being cheated. Her fantabulous new crown might be made from a cheaper metal, silver, concealed beneath a thin layer of gold. She asks Archimedes, the mathematician, to figure it out."

"Harriet," I said, "what are you talking about?"

"I'm coming to that." She looked at her plate as though she'd forgotten it was there. "By the way, a few rulers of the ancient world *were* queens. Etazeta of Bith—"

"Great, Harriet. What is your point?"

"Archimedes needs time to cogitate. To think," she said. "He goes to take a bath, and after soaking in it, the answer comes to him. That's the point. He leaps up, cries, 'Eureka,' jumps naked out of the tub, and runs through the streets of Syracuse, he's so excited."

I asked what Archimedes discovered, but Harriet said that was beside the point, too. "He figured out how the level of water in a container could measure the volume of an object, but never mind." She waved her hands.

"It's not *what* he learned," I said, as Harriet's meaning came to me, "it's *how* he did it, by taking a break to think in the bath, to solve the mystery. Without the naked running part."

"Correct," she said, "and yet, no decent firefly experiment has occurred to me. I exceedingly wish one good idea would."

"In a flash, like Archimedes," I said, "no pun intended. So take a bath!" I thought Harriet would smile. She didn't. "Listen," I added, "I do need to talk to you about fireflies. Really it's about Owen's sister. Remember the time you noticed Piper was interested in a firefly?"

"A *Photinus pyralis*," Harriet agreed.

"Thanks to that observation," I said, purposely using Harriet-ish language to keep her attention, "on the Fourth of July I put a few in Piper's hands. She got so excited, she talked. Everybody thinks she can't. But she did, I swear." It was only one word, and it wasn't even a real word, I explained, "but I did hear it, 'bug-fire.' Her parents thought I made it up. Her dad got super mad."

"Go on," said Harriet, when I paused to eat a quesadilla triangle. She was listening in the same intent way she sat through my firefly cake story. It was nice to have a second person, after Owen, take this seriously.

"I need your help making a video so I can prove Piper talked. It has to be outdoors, with fireflies," I explained. "Owen was going to, but we got rained out. If you'll do it, we can use the camera on your phone."

Then Harriet did smile and said something garbled. "Myuhroonhurenmurenhurf."

"What was that?"

"What do you think I said?" She sipped a long pink thread through her smoothie straw.

"Um . . . 'You can have my half'?"

"Exactly," Harriet said. "You're hungry. You've finished your food and would like to eat mine. I speak gibberish and throw in a *yuh* sound and a few *h* sounds, and you hear what you want to hear. If I had to guess, I'd say that's what happened with Piper. She makes random sounds, right? And screams and has tantrums? You told me that. You can have my half, by the way."

"Owen believes me." Even if she didn't, I thought, feeling indignant, Harriet could have gone along, as my friend, and agreed to help. Since it was important to me.

"Really?" She sounded surprised and drew another pink sip up her straw. Then Harriet pointed out that, without Owen, we had little chance of getting access to Piper at night. "You're not high on their list of evening babysitters anymore, am I right?"

After all the trouble I'd gone to for Harriet, to use Mom's darkroom and keep her stuff in my tent. I felt irritated. Also annoyed, because Harriet was right. Like other plans I'd made this summer—the move to the tent, taking care of Mom—this one was strong on big ideas and weak on small details.

I scarfed the rest of the quesadilla. It was my first meal of the day. I'd woken up too late to go in the house for breakfast, gotten dressed in the tent, and ridden straight to the pool. At the Phoebes' I didn't like asking for snacks. At home, I'd grown tired of peanut butter sandwiches for lunch.

Harriet said, "I'm afraid a video is a farfetched idea, without practical means of implementation, and it's an exceeding no-go without Owen."

"Thanks a lot, Harriet," I responded, not nicely. I stood up with my swim bag and walked to the lap pool. I wished it could reward me like Archimedes' bathtub had worked for him.

We had half an hour until the late practice. The coaches were running the early workout for the younger kids in four lanes, but two were free for regular lap swimmers. The only person in was an old lady revolving her arms and legs so slowly, it was a miracle she didn't sink.

I took the other lane and got in on my back. Every time I swam backstroke now, I felt the sky expanding overhead with no limits. It seemed like you could go anywhere. At the same time, you could count on where you were going, too.

Backstroke had opened up possibilities. My gold medal was sure proof. Backstroke and Piper went together that way, the two unexpected wins of my summer. Piper had talked to me, and even if Harriet refused to help, I was determined to find a way to prove it. I thought: I'm going to get my gold medal with you, too, Piper.

Resolved, happy, I walked home from the pool that afternoon to find Aunt Ruthie waiting for me in the backyard at the picnic table with Chinese carryout.

"I thought I timed this right," she said when I told her about the record board. "We're celebrating!"

After swimming, I was hungry again. She'd brought Chow Foon noodles, my favorite.

"Your dad took the boys out for dinner because I'm helping your mother pull some papers together. That can wait a few minutes, though." She spooned the flat rice noodles in spicy sauce with vegetables onto two plates.

The year Uncle Ahmed died, my dad used to go to Aunt Ruthie's on weekends to mow her lawn or fix a faucet. When she went back to school to become a teacher, we babysat Guy. This summer, I realized, Aunt Ruthie was taking her turn for us.

"How's it been, sleeping there?" She waved her chopsticks at the tent.

"I remember more dreams than in the house. There's one I have over and over. My parents, me, Mike, and Josh are in the tent, in a forest. Only we never went camping after the twins were born."

"I often have a similar dream. Your uncle and Guy and I are all together," she said, "except Guy is the same age he is now, not an infant like he was when your uncle died."

"I'm sorry," I said.

She gave me her kindest Aunt Ruthie smile. "I think it's natural to dream of your family being together. We often dream what we wish for. Which reminds me, your mom mentioned you babysitting for the disabled neighbor, who doesn't talk? And telling people she spoke to you? I'm sure everyone who cares about this child wishes that would happen. I think that when we wish for something a lot, we can sometimes envision— or maybe hear—it happen."

First Harriet, now Aunt Ruthie. "She *did* speak to me," I said. I was so tired of this.

"Well, I know your heart's in the right place, honey." She went on, "I can understand a mom who's new in town hiring a thirteen-year-old mother's helper, the first available pair of hands she meets." With an expert pinch, Aunt Ruthie tweezed noodles with her chopsticks. "Given what you've said about her daughter, though, I have to question her judgment."

"Piper's not hard to take care of, once you get to know her," I said.

"That mom is lucky, Alice, because you are an excellent babysitter. She's asking too much of you, though. It's only because I thought you'd rather be away from everybody for a while that I didn't bother you about babysitting our three guys at my house. I do want you to know how much I'm looking forward to your company, at home and at camp, after your big swimming competition."

It's funny how a person's feelings can fight each other, like two wrong fish put together in a bowl. As much as I loved Aunt Ruthie—and Chow Foon noodles—and as bad as I'd feel to let her down, I knew right then that I did not want, ever, to move to her house.

Mom might be able to make Dad, Mike, and Josh leave, like she wanted, but she wasn't going to do that to me. True, the tent had had no effect so far. Neither of my parents seemed to take me seriously when I said I wasn't moving back into the house until Dad did. I needed to think of something else to make them believe I was serious, and for that I needed more time. Plus, I had a second good reason to stay where I was. Now that Harriet had refused to help make the video, I had to wait for Owen, and he wasn't coming back to Cherrywood until the day after the meet.

None of this would make sense to Aunt Ruthie, I knew. She was only trying to be kind to all of us. That's why I changed the subject. "What's the paperwork, for Mom?" I asked.

Aunt Ruthie eyed me, as if she was trying to watch me think. "I have a friend starting a business, making skills-training videos for companies. She needs an office administrator. I'm going to help your mom write a cover letter and redo her resume to apply for the position."

"Does that mean she's better?" I asked. "Does that mean we won't have to sell our house, if she gets the job?"

"I don't know the answer to your second question," Aunt Ruthie said. "As for the first, never underestimate the healing power of meaningful work."

"That sounds like a fortune cookie," I said.

"Speaking of which." Aunt Ruthie handed me two of the four fortune cookies on the table and opened one of hers. "'You will pass a difficult test that will make you happier.' Not so far." She tried the second. "'You will spend old age in comfort and material wealth'—I'll take it!"

"'Good fortune takes preparation,'" I read out loud, and thought of swimming. The second slip I laid on the table for her to see: *It is not in your character to give up.*

I raised my eyebrows at Aunt Ruthie, and she raised hers back at me.

19
THE SWIM TEAM BANQUET

"NATIONAL GEOGRAPHIC HEADQUARTERS in downtown Washington, D.C., is seven miles from this house," Mom said later that night, after I asked about the job with Aunt Ruthie's friend.

She was drinking tea at the kitchen table and reading forms. I'd come inside for cereal.

"It might as well be seven million miles," she complained, "if I end up with such menial work."

"If you get that job," I asked, "can we stay in this house?"

"Oh, Alice." Mom sighed, as if that was a tiresome question, and didn't answer it.

I said, "Did you get the internet connected to fill out your applications?" At least we might have that back to the way it used to be, I figured.

No, she and Aunt Ruthie were driving to the library tomorrow to use the computers there, Mom said. "Take it from me, Alice, if you want to do anything with your life, think twice or ten times before you get married or have children."

The idea that if she'd thought harder, I might not exist, was too disturbing and strange for me to imagine. Never mind Mom's unhappy talk, I thought: she must be getting better if she was looking for a job. My trips to the pharmacy and work in the house must have helped, after all. I'd turn those chores into part of my argument against moving to Aunt Ruthie's.

It is not in your character to give up. I pressed the fortune cookie fortune between the last two pages of *David Copperfield*, at the happy ending.

Joanna needed me only two mornings during that final week of regular swim team practice. She was trying out adult sitters and a sign-language tutor, who, she said, quit after ten minutes. "I wish you were the tutor," Joanna told me. "How about taking a crash course in sign language, Alice?" Piper had refused even to look at the tutor's face. "That woman lacked your patience."

When Piper and I played together, I paid close attention to her squeals. To her grunts. To each syllable of her frustration when she wasn't allowed a snack. Nothing sounded at all like a word. If Harriet was right—that I'd heard what I wanted to—I would have heard a few, it seemed to me. On the other hand, maybe I didn't want to hear word-like syllables from Piper during the day. Was I so convinced that fireflies had inspired her to speak, I believed nothing else would draw speech out of her?

More than ever, Joanna's sadness made me impatient to do the video. "I'm beginning to worry time is slipping away," she said after the tutor's visit.

The night after the Sharks' final Saturday meet, the team held its annual banquet. Parents organized the usual pre-dinner games: a penny dive, with dollar coins for the big prizes, and crazy relays with floating watermelons and silly swim strokes. Coach B made a speech and handed out awards for Most Valuable and Most Improved. "And a special award to Alice Allyn," she called, "Best All-Around Sport, with appreciation for her help, daily and in a pinch." Proudly, surprised, happy all over again about the record board, I stepped up to shake her hand as people clapped and whistled.

Everyone got one of those participation trophies. Then we ate deep-dish pizza from the Pete's A Pizza's catering truck that came every year, with potluck salads and desserts that reminded me how my parents had taken care of signing me up and bringing food in the past. This year I'd filled out the form and paid with babysitting money and checked dessert for my contribution, since there were still two boxes of Girl Scout mint cookies in the freezer.

The season was over for everyone except the dozen of us who'd qualified for All-Stars. We had one more week to get ready. I'd stayed the third-fastest backstroker in our age group, behind Elise and Sinjin, "but your advice was right," I told Harriet as we stood in the dessert line, "to concentrate on backstroke."

"I forgot to account for the margin of error," Harriet admitted. "But you improved 19 percent!" She held out another one of those graphs she'd made on her phone.

"I never cared about being number *one*," I said. "I'm in All-Stars, I'm on the record board! It wouldn't have happened with freestyle."

When Harriet said nothing, I didn't think much of it. It was time to get in the water for the swim team movie.

Mr. Falco, Mario's dad, had strung a giant white screen over the front end of the lap pool to show the team movie he'd spent all season filming. The lifeguards switched on the underwater lights. The pool started to fill up with floating kids. Harriet and I grabbed foam noodles from the bin, and I balanced in the water on mine like it was the seat of a porch swing.

Harriet, riding hers like a saddle, was frowning. "This is dumb."

"Do you wish you were at the Loons banquet instead?" I said.

She merely shook her head no, but it was growing too loud to talk anyway. The more crowded the water got, the more I thought back to when Mom had avoided answering about selling the house. It sucked, it really did, that this was Harriet's first Sharks banquet night, and she didn't like it, and I loved it, and it might be my last.

Coach B and Mr. Falco called for quiet. The movie started with short clips of individual kids diving for their races, set to the music from the beginning of *2001: A Space Odyssey*. Trumpets, organs, and pounding drums climbed to the same tip-top point of sound, five times in a row, as five swimmers dove. It was so melodramatic and wonderful that I forgot my worries and laughed and nearly fell off my noodle.

"I don't see why that's funny," Harriet half-whispered beside me in the semidarkness. "The music isn't supposed to repeat like that."

"So?" I said.

"You know what this is, right? Strauss's 'Sunrise' fanfare from *Thus Spake Zarathustra*. My oboe teacher in Minnesota made us listen to it, to learn the importance of playing in an orchestra."

"Maybe you can visit sometime," I said, thinking I'd been right about why Harriet seemed to be in an increasingly bad mood.

"It's famous for the four trumpets. The flashy instruments get the credit," she said. "But he wrote in parts for woodwinds, too. There are three oboes. The trumpets need the oboes, and it shouldn't repeat."

"Harriet, but why does it matter? This is the swim-team movie," I said.

By now the same sound clip had played maybe fifteen times, each for a different swimmer. "It's dumb," Harriet said. She kicked on her noodle to the side of the pool and got out.

The pictures switched from diving to a panorama view of team parents. The music turned into an old rock song that had a lot of them smiling. Mr. Falco tried to include every swimmer on the team in his movies. There I was, lining up Eight-and-Unders to race.

I followed Harriet out of the pool to the grass behind the chair area. She looked as if there was nothing she hated more than the swim-team movie. "What's bothering you, Harriet?" I said. "Didn't the Loons have a banquet at the end of the season? Mr. Falco does this every year. It's just for fun."

"Look, Alice," she said. "I know you're going to be upset, but I can't swim All-Stars."

"What?" I felt like someone had bopped me with every floating noodle in the pool. "But that means—"

"My parents rented a house on Cape Cod," she interrupted. "I never knew exactly when it was for. It turns out the trip ends the day after All-Star Relays. My whole family will be there, and I have to go."

All I could think about was the no-subs rule. If Harriet couldn't swim, our relay was out.

"Can you come back early and stay with me?" I tried.

"I asked. The transportation is problematic and expensive, my mother says, and I'd miss a week of workouts before the meet, too, so, what's the point?" Harriet was looking at the grass.

"I can't believe you didn't tell us," I said. "We've been practicing for weeks."

"I only found out yesterday afternoon, when she reminded me," Harriet said. "I told the coach before the awards ceremony. It's only one race, Alice. The All-Star Relay meet doesn't even lead to anything else in swimming."

"Thanks a lot," I said.

"Don't you think it's more important to focus on your training goals for fall anyway?" she said. "Like for winter club swimming?"

Maybe if you were her. Or April or Sinjin or anybody else whose parents could afford the expensive fees for the private winter club team. If my parents couldn't pay for my cell phone, there was no way I'd be swimming this winter. No—if I was ever going to swim a great backstroke race at an elite meet in my entire life, it would have to be at All-Star Relays, and now—never mind.

I didn't look, didn't think. I dove into the only part of the lap pool that wasn't crowded with people, noodles, and floats. In about the time it would take a *Photinus pyralis* to flash, I figured out why that space was open water: Mr. Falco had raised his screen there, on the poles where the backstroke flags usually hung.

My foot knocked loose part of his rigging. I felt the unplanned *clunk* as my body breezed past and down to the water. By the time I surfaced, the left end of the screen had fallen, kids and parents were screaming, and pictures from Mr. Falco's movie were flickering into the dark trees.

He was first to call from the edge of the pool. "Are you hurt? Can you swim to the side?"

"Clear the water!" Coach B shouted. "Everybody clear the water!"

My view was partly blocked by the screen, which hung slantwise across the pool. One end was still attached to a pole. I waited for someone to start yelling at me, like Mr. Phoebe had.

Please nobody be hurt, I thought, repeating it like a new mantra, *Please nobody be hurt.* Then Mario's dad whipped off his T-shirt to dive in to rescue me, and I called out, "I'm fine, I can swim. I'm so sorry, I didn't mean to."

"Of course not," Mr. Falco said. "Come to the side so we can make sure you're okay. There's insurance on the rental. No worries."

On the deck, it was hard to stand on my right ankle. The outdoor lights remained low, which thankfully made me feel less stared-at. Mr. Falco helped me into a lounge chair. I was glad to hear that the busy crowd had resumed talking, like this was an intermission. "Hey, Maureen, you're a doctor. Take a look at Alice's foot," Mr. Falco said.

I had no idea whose mom Maureen was. She gently pressed my ankle, foot, and toes, and said I'd probably have a bruise and should take it easy in the chair the rest of the evening. A bunch of kids helped raise the screen. The only sign of my accident was a crease at the lower left-hand corner.

Everybody was so nice about it. Another parent brought me lemonade, and people settled down; a full-length Disney feature always followed the team movie. I was just about calm again when Harriet knelt at the side of my chair.

"The doctor says your foot isn't broken. Can I sit on the end? All the chairs are taken."

"Please go away, Harriet," I said. But she didn't move. "What, do you have more bad news?" I asked.

"Alice, the fact is that these All-Star meets don't use regional or national cut-off qualifying times. They're a capstone activity within this league." She was talking like she was explaining a math concept to Owen. "Many of the relay events don't even exist in U.S.A. Swimming. They don't count for anything beyond that one day."

"I know, Harriet. I don't care about that. They're fun. It's an honor. You've never been to All-Stars, and you don't care that I care." I didn't look at her. I watched the team movie credits scroll.

She stood up. "I think I'll see if Lydia's available," she said.

"Good idea," I replied, and she left.

20
ALL-STARS

COUNTY ALL-STARS are held at the municipal aquatic center, in an Olympic-size outdoor pool. They run for two days, the final weekend of the summer league season. This year's calendar bumped the meet from the end of July into August. Saturday was for relays, Sunday for individual events.

April had qualified to compete on a second relay, whose four swimmers actually could make it, so I got a ride from her and her mom just to watch. The Sharks had one of the later call times for warm-ups, and the place was packed when we walked in at 7 a.m.

There were tables filled with T-shirts for sale, reps handing out brochures for winter swimming clubs, and a snack bar selling muffins, doughnuts, bagels, and made-to-order omelets on a grill. There were hundreds of parents, swimmers, coaches and their bags, cameras, phones, tablets, coffee cups, towels, folding chairs, flip-flops, team clothes, and team signs. The air smelled like sunscreen, chlorine, and wet grass.

We made our way through the crowd, down into the bleachers, where Coach B had staked out half a row for our team. I felt sad all over again that I wouldn't get to race, even though it was so exciting just being here. "Got a minute, Alice?" the coach called as soon as she spotted me.

My eyes caught on the patch of grassy hill rising behind the spectator stands. A man was carrying folding chairs at a slower-than-normal pace, alongside a woman walking with a cane. It took a second to realize: this was the astounding sight of my dad and mom together.

"Alice?" Coach B repeated.

I panicked. She was waving, so I followed her direction, definitely a lot easier than meeting my parents to confess that, no, I was not scheduled to swim. I squeezed down the row, high-fiving as I went, with Joey and my other Eight-and-Unders who'd made it into the meet.

Then it occurred to me. I might be in trouble about the movie screen. Up the hill, down the hill, my mistakes trapped me.

"I meant to ask you at the banquet," the coach said when I reached her. We were crammed close to each other on the bench; she clutched a clipboard and tablet to her chest. "Because I didn't expect to see you today. I want you to consider becoming a junior coach next summer. I'd love to sign you on to work with the pre-team. Interested?"

Junior coaches were typically tenth graders or older. I'd be a rising freshman.

"Oh, yes!" I was too surprised to say more. "Thank you!" Pre-team meant the littlest swimmers, usually five and six. I breathed relief—and disbelief. "Sure, of course, yes." It was an honor. "Thanks, Coach B," I repeated.

"Fine. We'll talk more later. I'll be emailing you in the fall," she said. "I'm glad I got this chance to ask you. Excuse me, for now." She acknowledged a meet official on the pool deck down below who'd been trying to get her attention, and slipped away.

I hadn't expected anything good to come out of today. I felt better now, confident enough to climb the hill to my parents. I squeezed back along the row to the central stairs up the hill, which is when I remembered. If my parents sold our house, by next summer I might not be living in Cherrywood.

"Triple A!" Dad called. He was securing the feet of a folding chair in the grass, despite the angle of the slope.

"I didn't know you were coming." I couldn't help sounding disappointed. It had never occurred to me that they would.

"We decided to surprise you," said Mom, lowering herself carefully onto the canvas seat while my dad held the back of her chair steady. "Where's my sunscreen?" she added, dipping into the bag he'd toted with the chairs. "You always forget, Alice. Here. Better put some on."

"I did." I was thrilled they were together and the exact opposite that they'd come. I wanted to tell them what Coach B had said, but I didn't want to tell them I wasn't swimming.

"Are you just saying that?" Mom laughed.

"A few minutes ago," I answered, which was true.

"I don't see you on here, Triple A." Dad was examining the copy of the meet program. The gravity I felt at that moment was the usual kind. Like a rock, when you drop it, thudding to the ground.

"Um . . . it ended up Harriet couldn't swim," I admitted. "Our relay had to scratch."

"What?" Mom looked up from rubbing sunscreen on her arm. Dad started to speak, then didn't. He folded the meet program in thirds and stuck it in his back pocket.

"Thank you for coming, though," I said, trying to make that the important part. "I really appreciate it," I added, as if me swimming or not swimming was a detail. "I never thought you would."

"No, I bet you didn't," said Mom, like she'd figured out the whole story. "How long have you known?"

"Harriet only told me last week." I talked like our subject was the weather, or grocery shopping. The way I tried to hold off a Code Mud. "And you know, all summer the coach asked me to help her at practice. So I kept going, and I came today to cheer everybody on." I added, "The great thing is, she invited me to be a junior coach next summer!"

Mom looked at Dad like the situation was his fault. He returned her gaze with disapproval. I couldn't help thinking their eyes were like dueling swords of laser light in a movie. The hope I'd felt, seeing them together, burned off like the morning sun evaporating the dew on the grass beneath our feet.

"The deal was," Mom said to me, "you didn't move to Ruth's three weeks ago because you had an All-Star race to train for. If that wasn't the case, you should have told us. Why didn't you?"

"Dad," I appealed. His eyes had locked on the empty seat of the chair he'd set out for himself. "I really did expect to be swimming." Forget my disappointment about the scratched relay; now I was going to have to feel guilty about it. "I'm very sorry you went to so much trouble," I added, since I guessed coming here was his idea.

"I wish you'd kept us in the loop," Dad sighed to the chair.

"Get your things, Alice," Mom said. "Sam, if my sister is home, we are driving Alice straight there. No more delaying. Please try Ruth's cell."

"I don't see why this means I have to move," I said.

"Triple A." My dad looked up at me. "I have to agree with your mother on this one. I think the change might do you good."

At that moment, an announcer broadcast a request to rise for the national anthem. Dad and I fell in with the automatic response of most people, turning toward the flagpole on top of the pool house. Mom, who remained seated, motioned to me to get moving while three girls harmonized over the loudspeaker. In protest, I stayed put until the song ended.

The crowd whooped, the officials took their places to begin the meet, and I returned to the stands to collect my bag. I thanked April and her mom and said it turned out I was unable to stay to cheer on the Sharks. My mom wasn't feeling well, I said. Sort of true.

Dad had had to park several blocks away and had gone ahead to pull the car up to the entrance. I folded Mom's chair and carried it with us to the parking lot.

I tried the reason I'd saved up: "Mom, if you let me stay, I can keep on doing all the chores to help you."

"I've appreciated that," she said. "But your father and I have been talking again about the night the police came. Then that phone call from the neighbors—you never told me you also called him that night."

She paused as cheers erupted behind us. The racing had started.

"He said you were already worried you'd done something wrong," Mom continued in that accusing tone. "Then the pharmacy episode. Now this? It's too much."

Vacant cars stuffed the parking lot, baking in the sun. My mind felt empty, too. I could think of nothing to say. The buzzer blasted the start of another relay from the pool, on the distant side of the building. I opened the chair for Mom to sit near the handicapped cut in the curb.

". . . this ridiculous setup in the tent," she was saying. "I've gone along with it because your father wanted to humor you. We should have done this sooner."

An idea flashed on me, though I'd have to get over being annoyed with Harriet. "If you let me stay there," I began, "next week I can introduce you to Harriet's mom. She buys stuff to decorate people's houses." There was no logical connection between the tent and meeting her, but I went on anyway, chattering about the sand dune pictures in the Barclays' hallway. "She'd love your plant photos. She might buy them for her clients' houses."

"Clearly," said my mom, cutting me off, "you need more structure and supervision than I can give you, until school begins and your father and I sort out our arrangements."

"What arrangements?" Had I missed some news?

"We'll discuss that later. Here he comes." She pointed and pushed herself up, using her cane. "Please get in the car." I had to fold her chair up first.

They waited for me in front of our house while I stuffed a duffel with clothes from the tent. The sleeping bags I knelt on felt extra soft; the striped, oatmeal-colored canvas and high ceiling, so familiar. My summer bedroom. *Goodbye tent*, I thought. It felt like a large, thick scab was being ripped off of me before my skin had healed. It crossed my mind to refuse to leave. Until my parents tired of waiting and came to investigate and had to drag me out by force. Piper might behave like that. I couldn't. Maybe I understood a little better why Owen went along with where Mr. Phoebe sent him to visit. If you weren't in charge of where you lived, you could become very tired of trying for what you wanted. Maybe if I practiced not wanting something else, there would be no scab to rip off. It wouldn't hurt so much.

I zipped up the net screening and the outer door. My heart lay behind in my sleeping bag. So much for staying out here till Dad moved home. I left nearly everything I'd carried out of the house where it was. I left Harriet's stacked, plastic crate shelves, full of her stuff. Her problem now. My dad would break down the tent, I guessed, next time he came to mow the lawn.

Goodbye tent. Goodbye picnic table. Goodbye fireflies.

"You should have listened to me, Sam," Mom was saying as I slid back onto the rear seat of the car with my duffel.

"What if I agree to sleep inside the house, in my bedroom? Can I stay here?" I asked. That way when Owen came back, at least we'd have a chance to make a video. Remaining at this address—inside or out—was all we needed. "Aunt Ruthie's house is small," I argued. "There's only one bathroom, and two bedrooms." I could hear my voice get whiny with defeat as Dad steered around the corner and our front lawn disappeared. "I'm really sorry I didn't tell you about the relay."

"Alice, I need days when I don't have to worry about you," Mom said. "I've had enough. Period."

Dad met my eyes in the rearview mirror, which I could barely see through tears. It felt like I was being kidnapped. This is what a firefly feels like in a jar, I thought.

"Triple A," he said, "you can move in with me the rest of your summer vacation, if you don't want to go to your aunt's."

"Don't be ridiculous," snapped Mom. "How will you supervise her while you're at work? You live in a slum student building off a busy strip. There's nothing except fast-food restaurants, gas stations, and crummy motels. What would she do all day? We know we can't trust her to stay where she says she'll be. She wouldn't be safe."

I unzipped the duffel and took out *David Copperfield*. It was the longest book I'd ever read, and I had hundreds of pages to go. I turned to the final scene and reread the slip of fortune cookie paper pressed there: *It is not in your character to give up.*

Maybe Aunt Ruthie had given me the wrong cookie.

21
MORE LIES, AND
HARRIET'S JOURNAL

"IT'S A TOUGH SUMMER, Alice," Aunt Ruthie commented after my parents dropped me off. I was grateful she said little. I managed Hi, how are you, I'm fine, still stunned at the speed of my arrival here. I could feel how the tears streaked on my face, and I left them there. So what if that fell into the category of Lame, I thought. I don't care. My family doesn't exist. I wanted to count on my family like I could count on the flags, five strokes, the wall. Why was I the only one who cared about that?

Aunt Ruthie put her arm around me and gently dried my cheeks with a tissue, as if to say, *It's all going to be okay, Alice.* Then she asked, "How about helping with these sheets?"

We made up the pullout couch in her living room. I borrowed her phone, pulled myself together to cut the quaver out of my voice, and left a message for Joanna, apologizing for not being able to help her out in the mornings the rest of the summer. I'd never bothered to get Owen's number. He'd figure the situation out from Joanna when he returned from his trip.

The Guys and Guy distracted me with video games and a fleet of Lego spaceships they were building, and Aunt Ruthie ordered Chinese carryout for dinner, including Chow Foon. Going to sleep, it felt like an error, lying on a platform elevated from the ground. I missed the crickets. In the middle of the night, I pulled the thin mattress off the lumpy springs onto the floor. Any time I started to feel that pressure around my eyeballs, like tears were coming, I thought of the record board: my name was there to stay.

At Aunt Ruthie's day camp, a different group of kids trooped into the arts-and-crafts room each hour between nine and three. I started out numb, wishing I was with Piper and Timmy instead. But by the second day of camp, I began to enjoy it. This week, the kids were making pop-up books. Glitter, pens, glue sticks, scissors, and construction paper littered our worktables.

Each camper had written a five-sentence story, one sentence per pop-up page. Now they were illustrating. "Alice, can you help Gabby and Bruno? They look ready to glue their pop-up pieces," Aunt Ruthie said to me at one point.

"'The bear got out by a portal,'" I read on Gabby's opening page. Portals were a popular subject for these kids, for some reason. "Is that a forest your bear landed in when it escaped from the zoo?" I guessed. "Fix her on the tab like this, without too much glue, so she can jump out. That's it. Okay, Bruno, let's see yours."

Bruno was busy flipping through the book of the boy next to him. All Joanna wanted, I couldn't help thinking, was for Piper to be able to sit at a table like this and share her story with the camper beside her. A lot of happy chattering was going on among our artists.

"Hey, Bruno," I interrupted. "Let's finish up your robot. Then you can glue your whole book together."

I had to admit, I liked having this break from home. Aunt Ruthie discussed the art projects and campers, nothing else. It was a relief not to talk or think about my parents, or about Harriet and All-Stars, or about missing my chance to make the video with Owen. I was too busy solving problems like how to keep Bruno's pop-up robot from sticking to the side of its page.

Thursday evening after camp, Aunt Ruthie got a voice mail she had me listen to: "Hello, this message is for Alice Amary Allyn's Aunt Ruth from Alice's Cherrywood Sharks age-group teammate and Cherrywood Middle

School Science Fair project collaborator, Harriet Barclay. Please forgive my ignorance of your surname. Your niece, Alice, is a vital member of a three-person team studying Lampyridae. Alice's participation is an essential component of our research. I would be exceedingly grateful if you could spare Alice for an hour, at the conclusion of her workweek, for a meeting on Friday afternoon at 4 p.m. at Cherrywood Pool in our regular conference space to discuss our project. Thank you. Please text an RSVP to my phone."

Aunt Ruthie found Harriet's message amusing. Me, not so much. "Do you want to?" she asked. Aunt Ruthie didn't see why I shouldn't spend time with friends. She could drop me off, she said, and let the boys swim or take them grocery shopping and come back for me.

All Harriet ever thought about was winning the science fair. Didn't she get that, if you let a friend down and don't care, you don't turn around and ask that friend to help with your experiments, like nothing happened? Plus, I refused to kill any more fireflies. Or maybe she just wanted her stuff back from my tent.

On the other hand, I had a feeling Harriet was trying to tell me she had something specific to communicate. The one-hour time element struck me as odd, and she'd gone out of her way to let me know Owen would be there. Something was up, I decided. I told Aunt Ruthie yes.

Harriet had a quesadilla, fruit smoothies, and an order of curly fries waiting in the snack bar. "You're on time," she exclaimed happily, half-smiling at me, half-checking her phone. She hunched her shoulders and let them go repeatedly, as if she were prepping for another one of her performances.

"What's up, Harriet?" Seeing her again, in the usual pigtails and Sharks scrunchies, I was unsure how I felt about her. I wasn't quite mad. There was no one but myself to blame for what happened at the All-Star meet. Even if our relay had competed, my parents would likely have moved me to Aunt Ruthie's. And so far Aunt Ruthie's house had been a little like lemonade you add to an awful medicine in order to drink it.

"Thanks for the food," I said. "What do you need for your project, and where's Owen?"

"He'll be here in fifteen minutes, and it's not about fireflies. Just let me do this." She laid her hands palms down, fingers fanned, on the table, and spoke, looking at them. "Remember that night you asked if I used to do experiments with friends in Minnesota? Shhhh!"

She flashed her hands up to cut me off when I started to say yes, and I recalled that she'd never answered the question. "That was my rhetorical introduction, okay? Don't interrupt. So. That night. I did not reply, Alice, because it's fair to say I *didn't* have any friends in Minnesota. I probably actually haven't ever had a good friend before. Fast-forward to the middle of last week, in this ginormous house filled with an exceeding number of cousins, some of whom are my age and precisely none of whom I actually particularly like all that much, and it dawned on me, you are the first friend I have ever felt close to in my entire life. In fact, I don't think I knew what a friend was before I met you. I've never been good at making friends. You are, since you made friends with a girl who can't even talk. I doubt I could have survived being forced to move here if I hadn't met you, Alice. When I was with the cousins, it occurred to me that . . ." Here she paused, and took a deep breath. ". . . there are times I have been a shabby friend to you. I arranged for you to arrive ahead of Owen so I could say I'm sorry. Also I apologize if this isn't how normal friends apologize."

A tear leaked down her cheek. The only other time I'd seen Harriet cry was also in the snack bar, the day we met and she embarrassed me by transitioning from fake-cackling to fake-sobbing. She wasn't acting now, and though I was still embarrassed—people at the other tables had turned to look—I understood. The infinity between those tears and this one was huge. I leaned in. "Harriet. There's no way you can be shabby with all those clothes in your closet."

She shook her head to stop my lame joke.

"I was mean about All-Stars, because I was disappointed," I said. "I'm sorry. I'm very glad you're my friend." I told her what happened with my parents, but admitted I was kind of enjoying working at Aunt Ruthie's camp. "And if you hadn't kept telling me I was going to improve in backstroke this summer, I might never have put so much into it," I said. "Winning at Relay Carnival got my name on the record board, and the extra stroke training for All-Stars developed my backstroke skills even more," I added. "I've decided that from now on, I'm a backstroker. Thanks to you."

"So you're not mad?" she said.

"Not *exceedingly*." If being friends with Harriet did have its strange moments, well, they were strange in a usually good, mind-expanding way. "Who else would have taken the trouble to read through five hundred pages of swim-meet results to find something positive to tell me? Or taught me to talk to fireflies?" I smiled. "No, I'm not mad at all," I reassured her. "Especially since you bought these." I ate a curly fry.

Owen walked into the snack bar then, and like always the crush hit my whole body. Annoying.

He began telling a story about this exotic sushi restaurant his grandfather had taken him to in New York. "We ate garlic Taipei crickets and fried white sea worm sushi, with ginger, chili pepper, peanuts, lime, and tamarind." He bugged his eyes out until we laughed. "When the chef came to our table, I couldn't resist asking . . ."

"You didn't," I said.

"No worries, Alice. He said fireflies would make terrible sushi."

"Let's proceed to business," Harriet said, "before the hour is up and Alice turns into a pumpkin."

Owen looked from me to her. "I assume you guys are good? Harriet said she had to clear something up with you."

Yes, we said, and Owen asked Harriet, "Did you tell her the plan for the video?"

I was confused. "I thought we were here for your next science fair project."

"That would be incorrect," she said. "I considered my failure in your basement for some time. What most interests me about fireflies, I've concluded, is their cold light, remember? How they don't waste energy because their light gives off no heat. So I'm designing a new experiment about a fuel cell that will be like a firefly because it will create energy without pollution." She waved her hands as if brushing the subject out of the way. "That's for later," she said. "We are assembled here today to make the video you wanted."

"Harriet, I thought you didn't believe me," I said.

"I changed my mind, for a few reasons," she answered vaguely. "Also, Owen called, he didn't know how to find you, and insisted. When we started sketching out potential solutions to the obstacles, it got fun, like a detective novel."

"If we can pull it off, Alice, I think your mom might be almost as impressed as my parents," Owen said, which I doubted.

The plan they described contained so many *if*s, it was like a line of dominoes arranged standing up to be tipped over. Each step had to be completed for the next part to work. If one failed, the whole plan came to a halt. But I was feeling so moved by Harriet's apology, and her and Owen's insistence that it all depended on me, I kept my hesitation to myself.

"There's a final catch, too," Owen said, "We have to do it tonight or tomorrow night." His plans had changed. He was flying home to Denver on Sunday morning instead of two weeks from now. He added, "Today it's a little late, but I bet I can persuade them to go out for dinner Saturday."

He rose immediately to leave, to check with Joanna, saying he'd text Harriet's phone to confirm. As soon as he disappeared into the men's locker room, which he had to pass through to reach the front entrance, I told

Harriet, "Wait here," and ran through the women's side to catch up with him.

"Owen!" I called. He turned. "What happened? Why are you leaving in two days?"

He grinned. "All thanks to you."

"Me?" What had I done? Why was he smiling?

"This summer, I wanted to hang out with Riko in Denver, work at the restaurant, and improve my knife skills," he said. "But—I went where my parents told me. I always have."

Owen studied his feet like he was either sad or laughing at himself, I couldn't tell. It surprised me how often with him I couldn't. "It's because I never forget that I'm extra for both of them," he said. "I mean, I figure, in the whole universe, what does it really matter what I do with my time?" He looked up at me and shrugged. "It's less trouble if I fit into what works for them."

Owen stuck his hands in the pockets of his jeans and took a deep breath that was like a sigh, and looked out at the parking lot. He said, "I've always thought it was my fault my mom had to delay getting her degree, and my dad had to make special arrangements for me every summer, and even moved here for a job I'm pretty sure he doesn't want, to make more money to pay for three kids and Piper's treatment." Now he looked straight at me. "When I heard your deal with your parents and the tent, I finally realized it's not my fault. But it is my life to take care of. That's why I'm going on Sunday."

Maybe what I'd thought of all along as the "twist" in Owen's voice had to do with what he was telling me now. Stuff coiled up in him because he hadn't been ready for it.

"Their lives are what happened to them and how they chose to respond to that," he went on. "Like your mom's accident and your parents' splitting up." Owen paused. "I decided it was time to quit tiptoeing—I don't need to do what everybody else wants all the time. I don't need to apologize for existing."

"No, of course you don't," I said.

"My relatives are good, nice people," he continued. "But I miss home and Riko. I want to be a chef. Okay, I do need to graduate from high school, but I looked it up—the advanced math track isn't important for getting into culinary school." His voice took on a new strength. "I'm ready to go home. After that night in your tent, I decided to. I bought the ticket myself and then told Dad. He and I had a long talk. From now on, I'm going to have a lot more say about where I go and when."

Owen looked so happy, all I could tell him was that I was glad, though I wasn't totally. A single night for carrying out the plan he and Harriet came up with made it seem nuttier than ever. Plus, I would miss him.

"Onward to Joanna," he said, raising a hand to high-five.

"Good luck, Owen." Our high-five melted into a quick two-fisted clasp. Then he sprinted across the parking lot.

"My mother says 'What a darling idea' for you to spend the weekend at my house," Harriet reported, without looking up from a Sudoku puzzle grid she was filling in. "I had to restrain myself from saying we're hoping it's 'memorable,' too. Your turn." She passed me her phone.

"Hi Aunt Ruthie," I said when she answered, explaining that Harriet had invited me to sleep over tonight and tomorrow, to have enough time to finish our project. "Her mom could bring me home Sunday morning. Can I? Would it be okay if Mrs. Barclay calls you about it?"

Aunt Ruthie was at an ice cream parlor with the Guys and Guy and said she'd be glad to speak with Harriet's mother and then would let me know. "Let's not bother your mom, who besides having too much on her mind, has a late-afternoon interview with the owner of that company I told you about."

"Perfect, and more perfect," said Harriet. She and Owen had tested their phones. Neither of them took decent night video, so another piece of the plan

involved borrowing a camera from my basement that
could film at night.

"We should walk to your house immediately."
Mom's interview eliminated a step; Harriet and Owen
no longer needed to distract her while I snuck into the
basement.

On the way, Aunt Ruthie called back to let us know
she'd talked to Mrs. Barclay and it was fine.

"Thank you," Harriet said. "You and Alice are doing
me an exceedingly huge favor. My mother gave you our
address and home number? Here's her cell phone number, too."

Technically, the only lie I told was when I reassured
Aunt Ruthie I kept a toothbrush and change of clothes
in my swim bag. Harriet preferred the phrase *diluting
the truth*. Tonight, Friday, was a legitimate sleepover.
And so long as we woke up at her house on Sunday
morning—even if we slept there thirty minutes—
Harriet said that qualified as a sleepover. She revealed
she gave Aunt Ruthie Lydia's cell number, which
differed from their mom's by two digits. That was part
of the plan. "Oops—I misremembered, oh well!"

I hated taking advantage of Aunt Ruthie's kindness
and trust, but I told myself the chances of her calling
that number were slim. If we succeeded with the video,
maybe a few sort-of wrongs would add up to one very
right.

Then came good news from Owen. He'd convinced the Phoebes to let him babysit Saturday night while they went out for a quick dinner, because who knew when they'd have another opportunity.

The plan was falling into place.

Harriet and I snuck down the less-used path, on the opposite side of the house from both Mom's bedroom windows and the Phoebes'. To my surprise, the tent was still standing, though the ropes I used to tighten every few days had loosened, and the canvas sagged. I unlocked the back door, turned the handle, and opened it in slow motion, as quiet as possible, in case we were wrong about Mom being out. Inside the house where she didn't want me to be, I got a feeling like I had the night I ran home from the pool and met Piper. As if I were trying to keep away from ghosts, even though I knew they didn't exist.

In two minutes, I was in and out of the darkroom with the video camera my mom used to bring along on our Fourth of July picnics. I grabbed extra clothes from my tent, and we crisscrossed along back streets to Harriet's house, to shrink the chances of Mom driving by.

What had started to feel like charmed good luck ended when we reached Harriet's bedroom and discovered the camera was broken. It was an old model that used miniature tape cassettes, and a stuck cassette refused to eject. We tried a toothpick, a Q-tip, a hairpin, a knife. Harriet's family no longer owned cameras besides their phones; neither did the Phoebes, according to Owen. I knew of nobody to borrow one from. By the time we called camera shops and learned our best option was Suffern's Repair, it was about to close. For same-day service, we were told to be there when they reopened the next morning.

"I'll ask Lydia to drive us," Harriet said. "She usually works Saturdays, but she has tomorrow off."

Lydia wrote back right away. "Nope, meeting James for breakfast. Whole day booked."

"It's incredible how within seconds of moving to a new town my sister has a boyfriend and is hanging out as if she's lived here her entire life," Harriet said.

"What about a taxi?"

"An hour's worth of cab fare, on top of paying for the repair?" Harriet said. *"Ka-ching."* From her back pocket, she pulled out the small spiral notebook I'd sometimes seen her writing in and waved it in the air. "I've been saving this for an emergency. Believe me, Lydia will drive us."

Mrs. Barclay fed us mushroom risotto, salad, and homemade chocolate chip cookies for dinner. Infinitely more tasty than my usual mac and cheese. Dr. Barclay was on a business trip, Lydia was still out. Harriet practiced her oboe after that while I read more of *The Hobbit*. Then we watched my favorite movie, *The Parent*

Trap, which made me wish Harriet and I were identical twins and the plan we were working on was to convince my dad to move home. The whole night felt like it was just waiting for the next day to begin.

After midnight, Lydia showed up. We found her downstairs on one of the white couches in the family room. "Alice needs to talk to you," Harriet said, and I gave her a *What?* look.

"Hi, Alice," Lydia replied without moving her eyes from her laptop. "Hang on a sec." Her phone buzzed. She glanced at it without answering and kept typing.

Harriet nodded at me, like I was supposed to say something. I began a short version of Piper and fireflies. When I got to the part about her speaking for the first time in two years, Lydia looked up. "That sounds impossible."

"Owen Phoebe believes her," Harriet said. "He wants Alice to try this."

Harriet certainly knew how to get her sister's attention.

"Owen Phoebe?" Lydia said. "Okay, tell me again Owen's connection to this girl?"

I had no idea they even knew each other. Harriet was right, her sister made friends fast. It turned out Lydia had met him at Noah Gaines's. I explained Owen's family.

"Does it have to be tomorrow?" she said.

"Actually, today," Harriet said. "Eight hours and fifty-five minutes from now."

"It's a sweet idea, Alice, but I can't change my plans. My boss has a meeting in Atlanta, so it's my last day with James before he leaves for college."

"*Lydia!*" Harriet said in her commanding voice. She whipped out the notebook. "Pay attention: St. Paul, Minnesota, March twenty-fourth, four-thirty p.m. Ran a red light at Woodshole Avenue and Chestnut Street. Minneapolis, Minnesota, March thirtieth, seven-fifteen p.m. Stopped for speeding by police two blocks from home, given a warning by Officer Stephanie Orlickson. Cherrywood, June seventeenth, three-thirty p.m. Ran a red light at East West Highway and Beach Drive. Stopped by police and given a seventy-five dollar ticket which you secretly paid by sending a money order knowing it won't show up until Mom and Dad's insurance plan comes up for renewal next winter. . . ."

"What is that?" Lydia said. "What are you doing?"

"It's my complete log of your driving infractions, and these are only the ones while I've been your passenger. If you don't agree to help Alice—help us—I will turn this over to Mom and Dad and they will revoke your driving privileges as per your Official Parent-Teenager Driving Contract." Here she turned to me. "Lydia totaled a car our parents gave her for her sixteenth birthday. As a result, she had to sign a contract promising ixnay on tickets and accidents until she goes to college, if she wants a new one."

"Ooooo—you little spy! You promised not to tell, and those things aren't even serious," Lydia said. "I'm never taking you anyplace again."

"If you're even still allowed to drive, Mom will *make* you drive me so she doesn't have to, so you have no choice," Harriet replied calmly, "and I have not been spying." She drew herself up in mock-professor mode. "I declare my experiment on the exceptional value of meticulous notes an unqualified success."

I restrained myself from pointing out the obvious about *Harriet the Spy.*

"I hate you!" Lydia said. "This is blackmail."

"Be ready at nine-fifteen a.m. With luck, we'll be home by noon." Harriet plopped down and put her legs up triumphantly in an armchair.

Lydia texted, typed on her laptop, received a text, texted again. "You're lucky Turbo Thai serves lunch till three. Promise you'll hand over that notebook afterwards."

Harriet crossed her heart sarcastically with her index finger. "Thank you, Lydia," she said with a sweet singsong.

Lifting her hands like claws, Lydia pretended to cat-scratch us. "Go away, bug ladies. Seriously."

"Lydia, this is so nice of you," I said.

"No, it's not," Harriet said.

"She's right, I don't mind . . . really." Lydia rolled her eyes.

We set Harriet's phone alarm, and I covered myself with a throw blanket from her bed and curled up on her carpeted floor. The night air in Harriet's house was as smooth as an ironed pillowcase. "What *were* you saving those notes for?" I whispered. But Harriet, above me in her bed, was already asleep.

22
EXCEEDINGLY MAGIC

I HAD TO ADMIRE Lydia. Once she agreed to Harriet's bargain, she quit complaining, got us to Suffern's at ten minutes to ten, and waited at a Starbucks at the other end of the strip mall. She also agreed to cover for us if my aunt called.

The charge was sixty-five dollars to remove the tape and unjam the release lever, and another twenty-five for a pack of blank cassettes, which Harriet reasoned we should buy because there were no extras in the camera case, and tapes were so out of date, they would be hard to find someplace else. Spending a chunk of my cell phone fund to help the Phoebes felt good, since Joanna had so generously overpaid me. There was also a kind of justice, I thought, in paying a literal price for all the lying. Maybe it would keep me out of trouble.

Back at the curb by the Barclays', Lydia rolled down the driver's-side window and extended her hand to

Harriet. They didn't speak a word. Harriet placed the evil notebook on her sister's palm.

I said, "Thank you, Lydia. I promise to keep your sister from spying on your driving." I looked at Harriet. "I mean that, too."

"No problem, Alice," Lydia said. Harriet waved like a queen dismissing a servant. "Mission accomplished."

Lydia answered by squealing the tires as she headed off to Turbo Thai.

"She may have thousands of friends, but she's strikingly moronic," said Harriet, and held up a tiny USB flash drive.

We had hours to go, and all I wanted was for it to be night. But we made good use of the time. Harriet taught herself to work the camera by googling the instruction manual and practiced filming me in her room. It felt like her postcard of Tim Berners-Lee was staring at me, and I couldn't stop thinking you needed a smarter mind than mine to conjure up a complex miracle. "What if the new tape gets stuck?" I said.

"What's that idiot chant of Coach Bowling's," Harriet replied.

"Be positive. Okay." Calm down, I told myself. "What if I succeed, but Mr. Phoebe suspects I dubbed a voice onto the tape? He could call my parents, accuse me of cruelty to his family for adding fake audio, take legal action and sue."

"Alice? See why people think you make things up? Do not go wacko on me."

Fortunately, I had my bathing suit. I told Harriet I needed to go to the pool. If anything could calm me down, that would. "See you soon," she said, muffled behind the camera, and I was out the door.

It was a longer walk from her house than mine, but as soon as I dove in, everything seemed a little better. Backstroke, sky . . . flags, five strokes . . . the wall. Were we crazy to think we could pull this off in a night? Piper had not seen me in eight days. Out of all the times I'd babysat, she'd spoken once—unless, of course, I *had* imagined it. . . . Also, what if Mom decided to look out her bedroom window facing the evergreen trees between our house and the Phoebes'? It would be out of character, but if she did? The Phoebes' deck was unlikely to be visible through those trees at twilight. Still. We had to change the plan.

It took half an hour of texting, between Harriet's phone and Owen's, before they agreed that instead of the deck, with Harriet filming by crouching at the side, we would risk the tent. Instead of heating water for accelerator jars in Owen's kitchen, we would transport thermoses from Harriet's house and a stepladder for her to stand on, to film through a tent window.

At dusk, as planned, we caught fireflies in the woods near the public library. We needed five or six, I thought, but I went along with Harriet's insistence on two dozen because she promised we'd let them all go.

As we approached my house, I saw that a light was on in my mom's bedroom, and I halted us several houses away. "Harriet, tell me why you and Owen think this will work on the one night we have, in the few minutes we have."

She studied my face with the expression I'd seen when she was sizing up her competition at swim meets. "Fact one: sometimes things just happen. Fact two: if you don't try, they can't. Fact three: if you do, they might. For evidence, I give you Relay Carnival." I leaned against a tree. I wished it was next summer, so the hours ahead would be long behind.

Harriet put down the bags she was carrying and unslung her backpack. "If you try, you open up the possibility of succeeding." She could be talking about why I moved to the tent, I thought.

"Therefore, the choice is between sure failure and the possibility of success," she concluded. "That's why."

Our roles had switched, I saw, as we made our way into the backyard. I was the doubtful one. She was all in, being my true friend.

Unzipping the tent door, I felt a mixture of anger, danger, and excitement. It had been a whole week since I'd been inside. None of the old crop of fireflies were visible, and I guessed if they hadn't crawled out those days it rained, they'd left while I was away. Or found a way to mate and complete their life cycles.

Harriet rigged the opening she needed for the camera to poke through while I moved my bike to a far corner, arranged flashlights, and figured out where Piper and I would stand.

Owen met me at the Phoebes' deck door. He happened to be wearing the I AM SUSHI, YOU ARE SUSHI T-shirt from the day we met. "What's the frown for?" he said, letting me in.

"What does your shirt mean?" I asked.

"Dunno. We are all raw fish? What *is* wrong, Alice?"

"I guess I'm nervous." The faster we got this over with, the more time I'd have to think up apologies for disappointing him . . . and everybody.

Piper lay on her stomach, watching TV on the rug, knees bent in the air, toes pointed like a ballerina's. Before going out, Joanna had put both kids to bed; Owen had gotten Piper up again. "She's all yours," he said, and with two fingers he nudged up the corners of his mouth. "It's gonna be okay, Alice. Go for it," he said.

We had forty-five minutes, an hour at most, before the Phoebes got home. Fortunately, Piper did not protest when I switched off the TV or squirm as I carried her down the deck steps in the dusk or squeal as we traveled the long way around the front of my house.

When we reached my backyard, she wriggled for me to let her down.

"I hope that wasn't my first mistake," I whispered after her as she ran to the swings and slapped one of the two hanging seats to indicate she wanted a ride. No light had come on in the kitchen window, Mom had not appeared at the back door, so I set down the ball I'd brought along, lifted Piper onto the swing, and pushed. Out and back, out and back she went from my hands, her feet reaching into the air over the lawn, toward the tulip tree.

Two flashlight beams switched on in the tent: Harriet's signal that her setup was ready and that she was taking up her position at the camera.

I abandoned my usual practice of talking out loud to Piper as I lifted her down from the swing. How long ago it seemed, that first night I'd carried her wrapped in my towel. *Please,* I thought now, with each step we took hand in hand across the nighttime grass as I led her to the door of the tent, *please, please—please speak.*

Harriet was right to have made a fuss about needing a camera that worked in the dark. Shadows filled the tent as we entered; the light was low. I heard the video camera click softly into record mode and set Piper on her feet. "Do you remember being here, Piper?" I asked, and bent slowly, so I wouldn't scare her, and picked up one of the flashlights and held it out.

She jerked her hand away, moved to the tent wall, and spread her ten fingers like two sets of tree branches against the textured fabric. She seemed to be watching how it moved, or maybe how the shadows moved, while she pressed the canvas in and out.

It felt odd, being filmed. I got that stiff feeling, like when you have to get up in front of a class. We had to do this now, or never, and I had a moment of thinking I could go with never. But no—like Harriet had said, sometimes things just happen. This was a choice between sure failure and possible success. The only way it might work was if we tried. "Piper, how about this?" I held the ball into her angle of vision. She hesitated.

"Fun!" I said out loud and, waving the ball, sat with my legs in a V, like we did in her family room, and she copied me. Thank goodness for our old game.

Every millimeter, ounce, hair, muscle in my body concentrated on her. Her glad face seeing the ball, her curls, her purple flowered pajamas, the orange plastic sandals I'd slipped onto her feet to leave the house. She bounced the ball to me, I rolled it back. In the jars, the fireflies were still blinking, but the air inside must be cooling.

Piper sent her next roll over the bumpy ground cloth to an empty spot. I took that as a signal she was engaged and stopped the ball with my hand. Then Piper climbed onto the sleeping bags. She liked soft, squishy seats, like the beanbag chair in Owen's room. I picked up a jar of fireflies and sat beside her, scooting the sleeping bag a few inches closer to the masking tape, where the camera was focused.

I held out a jar and Piper's chin lifted; she was curious.

"Here are my fireflies," I said. "Well, they're not mine. They belong to summertime, but I know you liked them before. Maybe they're your friends, Piper."

She stood up, so I stood up, moving us to the masking tape X. She held her hands out for the jar and came toward me as I chattered on about magic flying lighted bugs, until we were in the right place. "Piper, can you hear me?"

Nothing.

"Do you remember that night, Piper, here in the tent?" I said as I unscrewed the lid and squeezed my hand down into the jar to gather fireflies. "It was darker than now. Remember you said a word, when you saw fireflies glow? A light came from inside them, and a word came from inside you. I know I heard you, Piper. Was I right? Did you say 'bugfire'? Can you say 'bugfire' again? Bugfire, bugfire, bugfire."

Nothing.

Piper moved her right hand forward, turned the palm up as if she were asking for what was in the jar, and waited as I withdrew my hand from the container as fast as I could. I uncurled my fingers to show her the fireflies. One of them blinked; another blinked.

"Piper?" I said. "Bugfire."

Her arms and legs grew still. Her eyebrows lifted; she looked surprised. Her eyes stayed on the fireflies. Her lips parted. It came out fuzzy: "Ahye wahn thahdt," but I understood her. She was saying, "I want that."

It was, to use Harriet's word, exceedingly magic.

23
A SMART GUESS

FOR A MOMENT, I had to consider whether Piper's words fell into the category of Maybe Not. As in, had I heard what I wanted: sounds imagined into words?

But behind the lens, in the window opening, Harriet was grinning.

So it was true.

I tried to make Harriet understand we should get more words on the tape. We communicated by eye and hand, as if our voices might break the spell cast by Piper's. Harriet pointed to her phone, meaning either she'd received a message from Owen that we needed to stop, or her clock showed time was running out.

Piper was still watching her hand. I slid three more bugs onto her palm, but two spread their wings and flew. The other was motionless. None of them flashed. A silent minute passed that felt like an hour. "Okay, Piper," I said. "We're done."

Harriet texted Owen; I slung the camera bag over my shoulder and carried Piper through the side yard, chancing the path under Mom's window. In my arms, Piper shook the remaining firefly off her hand into the moist grass.

"Fantastic, Alice!" Owen called in a loud whisper from the deck doorway. "You are amazing, and I want to hear how you did it, but ten minutes ago Joanna called to say they'd be here in ten minutes."

At the top of the deck steps I lowered Piper, who passed by Owen into the family room. It felt like we were in the middle of a dream.

"Thank you, Owen," I said. "It was the fireflies, like I told you." I handed him the bag with the tape, camera, and a printout Harriet had made of the user manual, since the Phoebes would need to operate the camera to watch the tape. Our plan called for Owen to leave the bag with a note on the dresser in his room before Mr. Phoebe drove him to the airport. In twelve hours, I guessed, they'd be finding it.

Half in a daze, still, when Owen slid the door shut behind me, the lock clicked, I realized we hadn't said goodbye.

The motion-detector floodlights above the Phoebes' garage popped on at the same time I stepped off the backyard deck. The brightness spilled into the side yard. The Phoebes were back, and their headlights

illuminated the area where I needed to walk. The best
choice seemed to be to wait for the lights to go out,
and the sounds of the Phoebes exiting their car and
entering their house. For some reason, the Phoebes
were staying in their car. Then the headlights switched
off, but I heard no doors open.

If I hadn't grown impatient, if I hadn't been
half-distracted and now half-wishing I'd watched the
tape before handing it over to Owen, to be sure it was
true, I might have stayed calm. But I needed to get
out. I dashed from the edge of the deck to the base of
the tall evergreens, inching in a waddling squat backward, as far as the rosebush, which grew deep enough
down the yard to be out of the range of the floodlights.
The Phoebes kept their side trimmed. My side was the
challenge.

This is going to hurt, I thought.

Eyes shut, lips pressed, I parted the clipped stems
on the Phoebes' side and toed up the metal. Only a
person who'd traveled over this fence dozens of times
could do so without a sound. I pretended I was about to
dive. My goal was to pitch myself up, over, and forward
headfirst, aiming to land in a curled forward roll.

Near the top, with my ankles in the stems I'd
respectfully maneuvered to make space, and my flip-
flops scrunched into the metal diamond holds, I stood

and envisioned the pool. The pool. Not the wild scrawled bush, the soft pink blooms backed up by evil thorns, that lay between me and the grass in my backyard.

The mess of the bush, as I leapt outward and attempted to clear it, snagged me into its full, thorny summer growth. The fence shivered. I'd made it. Now the hard part was not screaming.

I became aware of lying on my right arm, facing the tulip tree. I tried to make my breathing soundless, but this was difficult because I was crying.

The Phoebes' deck lights came on. I heard the door slide open. "I don't see anything." It was Joanna's voice. The door shut, the lights went dark again.

My brain registered Harriet running to me from the picnic table, then away. Where was she going *now* of all times? Using my left thumb and forefinger I raised the sticking stems off and sat up. The rosebush had scratched tiny heat points of pain all over my body. Then Harriet was back, kneeling in the grass next to me with an enormous white box with a red cross on it. I had no memory of a first-aid kit from the day we'd unpacked her suitcases. She whispered, "Keep still."

The tweezers were the worst. With each thorn she pulled, I gasped and she repeated "Shhh!" If I lifted an arm or a leg, Harriet commanded, "Don't move," in an enthusiastic whisper that made me wonder if this was her idea of a fun practice for her potential future career as a surgeon. She must have used up a whole box of Band-Aids.

My right ankle would not bear weight. The same ankle I'd crashed into the movie screen. Harriet felt it and declared a sprain. She helped me hop to my sleeping bag in the tent, rearranged the flashlights, and pressed an instant cold pack against my foot. She held out a water bottle and a white pill. "Non-aspirin pain reliever dose for age thirteen," she said, checking her phone. "Lydia is refusing to pick us up. Let's rest your leg a few hours before we walk to my house."

"Okay. Thanks, Harriet. For now, and for before," I said.

"I did not expect what happened, Alice. It was astonishing."

"You heard the words, right?" I wanted to add something clever, that Harriet would appreciate. My happiness about Piper speaking made a kind of weird oxymoron with the pain from the rosebush, I was about to say, when Harriet removed a three-inch stack of paper from her backpack and handed me the top pages.

"In light of your success," she said, "I think it's fair to say Piper may have a rare brain disorder."

Now who wasn't making sense?

"I followed a few links online," she continued. "I had a little trouble locating the original article that identified it. Fortunately, the National Library of Medicine is near my dad's office. You have to be sixteen to use the library alone, so his secretary took me. I copied a bunch of stuff."

I sat up on my elbow—*that* hurt—and quickly lay down again and held the papers above my face. Harriet aimed the light. "'Syndrome of Acquired Aphasia,'" I read out loud. "What does that even mean? 'With Convulsive Disorder in Children, by William M. Landau, M.D., and Frank R. Kleffner, M.D. *Neurology,* Minneapolis, August nineteen fifty-seven, volume seven, number eight' . . . Minneapolis?"

"Coincidence," Harriet said.

"You understand this?" I shook the article like it was a baby's rattle.

"It's not hard if you use a dictionary," she said. "It's about kids who started out normal, lost the ability to hear and speak, then regained it."

"It came, it went, it came back?" I said.

She nodded. "Plenty of later studies confirm this is possible, especially with treatments. It's named Landau-Kleffner Syndrome, LKS, after those two doctors who first described it. Some kids recovered, some didn't, some improved a little. It's all due to electrical activity in their brains. Very cool, right, brains use electricity? I might want to be a neuroscientist. The point is," she said, "if Piper can say words again, and if she has LKS, she could be one of the lucky ones. Our tape may prove she's spontaneously recovering."

"Harriet, if a thirteen-year-old kid can find this online—okay, not a typical thirteen-year-old, but still—wouldn't the Phoebes have seen it, too? Even if they didn't, wouldn't Piper's doctors have told them?" I handed back the pages. "My dad says some people who read medical dictionaries never fail to find symptoms of illness in themselves. Of course, he was talking about my mom. But what I mean is, aren't you jumping to conclusions? A person's imagination plus random medical facts can make people think they have horrible diseases." That was why I hadn't googled Piper's symptoms on the library computers myself; it had seemed like a waste of time.

"All I'm saying is, it's *possible* the Phoebes haven't considered LKS for the simple reason that they haven't *happened* to visit a doctor who told them to," she said. "One of the best-known facts about LKS is that it is so rare that it is commonly misdiagnosed."

"So rare that it is common," I repeated slowly. These oxymorons seemed to keep following us around.

"Most commonly misdiagnosed as autism, by the way," she said. "Isn't that what they think she has? LKS is exceedingly rare. In fifty years, maybe a few hundred or a thousand kids have had it out of billions of people on Earth."

"And trillions of insects."

"Ha ha," Harriet said.

"How do you suggest we prove Piper has a rare illness you happened to read about on the internet?"

"I'm not suggesting that, and we can't," Harriet said. "And I didn't say I'm right. I said it's possible. We can show them it's a possibility."

"So I'll go knock on their door after Owen leaves and say, 'Pay no attention to the fact I look like six cats attacked me, but by the way those adult doctors with all those years of medical training gave you the wrong info, and my thirteen-year-old genius friend thinks she may have correctly diagnosed your daughter's illness!' Mr. Phoebe will love that. Also, why didn't you tell me before?"

She waved a hand. "It felt relevant only if you got her to talk. You have to admit, the wishful thinking theory sounded plausible."

I didn't answer.

"Anyhow," she went on, "I stuck copies of a few articles in the camera bag, under the instruction manual. The Phoebes should see them when they open the bag. The truth is," she added, "I only read about LKS a few days ago, when I went online to escape my cousins on Cape Cod. Like I told you at the pool, I was thinking what an exceedingly good person you were to go the trouble to make friends with a girl who couldn't talk, and with me, who . . ." She trailed off, and I thought: this'll be good, Harriet's description of her own weirdness. But she only added in a sincere voice: "I wished I could do something so you'd still be my friend, so I tried searching the symptoms you'd told me. I'm not a doctor. But I'm sure this is at least a smart guess."

"What other kind could it be, if it's yours?" I joked. "This is like that time Coach B dropped a box of paperclips in the grass and we're all picking them up but you start reciting random facts—do we know the paper clip was invented in eighteen-something by a Swede named Yon—"

"Johan Vaaler in eighteen ninety-nine, yes. He was Norwegian. Alice, you're missing the main idea. The articles are meant to be helpful, they could be wrong. My guess about why she lost the ability to talk is a guess. Whatever the problem turns out to be, thanks to you, there's proof she can."

24

CODE MUD

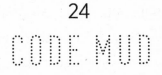

THE SUN WAS UP. We had overslept. Harriet was on the phone. "Excellent," she was saying. "Double excellent."

My watch said 8:15. Owen was leaving at nine. "Harriet, we need to go." I pushed out of the sleeping bag and stood, able to place decent weight on my right foot.

She lifted her hand for me to hold on. "We'll be waiting," she said into the phone.

"Waiting? Mom will kill me if she finds me here," I protested. From all angles, sun filtered in with a lamp-like glow, the effect I loved about waking up in the tent, and would have loved more if my scratched skin hadn't also woken up with me. And if I hadn't led Aunt Ruthie to believe I'd be waking up at Harriet's.

"Apparently, Owen already showed his parents the tape instead of waiting for them to find it. He has to leave for the airport very soon," said Harriet, who had planted herself on top of the pillows, blankets, and sleeping bags I thought of as my couch. "The entire Phoebe family will be here to slather you with gratitude in five minutes. Your face isn't so bad." She handed me a mirror and a dose of non-aspirin pain reliever and went off behind her shelves to call Lydia to pick us up.

With the help of the mirror, I began peeling Band-Aids off my arms and cheeks and pulled a pair of sweatpants over my legs.

Owen arrived first. A last-minute diaper change for Timmy had delayed the others, so he came ahead, he said, for a longer chance to say goodbye.

I reached for Owen's free hand and squeezed it. That curious sensation of sideways gravity pulling me toward him was missing. I thought this must be because I understood how happy he was to be returning to Denver and Riko. So it surprised me when tears bulged the corners of my eyes and rolled down my face, stinging wherever they crossed a thorn-clawed line. "Thanks for not minding all the dumb things I told you this summer," I said.

"Alice, they weren't dumb. I told you why I'm the one who should thank you. And now my whole family has a reason to thank you too." Owen kissed my forehead, and my lips missed his cheek and brushed against his hair and ear as he leaned in. "A small token of thanks, washed. It's from Riko's family's restaurant. I'll get another one," he said, holding out the sushi T-shirt, folded into a neat square and tied with a piece of string. "So you can remember we're all raw fish," he added with that twist he had. I laughed because the words made no sense but gave you something to think about, and he laughed, too.

"Problem, Alice!" Harriet called out.

Owen and I stepped away from each other as she circled the end of the shelves to join us.

"Hey, Harriet," he said.

"Hi, where's the rest of your family? Alice, we have a situation," she said. "Lydia failed to cover for us. It's my fault. I didn't text her last night, since I thought we'd be walking to my house. That was before we fell asleep. Mother discovered my bed not slept in and wondered if she'd misunderstood our plans and called your aunt. To Lydia's credit, she hedged: you and I got up early for our 'project,' walked to the café on Brookville Road for breakfast, and I must have made my bed dutifully before we left. I've just texted my mother to say we might stop by your house and that Lydia is bringing us home, but she hasn't answered."

There was no time to think much about this mix-up because we heard Timmy's voice outside the tent. "It's a tall one," he was saying, and Owen folded back the door panels for them. Joanna was carrying Timmy, his blue basketball in his arms.

"Oh, Alice, my goodness, thank you! *Thank you.* However can we thank you?" exclaimed Joanna. "We had to stop by as soon as possible to tell you girls in person. My, this is bigger than it looks from outside. . . . Oh but Alice, what happened?"

"Nothing, I'm fine," I said. Joanna's face appeared to register some understanding all of a sudden, but she asked no more questions.

"This is our friend who took the video, Harriet," Owen said.

Harriet said hi as Joanna lowered Timmy, who managed to hang onto his ball while he climbed onto the pillows and sleeping bags. Then Mr. Phoebe walked in, holding Piper. An appreciative grin replaced his usual slight nod. "Hello Alice, and . . . ?"

"My friend Harriet Barclay," I said.

"Good to meet you, Harriet. Jo?"

"We're still at 'thank you,'" she said.

"Yes, thank you, all three of you," he echoed, including Owen with an enthusiastic nod. "Alice, let me also say I regret doubting you before, and I hope you'll understand how unlikely it sounded. Where

Piper's concerned, the news from the professionals has been gloomy for quite some time. You haven't said your lovely words to Mommy and Daddy, have you, sweetheart?" He held Piper's face close to his.

She laughed and squirmed to get down. She gave no indication she'd heard him or that she was responding to anything besides his movements and facial expression. Or that she remembered last night. Piper did seem unafraid to be here, I thought. So it must have felt familiar. She lay on her back next to Timmy and waved her arms and legs as if she were making a snow angel in the sleeping bags.

"We've been discussing this morning that it could be a matter of us not paying close enough attention," Mr. Phoebe continued. "I'm afraid our move has consumed the better part of mine, at any rate, these last six months."

"I'm embarrassed to say I hadn't unpacked the box of Piper's medical files until last week," Joanna said. "We've been up most of the night going through our notes."

"And we have heard of LKS," Mr. Phoebe added, drawing Harriet's photocopies from the camera bag slung over his shoulder. "It wasn't suggested for Piper. Obviously, we need to rethink." He flipped through the pages. "These sources are quite sophisticated," he said. "So, the two of you have been working together on this?"

"That's Harriet's research," I said. "She should already be in college."

Harriet rolled her eyes, but I had the impression a teeny tiny part of her didn't mind. "Mr. Phoebe, Alice is my best friend. However, when she told me she heard your daughter speak—a logical, if made-up word—for the first time in two years, frankly, I shared your reaction. The tipping point for me was that Owen believed her, or at least gave her the courtesy and benefit of a doubt. I zeroed in on LKS merely because, using information Alice provided, it fit. I'm well aware those studies may represent theoretical, incomplete, or even, if you want to call it such, wishful thinking."

Mr. Phoebe smiled. He asked Harriet a couple of detailed questions about the articles and how she'd positioned the camera. You could almost see him calculating her nerd quotient as she talked.

Finally he said it was time for him and Owen to drive to the airport. We had final hugs and said goodbye, with promises of video-chatting soon. Harriet's phone had been beeping repeatedly, and she excused herself again to the back of the tent behind her plastic shelves.

"I'll follow you and the kids in a minute," Joanna said to Mr. Phoebe, and when the others were gone, she squatted on the ground cloth near me. "I wanted to let you know, Alice, that at first I refused Owen's offer to babysit. It was going to be his last evening. Then, I'm afraid, he explained your plan. He pleaded with me, and I was quite moved. I called Eric and convinced him it was Owen's parting summer wish for us to have a dinner out, without going into the details. You had your friend, and Owen was there, and I knew your mother was usually home, too. I decided Piper would be safe. Not that I expected anything to come of it."

"Owen didn't tell us," I said.

"No, he thought it was better that way. He didn't explain why, and I figured that was something between you. I didn't ask, since he agreed I could tell you now, and I made him promise to tell his dad." Joanna reached out for my right hand, with two long and three short scratches etched across it. "These don't look too bad." She gave one of her sad-around-the-edges chuckles. "Oh, Alice, do you remember the day I told you about visiting Cherrywood, with the trees in bloom, that I'd mentioned to Eric it looked like Wonderland? Little did I know *you* would be our wonder, Alice. You have quite a talent for getting through to people. You've renewed my hope. *Our* hope." Her eyes teared up—mine did too—and she patted my hand and let it go and stood to leave. "I'm not sure yet what it's hope for, but we haven't had much for anything in a long time."

I was about to say I was glad, but I didn't get the chance, because Mom opened the tent flaps and walked in. She was in her bathrobe and slippers, without her cane, and clearly hadn't expected to find another adult.

"Oh, hello! Pardon me, please excuse us for visiting Alice so early," Joanna said, introducing herself. "I hope we haven't disturbed you. We wanted to thank your daughter as soon as possible for her beautiful help to us last night. Has she told you about it?"

"Hi." With a glance of disapproval in my direction, Mom said to Joanna, "I did see you and your family when you got here, so I assumed Alice must be the reason, and no, she hasn't shared anything with me yet."

"Well, you'll forgive me, then, if I let Alice fill you in, since we're on our way to the airport. Thank you, though; we're extremely grateful to Alice."

All my good feeling about Piper had been replaced with terror that Mom was about to start yelling. I was too distracted to hear whatever she said to Joanna. I went to the back of the tent to warn Harriet. "I think you should go," I whispered.

Harriet seemed not to have heard anybody come in. In her regular voice, looking relieved, she said everything was fine, and Lydia would be out front in five minutes.

"Harriet," called my mom, sounding as if she'd expected to find my friend with me. "Did I hear you say somebody is coming for you? I'd be grateful if you'd wait for your ride out in front of our house, while I speak to Alice."

"Of course. Hi, Mrs. Allyn," Harriet answered, with a slight *Oh no* in her eyes to me. "See you later at the pool, Alice? Like we agreed? Thanks again for sleeping over and walking from my house to the café for breakfast with me before we came here. Bye!" She squeezed my hand on her way out. "Sorry if that was weird that I squeezed your hand!" Then it was just me and Mom.

The scratches I'd been ignoring started to ping reminders of themselves. My ankle ached. I was exhausted. I had this hollowed-out feeling like I was an old tree, and a storm of angry wind was coming, and I didn't know if I could stand it, but being a tree, I had to.

Mom looked unhappily around the tent. I guessed at least one of the reasons and said, "I'll get you a stool."

I emptied Harriet's library books out of a top-row crate, brought it to the sleeping area of the tent, and turned it over, and Mom sat down silently. Because she always thanked me for bringing her things, the small neglect sharpened my sense of bracing for trouble. But the tent was my territory. Whatever was coming, I was going to be standing up.

Mom's eyes fixed on her camera bag. Mr. Phoebe had left it behind after removing the printouts. The Phoebes had kept the tape, too, of course, which they planned to digitize. "On top of everything," Mom remarked, as if she'd located a rotten cherry on a moldy cake. She inventoried the contents, frowned, zipped the bag up, and set it beside her.

She said, "Half an hour ago, I happen to be in the kitchen making coffee, when I see the neighbors stepping into this eyesore, which, by the way, I've been waiting for your father to take down. Why, I ask myself, would they trespass on our property at eight twenty-five on a Sunday morning with their young children? It must be because you are here, although you are supposed to be at my sister's house. I phone Ruth and find out she thought you were at a friend's house—I'm not going to dispute her judgment about granting permission for that—and believed that's where you were, until a few minutes before my call, when your friend's mother had found the two of you missing."

For the moment, I decided not to contradict Harriet's story. It was a good one.

"The neighbor said you helped her 'last night,'" Mom went on, "which leads me to conclude you and your friend slept here without permission, without any adults knowing where you were, using a camera of mine, also without permission. I wonder if I ought to call Harriet's mother to tell her that café opens Sundays at nine a.m.? Or ask why your arms and face are covered with scratches, while her daughter's are not?" She shook her head as if the situation were hopeless.

My impatience had been coming on gradually, and by now it felt like a balloon filled to its popping point. "I can explain," I said. "We used the camera to prove Piper *could* speak words, like I'd discovered on July Fourth." So I shouldn't be accused of having made that up, I added. I began describing why Harriet and I hadn't returned to her house, like we'd planned, and she interrupted.

"Tell me why, instead of being good at your aunt's, and doing what I ask, and giving me some peace and quiet, you disobey me again, deceiving adults who trusted you, having decided for some reason that it's more important to help the neighbors than your own family?"

Strangely, this was the first comment of my mother's that contained a fraction of sense I agreed with. I said, "A person can do a wrong thing to protest something bad, or to try to fix it. I know that doesn't make the wrong thing right." But what had I done that was so wrong, especially compared to what some teenagers might get into on a free night? "Mom, what have I done that's so awful, besides falling asleep twice in one summer in the wrong place?" Hadn't I, in fact, done something very right? Isn't that what Joanna had just said?

Mom closed her eyes and pressed her index fingers into the corners at the bridge of her nose. "This is just the sort of behavior I can't handle at this point, Alice. It's another symbol of how poorly your father's managed things while I've been ill and how I never should have listened to him about allowing you to spend so much time alone this summer. Your worst tendencies are taking hold. This is exactly the reason I wanted you at Ruth's. I thought I could count on my own sister."

"Joanna says I have a talent for getting through to people, and so does Harriet," I responded. "Didn't you hear what *I* said happened last night? Why is it, the only person I can't get through to is you? Won't you ever stop being so negative?"

Code Mud. Owen said: *Their lives are what happened to them and how they chose to respond.* I was done with trying to fix Mom, and I was done with being mad about it, too. It was up to her. I was finished with Code Mud.

"You need to stop talking like that," I continued, "at least in front of me." Mom opened her eyes and was paying attention. "I'm sorry for making you and Aunt

Ruthie worry. I didn't mean to. But Piper is a kid with problems, not me. All I did was prove there's hope she'll get better. I've tried saying that to you, over and over, and you refuse to listen."

Many little stitches, binding me to my worries about my parents, snipped away. I felt lighter, better, almost as if I were swimming. "Right now, I'm going to the pool to meet Harriet," I said.

I had nothing more to tell her than what I could get across in a hug, and so I hugged Mom and left her sitting in the tent, and made my way to Cherrywood Pool.

25

IN THE BUGFIRE
CATEGORY

THE FIRST THING I did there was borrow the phone at the front desk to apologize to Aunt Ruthie. She'd had a second chat with Mrs. Barclay, who had heard all about the video from Harriet. Aunt Ruthie accepted my apology. "I understand you intended to return to the Barclays' last night and why you didn't. I won't say I approve of all your methods, but I was never too worried. You're not the troublemaking sort, Alice. Believe me, I know those kids. I've learned a lesson from you, as regards your neighbors." She asked me to be back at my house by six, when she was stopping by with the boys and her usual Chinese for dinner. In the meantime, she said, "I know your mom's upset, she gets overwhelmed easily. I'll talk to her."

It was perfect pool weather: hot but not too hot, blue sky, white clouds, no sign of possible late-afternoon thunderstorms. The lap pool was practically empty. A lot of people were probably away, since it was the second weekend in August. Swimming on my back, in my full-body suit, the scratches stopped stinging.

When you're a kid, I thought, the adults who raise you give you a situation. You expect life will be that way: the five of us, in the house, in Cherrywood. Then they end it, say it's over. It's like they lied. Nothing I had done wrong *or* right this summer had made Mom better or brought Dad home, and in two weeks, school was starting again.

I was racing, but I was also relaxed. Fast, fast. Fierce but smooth, and dry air above my face. The flags, five strokes, the wall.

My life was what happened to me and how I chose to respond, and here, in the pool, racing between walls I couldn't see, I knew exactly what it was I wanted most, that mattered most: bugfire. The real magic you could gather up from inside yourself to change you.

By then, I'd swum four hundred meters. Harriet was waiting at the end of my lane.

We ordered smoothies, quesadillas, mini cookie ice cream sandwiches, *and* curly fries. Harriet's box came

with a six-curl fry and mine had a five. I said, "We
have eaten many, many, many, many curly fries this
summer."

We untwisted them and let them boing. Harriet
launched into a discussion of how machines sculpt
potatoes into corkscrews. I said the potatoes must be
mashed, then frozen like ice cubes in spiral molds.
Harriet insisted mechanical peelers cut potatoes into
naturally curling strings.

"Harriet," I said, because that was enough Harriet-
talk for me, "the video never would have gotten made
without you. Thank you for working out that plan with
Owen and persuading my aunt and your mom to go
along."

"Correction, Alice. It depended on you and only
you, and—as observation confirms—fireflies. Working
out the details was enjoyable. This morning exceedingly wasn't, but I've managed to smooth things out."

"You are a good friend, Harriet, in case you're
interested."

"Thanks." She blushed. "Anyway, based on last
night it seems reasonable to be cautiously optimistic
that Piper's speech could return. If this is the case,
it's safe to conclude Mr. and Mrs. Phoebe would have
heard it eventually. You and our beetle friends sped
up the process. So if the time you saved positively

affects the outcome of whatever course of treatment she takes now, you can say you've changed a person's life, Alice."

I couldn't resist. "After you changed so many firefly lives by executing them, now they're 'our beetle friends'?" I nudged her knee under the table.

"Going soft is a temporary deviation," she joked.

By this time, Lydia had arrived for us in the parking lot.

"I didn't see that," Harriet said when her sister accidentally drove through the stop sign at the corner of Summit Avenue near my house, and Lydia said, "Because nothing happened," and I said, "That stop sign has always been a figment of my imagination."

I had nothing to do the rest of the afternoon, so I decided to trim my enemy. Wearing garden gloves, long sleeves, and swim goggles, I filled a trash bag with rosebush stems. Then Aunt Ruthie appeared in the backyard with the twins and Guy, her bag of carryout, and the duffel I'd left at her house. Minutes later Dad showed up with a new croquet set.

"What's going on?" I asked.

"It's time for the pre-school-year family meeting," he said.

"That's the night before the first day," I objected. "There are two more weeks of vacation."

"Well, this year falls into a different category," he said as he unpacked the pieces of the game.

"Which category is this year?" I asked.

He said only, "I always meant to get you kids croquet," and began pounding in the wickets and showing the boys how to hold the mallets and hit the balls through.

Aunt Ruthie and I started setting the table, and I noticed she'd kept her purse on her shoulder and car keys in her hand, and she was dressed up a little in capris and sandals. "Aren't you eating with us?"

"I've got a date—dinner and a movie," she said. "It's with a teacher at my school. Sam is being nice and taking Guy out with your brothers. But before I go—how are you doing, honey? I wasn't worried, but . . . I've been wanting to check in with you."

"I'm fine," I said, actually feeling it.

"That four-letter word drives me as batty as the bad ones," said Aunt Ruthie. "If I weren't running late, I'd stick around to find out what's up. I promise to be a nosy, prying aunt next time."

"Honest, Aunt Ruthie, I'm okay."

She laughed.

"'Okay' can be two or four!" I said.

"Alice, in spite of yesterday, because of yesterday, I'm certain you are going to be fine and okay." She patted my shoulder. "Guy, Mike, Josh, come sit down!"

Aunt Ruthie went inside to get Mom, who I had not seen since our fight. Subdued was the best word to describe her. She'd put on regular clothes, didn't act sad or happy, and sat down beside me, at the opposite end of the table from Dad instead of across from him, like usual. It was the first time the five members of my family had eaten together since the day before Labor Day last year.

"Hello, Kim," Dad said to her. "Boys, Alice, we'll call this our Fifteen-Nights-Before-School Meeting, and since school doesn't start tomorrow, Guy, Mike, Josh, and I are going to the movies afterward. Alice, you're invited. A new tradition."

"Alice never goes," said Josh.

"It's up to her," Dad said.

"She gets to do whatever she wants, just because she's the oldest," said Mike.

"That is so not true," I sighed.

"First item on the agenda!" said Dad. "Josh, leave some noodles for the rest of us."

Half the Chow Foon container had spilled into a lump on Josh's plate. "I didn't mean to," he said. "They stick together."

"Don't worry, honey. Here." Mom reached across the table.

"Next item: basic model, nothing fancy, but you're back in business." Dad handed me a new cell phone.

"See? We don't get phones," Mike said.

"Thanks, Dad, but how are we paying for this? I thought you couldn't afford it," I said.

"This afternoon, your mom and I are officially agreeing we made a mistake with no phones for the summer. This will come in handy during the next two weeks, and, Mike, it's important for Mom and me to be able to reach Alice after school. We all have to stay connected. Internet service should restart in the house the first day of school, so you can do homework."

"Eww!" said Josh.

I slid out of my seat and went to the tent for the envelope of babysitting money I'd been saving, over eight hundred dollars. "This is for my phone contract," I said, handing the envelope to Dad. "Or for swim fees. I want to swim on a team with Harriet's club this winter."

He peered inside, raised his eyebrows at Mom, and passed the envelope to her. "Very impressive. And you stashed it in the tent? I'd say this confirms we've got a safe neighborhood. We can talk about swimming." He squeezed my hand, and I could tell he was proud of me. "The third item: to answer your question, your mom and I have some news to share."

"Is the house for sale?" I felt my body tense. "Do I have to change schools?"

A look crossed Mom's face like she might say something mean, but it passed. "Ruth's friend offered me that job, and I've accepted."

"Wow!" What a relief, I thought. "That's great news!"

"I'll have to leave at six-thirty a.m., which will take some getting used to, but I'm not exactly being left a choice," she said.

"What do you mean?" I asked.

She stared at her plate, and Dad added, "It's a wonderful opportunity for your mom, and what it means is that nothing's changed in terms of the house or school. Mike and Josh are in the after-care program and will spend Monday through Thursday nights with her and Friday, Saturday, and Sunday nights with me. We're not insisting, but you're welcome to do that, too, Alice. The mornings the boys are here, I'll come by to make breakfast and lunches and get them to the bus."

"I wish we had *two* schools, one for Mom's house and one for Dad's house," Josh said.

"How would you play on teams for two schools?" asked Guy.

"If they play each other, just go on the field at different times," Mike said.

"Or pick the school with the best team and be on that one," said Josh.

What was Dad talking about, "nothing's changed"? I wished, suddenly, that the picnic table wasn't covered with food boxes, so I could sit on it alone. "The only thing that *hasn't* changed around here," I felt like yelling, "is these Chow Foon noodles, because Aunt Ruthie's been getting carryout from the same place since Chinese food was invented!"

But my life was what happened to me and how I chose to respond. Theirs, too. No chores I did, no food I cooked, no words I said were going to fix Mom. The tent had not made Dad change his mind. What had changed was bugfire, I thought: that glow Harriet created in a mortar, that spark that allowed Piper to speak new words—maybe it could do the same for me. Harriet had made that light by mixing two important ingredients together. So I tried mixing mine—what I wished for and what was real. "I hope you like the job," I said simply to Mom, who kept her eyes on her lap. "Dad, I'm glad you'll be coming over in the mornings."

Everyone was quiet. Who knows if anybody heard the tremble in my voice.

I swallowed.

I kept breathing.

"If you don't mind, Sam, I'm tired. I think I'll go in," said Mom.

Dad gave her a look. But I could see she had reached her limit, and that she was trying, and that was more than usual. "Thank you for eating dinner with us, Mom," I added.

"I love you, Alice," she said, and she went inside.

The guys and Guy started whacking croquet balls. I stood up to toss trash from dinner into the garbage bag Aunt Ruthie had left us.

"Wait to do that, Triple A, sit down a minute," Dad said. "Look, it's normal to want things spelled out in black and white when you're a kid: your bedtime is nine o'clock, you can watch TV when homework is finished. But part of growing up means getting used to gray; most human relationships have gray in them."

"So by gray, you're saying you don't completely love us anymore, which is why you'll be here a few mornings a week but not live here?" I knew this wasn't true, but I couldn't help saying it.

"The love of a parent for a child falls into the category of Exceptions to the Rule, in my personal experience," he said. "Though, from what I hear, with teenagers a little gray may sneak in." He winked.

Then I understood what Harriet meant, really understood it for the first time. There was no line between hot and cold, or warm and cool, love and not love. Tiny infinities were always going to be there. You had to draw the lines in, yourself, like the lane lines in the pool, and make up your own mind about where you were going and how, even if you couldn't see straight ahead.

"How long until the movie starts?" I asked.

He looked at his watch. "Forty-five minutes."

"Guys and Guy," I called, "help me empty the tent. If we do it fast enough, we'll have time to knock it down."

"All *right*!" they shouted, and dropped their mallets on the lawn.

In about five minutes the boys and I had piled the sleeping bags, pillows, books, miscellaneous snack containers, and crate after crate of Harriet's stuff on the patio. I leaned my bike against the tulip tree. Dad finished clearing the table and sat and watched us, chin in his hand. I showed Mike, Josh, and Guy how to loosen the knots and stationed them at equal points outside. Then I went in and shouted, "One . . . two . . . three!" and the boys pulled the ropes free. I knocked the center pole loose.

I ran out in time to watch the gold flag soar down, and the cream-and-navy canvas collapse into folds. It was early evening, and as I spun around to the picnic table, I saw the flash of a firefly over the grass.

ACKNOWLEDGMENTS

An infinity of thanks to Steven Chudney, my wonderful agent, and to my exceedingly talented editor, Taylor Norman; likewise to Maggie Enterrios for her beautiful cover and to Alice Seiler, Marie Oishi, Carol Burrell, Binh Au, and everyone at Chronicle Books who helped to create this book.

Dr. Generoso G. Gascon, Professor Emeritus of Clinical Neuroscience and Pediatrics, Alpert School of Medicine, Brown University, generously reviewed an early draft of pages about Piper and gave me many invaluable suggestions. For Harriet's firefly experiments I am indebted to Edward Duensing's guide, "Talking to Fireflies, Shrinking the Moon," and to Terry Lynch's detailed instructions for recreating firefly bioluminescence. Thank you to audiologist Anne Oyler, entomologist Nate Erwin, naturalist Cliff Fairweather and Officer Melanie Brenner of the Montgomery County Maryland Department of Police for taking time to share their expertise.

Many writers and friends read pages and encouraged me in different ways: Susan Coll, Georgia Guhin, Lucia Annunziata, Dan Williams, Amy Reichert, Liz Steinglass, Rhys Kuklewicz, Jean Hanan, Joyce Schwartz, Ellen Butts, Lisa Greenberg, Helen Winternitz, Susan Luborsky, Mario D'Ambrosio, Patricia Tschiderer. A special thank you to Kathryn Freeman for translating Alice's summer into a magical painting, Bug Fire.

Finally: Infinities of love and gratitude to my husband, Jackson—a butterflyer at heart; and to my son, Sandy, who first introduced me to summer swim teams and kids who recite pi; and to my daughter, Caroline, another in a long line of Diehl family swimmers, whose fantastical "bugfire" drawing sparked my first glimpse of Alice and Piper in the tent.